DIVA RULES

Also by Amir Abrams

Crazy Love
Caught Up

McPherson High series
The Girl of His Dreams
Diva Rules

Hollywood High series (with Ni-Ni Simone)
Hollywood High
Get Ready for War
Put Your Diamonds Up
Lights, Love & Lip Gloss

Published by Kensington Publishing Corp.

DIVA RULES

McPherson High

AMIR ABRAMS

KENSINGTON PUBLISHING CORP.

www.kensingtonbooks.com

DAFINA BOOKS are published by

Kensington Publishing Corp.
119 West 40th Street
New York, NY 10018

All Kensington titles, imprints, and distributed lines are available at special quantity discounts for bulk purchases for sales promotion, premiums, fund-raising, and educational or institutional use.

Special book excerpts or customized printings can also be created to fit specific needs. For details, write or phone the office of the Kensington Sales Manager: Kensington Publishing Corp., 119 West 40th Street, New York, NY 10018. Attn. Sales Department. Phone: 1-800-221-2647.

Dafina and the Dafina logo Reg. U.S. Pat. & TM Off.

ISBN-13: 978-0-7582-9480-7
ISBN-10: 0-7582-9480-8
First Kensington Trade Paperback Printing: May 2015

eISBN-13: 978-0-7582-9481-4
eISBN-10: 0-7582-9481-6
First Kensington Electronic Edition: May 2015

10 9 8 7 6 5 4 3 2 1

Printed in the United States of America

DIVA RULES

Diva Rule #1: Keep it flossy-glossy. Always step out camera ready.

Diva Rule #2: Keep it cute. Never, ever, fight over a boy. No matter how much you like him.

Diva Rule #3: Serve 'em grace 'n' face. Politeness with a smile goes a long way. *Please and thank you* seals the deal in every situation.

Diva Rule #4: Read 'em for filth. *Snap, snap!* Never, ever, look for trouble. But if trouble comes strutting your way, give 'em a tongue-lashing before a beat-down.

Diva Rule #5: Keep a BWB—Boo With Benefits—on speed dial. Every diva should always have a rotation of cuties at her beck 'n' call.

Diva Rule #6: Love 'em 'n' leave 'em. Never, ever, get too attached to a boy. All that letting a boy be your life is a no-no. Getting cuckoo-nutty over a boy is for the ratchet! A diva has no time for that.

Diva Rule #7: Never kiss 'n' tell. Always keep 'em guessing.

Diva Rule #8: Say hi to your haters. Let 'em hate. Someone's gotta do it.

Diva Rule #9: Never let another chick steal your shine. You are your only competition.

Diva Rule #10: When in doubt, always refer back to rules number one through nine.

1

Diva check…
Hey, hey now! It's diva roll call…Are you present?
Rude, check…
Bitchy, check…
Spoiled, check…
Selfish, check…
Overdramatic, check, check…
Scrrrrreeeech! Hold up. That is *not* what *this* diva is about. No, *hunni*! Being a diva is all about attitude, boo. It's about bein' fierce. Fabulous. And always fly. It's about servin' it up 'n' keepin' the haters on their toes. And the rules are simple.
So, let's try this again.
Fiona's my name. Turning boys out is my game. Fashion's my life. Being fabulous is my mission. And staying fly is a must. Oh, and trust. I serve it up lovely. Period, point blank. At five seven, a buck twenty-five with my creamy, smooth complexion, blond rings of shoulder-length curls,

and mesmerizing green eyes, I'm that chick all the cutie-boos stay tryna see about. I'm that chick with the small waist and big, bouncy booty that all the boys love to see me shake, bounce, 'n' clap. I'm that hot chick that the tricks 'n' hoes at my school—McPherson High—love to hate; yet hate that they can't ever be me.

Like I always tell 'em, "Don't be mad, boo. I know I give you life. Thank me for giving you something to live for."

Conceited?

No, hun. Never that.

Confident?

Yes, sweetie. Always that.

No, boo. I don't *think* I'm the hottest thing since Beyoncé's "Drunk in Love" video. I'm convinced I am. Big difference. *Snap, snap!* Don't get it twisted.

Now who's ready for roll call?

Always fly, check...

Always fabulous, check...

Always workin' the room, check...

Always snappin' necks, check, check...

Always poppin' the hips 'n' turnin' it up, check, check...

Wait. Wait. Wait. Let's rewind this segment *alllll* the way back for a sec. Yes, I keeps it cute, all day, every day, okay? And, yes, I know how to turn it up when I need to. I'm from the hood, boo. Born 'n' bred. But that doesn't mean I have to *be* hood. No, honey-boo. I'm too classy for that. Trust. But know this. If I have to let the hood out on you 'n' introduce you to the other side of me, it ain't gonna be cute. So don't bring it 'n' I won't have to sling it.

If you wanna check my credentials, just ask the last chick I had to beat *down*. She'll gladly show you the stamp I left on her forehead, *okay*?

Soooo. Moving on. As I was saying, I'm from the hood. Lived on the same block, in the same house, all my life. I know these streets like I know the back of my hands 'n' the curve of my hips. They can be mean 'n' dangerous 'n' ohhh, so exciting. And, yeah, the streets might be praising me, but they ain't raising me. So I'm not about to serve you some effed up tale about a chick being lost in the streets, eaten 'n' beaten alive. No, no. I'm a hood goddess, boo. That chick the wannabes bow down to, 'n' the lil thug-daddies worship. But, trust. This ain't no hood love story. So be clear.

No, hun. I wasn't born with a silver spoon hanging from my pouty mouth, but that doesn't mean I can't dream. That doesn't mean I can't want more than what I already have. And, yeah, a chick dreams about getting outta the hood. Traveling the world. Bagging a fine cutie-boo, or two, or three, who I can call my own. And being filthy rich. One day I will be. Trust. But for now, that doesn't mean I can't wear the illusion like a second skin. And, trust. I wear it well, boo.

So if you're hoping for some sob story about some broke-down, busted, lil fast-azz, boy-crazy ho tryna claw her way outta the hood, trickin' the block huggers up offa their paper for a come-up—sorry, boo-boo. Not gonna happen. If you're looking to hear about a chick going hungry or sleeping on some pissy-stained mattress, or having her hot pocket stuffed in some dirty panties going to school smelling like a sewer, then go find you another seat, boo, because you're sitting in the wrong arena. That stage play is being run somewhere else. If you're looking to hear about some fresh-mouthed chick who got beat with fists 'n' locked in closets, that's not gonna be featured here, either. Sorry, hun. I can't tell you a thing about that. Well, I could. But that's not my story. So I'll save that for some other hood chick.

So who am I?

I'm that hot chick, boo.

I'm a diva.

I'm a boss *bish* . . . and *whaaaat*?!

2

Now, I'm not saying I'm a gold digger, but I'm not ever messing with a broke ninja, *okay*? And neither should you. I mean, c'mon. If his sneaker game isn't up, then what makes him *think* I'ma let him get up in heaven, huh? *Pop, pop!* Shots fired! Man down! He'll get his lil feelings hurt first. Trust. It's not gonna happen. Now. Hold up, boo. That's not saying we can't be friends. There just won't be any benefits along with said friendship. Well, okay, okay …aside from the benefit of being in my company. But the stairway to heaven is—and will forever be—off limits.

Amen.

Hallelujah!

Oh, *heaven*…? Yeah, that's what the boys call this wet-wet. It's where warm bliss and sweet waterfalls meet. Ooh, yes. Trust. And after we tear the sheets up, they all end up looking dazed and saying how they feel like they've died 'n' gone to heaven.

And most times they have.

Trust, honey-boo. If I don't know anything else, this sexy kitten knows how to make a boy forget his name. Curl his toes. And make his eyes roll up in the back of his head. Trust. And there you have it. But I ain't tryna read you my diary, so...

Meanwhile, back at the ranch...

Here I am, minding my own business, strolling down the Ave., keeping it sexy 'n' cute as a diva always should, when I approach two guys a few feet ahead of me posted up in front of Miss Moosie's candy spot—this lil corner store that sells all of your snack needs up front 'n' all your get-right (molly, weed, X, coke, you name it, she got it) in the back part of the store. Miss Moosie—oh, everybody calls her that 'cause she kinda gotta face like a moose, but I ain't one to talk messy about somebody else's moms so I'ma leave it at that. Anyway, Miss Moosie thinks nobody knows what kinda dirty operation she's got going on. But I ain't stupid. I'm young. Not dumb. Trust.

Besides, her three sons hustle 'n' been in 'n' outta jail since they were like eleven, twelve, for drugs 'n' whatnot. And her house 'n' store have been raided mad times. So who she think she fooling? Surely not *moi*.

Anyway...back to these two nondescript man-tramps up ahead. Of course, I size 'em both up real quick, way before I get up on 'em. The short round one, who looks like he has a water bed for a stomach, is kinda cute in the face 'n' he has nice eyes. They're kinda slanted. And he has nice thick lips. Ooh, 'n' you already know where my mind goes seeing them lips. Yes, *hunni*. Straight to south of the border, boo. Mmph. I have to snatch my thoughts out of the gutter.

I blink. Reel my senses in real quick. Then frown. Them

C-cup boy-boobs are just not it for me. Sorry, I like my cutie-boos in wifebeaters, not in need of training bras. Thick lips or not. Moving on.

Now the tall, lanky one standing beside him...well, he looks kinda fine. But it's hard to tell 'cause he's wearing a black Brooklyn Nets fitted waaay down over his eyes, like he's tryna be all sneaky 'n' whatnot. But I can see he's in need of a shape-up 'n' is looking a tad bit too scruffy for my liking. And at first glance his Timbs are dated. But don't get me wrong. From what I can tell, he does have potential if you're into fixer-uppers. Me personally, I'm not taking on charity work 'n' I'm not looking for a project. No, ma'am. I need my cutie-boos fresh, fly, 'n' already put together.

What I look like, tryna clean you up? Chile, boom! Not over here.

But that doesn't mean I have to be messy, either.

Soooo, as I pass by, the Pillsbury Doughboy says, "Yo, what's good, shorty? Where you off to wit' ya fine self?"

I force a smile 'n' slow my stroll. "Have we met?" I say, peering at him over the rim of my new Prada shades, compliments of my sister Leona, who—along with my other three older sisters—gives me all of her last season's hand-me-downs. How else you think I stay so fabulous? Honey-boo, they give me life, *okay*?! Trust. "Umm, do I know you?"

"Nah, shorty," he says, licking his thick lips like he's ready to chomp his teeth into my hot pocket. "We both tryna holla, though, if you wit' it. You got a name?"

Yeah. I got a name. First name: No Thank You. Last name: Go Away.

Always answer a question with a question. "You driving?"

"Nah, not at da moment, nah'mean?"

Yeah, I do, boo-boo. Translation: *I got my L's snatched for DWD—driving while drunk*. Or, *I don't have my L's 'cause I'm too dumb to pass the test*. Or, *nah…I'm good on foot, baby*.

But I'm not! "Where you work?"

"Here 'n' there, feel me? It's hard out here for a brotha, nah'mean?"

Oh, I know what you mean all right.

Translation: *I'm unemployed. I ain't beat for work. And I ain't looking for work 'cause I have everything I need right out here on this block*.

"Y'all in school?"

"Nah. We chillin', feel me?"

Oh yeah, I feel you. Trust.

Translation: *I'm a dropout! An idiot! I don't need an education! I sit around 'n' smoke weed 'n' play video games all day. The streets are all I need to get by!*

I shake my head. "Y'all can holla at me when you find a j-o-b or enroll in a school."

"Awww, damn, baby…it's like dat?"

"All day, boo," I say, thrusting my pelvis 'n' tossing an extra shake in my hips as I hit 'em with the peace sign.

"Damn, I'd crack dat back," I hear one of 'em say.

"Yeah, I need dat, baby."

"No, boo-boo," I say over my shoulder, catching them both staring at my phatty 'n' holding their crotches. "What you need to do is get yo' life."

High school dropouts?

Unemployed?

Hugging the block?

Deuces, bum-azz nuccas!

Please. What I look like?

You wanna get at me, then your wears better be up 'n' you had better be able to feed 'n' finance me, boo. Or there is no romance. Not that I need a boy to do anything for me, 'cause a diva is *never* looking for a handout. Trust. Besides, I have sisters who stay keeping me flossy-glossy. And I get a portion of my social security check to do whatever I want, while the rest gets banked. So I don't need a boy's change. I have my own coins. Trust.

Still…an unemployed, uneducated, unmotivated clown can't do nothing but bring me down. And Fiona isn't having that. So they can…*poof-poof*…miss me with all that.

Anyway, most boys don't know the first thing about bearing gifts. But they sure know a heck of a lot about givin' out false hopes. No, thank you, boo. Been there, done that. Trust. There's nothing worse than a boy with a pocketful of lint 'n' a mouthful of bullshit. Chile, *boom*!

Let me get home so I can get ready for my date tonight.

3

Keep it flossy-glossy…

I reach over 'n' hit the remote to my stereo 'n' turn up the volume. K. Michelle's "V.S.O.P." cranks outta my speakers as I pop my hips over to my dresser 'n' grab a bottle of smell-good from my vast collection of sexy scents. Yesssss, *hunni*. It's all about the fragrance. And tonight, since I'm feeling sensual 'n' enticing, I choose Midnight Heat by my boo, Beyoncé. Smelling good is a must. A musty funk-box is a no-no. And, like with handbags 'n' heels, smell-goods are another one of those essential accessories a diva never has enough of. Well, that's what my sister Leona says. So if the diva of all divas says it, then that's what it is.

And I'm a perfume junkie, *okay?* Trust.

A squirt here, a squirt there, I spritz some on my wrists, then just a taste in my sweet valley. I cup 'em, then shake 'em in front of the full-length mirror hanging on the inside of my closet door.

Yes! Come get 'em, boo!

I snap my fingers 'n' sway my hips as K. Michelle sings about lighting some candles 'n' doing whatever her boo likes. *Yasss! Yassss! Warm my bed, boo-daddy!* Only heaven knows what's in my heart! And even though there ain't gonna be no candles lit tonight, my new cutie-boo still might get a lil taste of goodness. Well...maybe.

My brain tells me, "No, boo, don't do it. Make him wait." It's also telling me to keep my behind home. But the firecracker poppin' off in my panties says drop it like it's hot 'n' put the heat up on him. Ooh, I hate it when I get to feeling like this. Frisky. Raunchy. Too hot for my own dang good. But I already know if I give him a taste of heaven, he's gonna start sweatin' me all hard, like they all do, 'n' want more 'n' then I'm probably gonna stop taking his calls. No. I will.

Chop.

Wait. Let me just put this out there for you now so that there's no confusion 'cause I don't do confusion, okay? Not that it's any of your business, but if you haven't already peeped it, I'm not a virgin. And I haven't been one since I was twelve. Sweetie, please. I gets mine. My first experience was outta curiosity 'cause my older girl cousins were all having sex 'n' bragging about how good it was, so I wanted to see what the hype was all about for myself. So I did it with this boy Dougie. He was sixteen. And probably a lil too grown for my young body, but I let him have my cherry anyway. And I can't say the first time was all that great. It hurt like heck.

But that didn't stop me from givin' him second 'n' third helpings of this cherry pie. And it got better. I liked it. And wanted more, but not with just him. If I was bored 'n' a cute boy with swag caught my eye 'n' said all the right things, he could get it. So what started out as curiosity soon bloomed into sort of a sporting event for me to see how many boys I could get with, whenever I was home alone 'n' bored outta my mind. So sex became my entertainment. And, yes, I'm seventeen now 'n' there's been lots of cutie-boos I've *entertained* over the last five years. But not all of 'em got the cookie. Oh no, honey-boo. Most of 'em got the hand.

Oh, don't judge me. I know I'm a ho. What can I say? Sometimes I like to sample the goodies, then toss 'em back on the shelf. Shoot. Boys are like toys. They're lots of fun when you first get 'em, then after playing with 'em a few times, they lose their excitement. And I get bored with 'em. Fast. Oh well. I like variety. That ain't no crime. And neither is givin' in to temptation. Well, not as long as it delivers me from evil.

Girrrl, don't even go there.

I sit at my vanity 'n' fuss with my shoulder-length hair. *This hair really needs to be washed*, I muse, picking up my flatiron. Mmm. I run my fingers through my hair. What look will I give it tonight? Slicked back into a ponytail? Or should I wear it slick-straight down past my shoulder blades? Maybe plumped up with a few curls? After a few seconds of mulling over the possibilities, I decide on an updo since my hair is slightly dirty 'n' updos tend to hold better when it is.

I flatiron my hair, then slick it up into a ponytail. Once I'm done, I spritz some hairspray on my fingers then comb my fingertips through my bangs, finishing it off with a feathery side-swept bang.

Next, I artfully spackle my lips with a layer of gloss.

Then I slip into my wears—a red silk cami 'n' pair of

skintight True Religion jeans 'n' very high heels. My eyes flick to the vision staring in the mirror in front of me.

Voilà!

Camera ready! Picture-perfect.

I blow myself a kiss, then reach over 'n' grab my cell. *Click. Click.* I snap several selfies, then post 'em up on IG and Twitter.

Ha! Hate on, hate on! How you like me now?

You mad, yet?

I throw my cell into my Gucci bag, flip off the lights, shut my bedroom door, then hit the stairs.

It's time to turn up, boo!

4

"**I**'m out," I say to my mother, more outta courtesy than necessity. Truth is, where I go or what I do is really none of her business. But to keep her from workin' my last nerve I extend her my good manners 'n' let her know—on those rare occasions when she's home, instead of being posted up at the hospital where she works crazy long hours—that I'm bouncin'. Like now.

"I know one damn thing," she starts in as I'm walking into the kitchen to get my jacket hanging on the back of one of the chairs, "those dishes had better be washed before you leave up outta here trollin'."

Trollin'?

Oh, she tried it. All I can do is shake my head. I swear. Misery sure does love company. Fortunately for her 'n' *it*, Fiona Madison is *not* the one to entertain it. Trust.

On cue, I roll my eyes up in my head.

"You hear me talking to you, girl?"

This chick better fall back! The only troll around here is her!

I stalk out of the kitchen 'n' head straight into the dining room, where she has her big, fluffy butt-cheeks pressed down into one of the chairs, a slice of lemon pound cake and a Diet Pepsi set before her.

Um. Know this about me. I'm never disrespectful. But I do believe in putting a chick in her place. Even if said chick happens to be my very own mother. For all intents and purposes, she might have given birth to me. But she hasn't mothered me. No ma'am, no sir! My four older sisters—Leona, Kara, Sonji, and Karina—have. They were the ones who practically raised me, especially Leona 'n' Kara since they're the two oldest. Let me see. Leona's thirty-four, Kara's thirty-two, Sonji's twenty-nine, and my sister Karina is twenty-six.

So don't get it twisted. I mighta got pushed outta my mother's womb, but it's no secret around these parts that Fiona 'n' Ruthie-Ann Madison don't like each other. Trust. Let her tell it. I was a mistake. Girl, *boom*! She's the mistake. As far as I'm concerned, she shoulda used a condom or popped a pill—better yet, kept her dang legs shut—if she didn't want any more babies.

But that's neither here nor there. So, moving on.

In spite of her ugly ways, this lady could be real fly if she fixed herself up. I mean. Jeezus. Can you say *fashion catastrophe*? Somewhere underneath her smocks 'n' all that evilness, she's hiding a very pretty reddish-brown-skinned woman with big, round, piercing brown eyes. And once upon a time—before slices of pound cake 'n' chocolates wrapped around her hips 'n' gut—there was a

woman with a sassy shape. But now? Mmph. It won't be
long before she'll be rolling herself outta here in a wheel-
barrow at the rate she's eating.

And let me not even get in on her hair. She has thick,
light brown hair that sweeps just above her shoulders. But
she does nothing with it. Nothing! Does she even realize
how many nappy, bald-headed souls there are running
around in the world slapping on wigs 'n' stitching in
raggedy weaves, desperate to have hair like hers? Mmph.
No. She'd rather wear hers either pulled back into some
god-awful, old-lady nun bun—a *bun* for Christ's sake! Or
like some frizzy bird's nest. Or she'll wear it like a wild,
stringy mop. Like right now. It's just hanging. No curls. No
bounce. No gloss. And all I can think is, *Please, God, don't
let that ever be me!* The lady needs a serious makeover.
But that's beside the point.

The point right now is, I'm done tryna be nice to this
fifty-year-old lady, looking like she's sixty. We will never see
eye to eye on anything. Period. Never have, never will. We
simply tolerate each other. And that depends on which
day of the week it is. Or whose cycle has come first. She's
evil. And nasty. And miserable. And downright hateful.
And if I was disrespectful like some chicks I know, 'n'
fought old ladies, trust. She'd be the first to get served. I
would give it to her good. Mmph. Ooh, I'd beat the wrin-
kles off her. Well, okay, okay . . . she doesn't have any wrin-
kles, yet. But, whatever! I'd yank her scalp. Yes, gawd,
hunni! I'd lay her out in a casket.

Anyway . . .

It doesn't matter to her that unlike almost every chick in
my hood, I'm not pushing a stroller, haven't been stretched

out on some clinic table getting my insides scraped out, am not running the streets throwing up gang signs, or strung out on coke or dope. Nope, she couldn't care less about all that.

And it doesn't matter to her that I've gotten straight As on every last one of my report cards since first grade—uh, well... with the exception of fifth and sixth grades, when I practically flunked everything. But, trust. I had a good reason for those Cs and Ds—okay, 'n' Fs. Still... I was going through a difficult time in my life. But we're not about to get into that. Not today. The fact is, nothing I do is ever good enough for this woman.

Never!

Instead of praise, she always has a way of finding something negative or derogative to say. And honestly, between you and me, I'm sick of it. She'd rather stress me out about dumbness, like dishes. *Dishes!*

I rapidly bat my lashes. "*Excuuuuuse* me?"

"You heard me. I said I want them dishes in that sink washed."

I raise a brow. Fold my arms in front of my chest. Then smack my lips. "How about *you* wash a dish for a change?"

"What?" she shrieks. A hand goes up on her wide hip. A tinge of anger seeps up from the back of her throat. "Girl, you had better regroup before you get knocked to the floor! I pay all the bills up in here 'n' make sure you have a roof over your damn head. And—"

"That's your *job*," I state, disinterested in her rant. "That's what you're *supposed* to do. Or have you forgotten? You don't get a medal or a standing ovation for doing what you're *supposed* to be doing as a parent in the first place. That's the least you can do since you don't do anything else for *me*."

"Fiona! I'm warning you! I want them dishes washed and that floor swept before you leave up outta here."

"Oh, now you want the floor swept, too. Ha!" I shift my handbag from one hand to the other, then toss my hair. She hates when I do it, which makes me love doing it even more. "Mmph. Well, I'm sorry to inform you"—I toss my hair again— "but Hazel the Maid is off the clock. You can check back later. But whatever dishes were put in the sink *after* I already did them will stay there. And whatever crumbs there are on the floor will stay there. Let the mice have at 'em."

"You heard what I said."

Finger snap. "And you *heard* what I said." I stare her down defiantly. And she doesn't back down, her wide eyes narrowing into tiny slits. She doesn't blink. And neither do I.

I can tell she's itchin' to wrap her lips around her fork and sink her pearly whites into that big piece of cake, but she dare not break her stare, even for her sweet tooth. No. She's stubborn like that. And so am I. But in this house, there can only be one winner.

She blinks first.

And tonight it's me.

"Don't you leave up outta here..."

I throw a dismissive hand up in the air. "Good night, ma'am."

"Your mouth is really gettin' outta hand, lil girl."

I twist my lips. "And so is yours."

She glares at me. "Don't try me, Fiona. I mean it. I will hop up outta this chair 'n' knock you in your damn mouth."

"Uh-huh. We'll see," I snap back. "Let me know how you make out with that." I toss my hair and head toward the living room.

"And who you goin' out with anyway?"

I stop in my tracks. Crane my neck in her direction 'n' give her a blank stare. *Since when she start questioning me, like she cares?* The one night she happens to be home 'n' all of a sudden she wants to know *whom* I'm going out with. Chile, cheese! She better go have several seats.

She's been working the night shift at Jersey City Medical Center as a registered nurse since I was eight years old. And more often than not, she stays working double shifts, going in at three in the afternoon 'n' not walking back up in here until after eight in the morning—when I've already gone to school—so I hardly see her.

And that works for me. With all of my sisters out of the house, and her hardly ever home, I parent myself. I take care of myself. And I answer to no one but myself. For five years, I've been doing me just fine without her breathing down my neck. And we're not about to change it up now.

"I'm going out with a *friend*."

She twists her lips. "Uh-huh. Well, make sure this *friend* has your hot-azz back up in here before two A.M., or you better stay where you at."

Chile, bye. I'll get home when I get home. Like I said, she's never here, so I have no set time as to when I come home. I make my own damn rules.

I swing open the front door.

"And you better not come up in here pregnant."

Pregnant?

I grip the doorknob. "Uh-uh...don't clown me, boo.

Where they doin' that at? Not over here, okay? I'm not you.
I don't do nothin' raw."

"Well, if you kept your legs shut. And what I tell you
about calling me your damn *boo*?"

Bam!

I slam the door shut, cutting the rest of her words off.
As usual, she is *waaaay* outta order!

5

"**D**amn, baby…"

"Boy, you ain't ready for this heat," I say all sexy-like. Of course, I'm all tease with very-little-to-no pleasing going on. Please. I'm not feeling as inspired to remove all my clothes as I had thought I would be before I slid into this boy's car.

"Yeah, a'ight," he groans low in my ear. "You stay playin', yo. You got me on rock, ma. When you gonna stop frontin' 'n' let me crack that?"

Okay, let me just put it on here now so we're clear: I have a weakness for tall, tatted, rugged thug-boos with swag. And if he has dreads and he's dark chocolate… whew! Yes, lawd…then it's about to be a situation. Every diva needs her a nice hunky chunk of dark chocolate to bite into from time to time.

But every now and again, like right at this very moment, my lil chocolate stud daddy winds up being a real lame. A dud. A terrible disappointment. And, sadly, a waste of my time.

And the only reason I have to try to bow out of this tragic predicament gracefully is because King's really, really a nice guy. Yes, King. King Matthews. He's eighteen and a freshman at Saint Peter's University. Six-three. Chiseled. Dark. Fine. And ohh so sexy!

I met him at a college party the Kappas were having two weekends ago at NJCU—New Jersey City University. I was lovin' his swag. And he was lovin' all there is to love about the fine, fly, fabulous me. Yes, boo. I'm a hottie. He knew it 'n' so did everyone else, which is why he stepped up to me in the first place, the minute he peeped me in my wears—skintight 7 For All Mankind jeans poured over my hips 'n' a cute lil low-cut T-shirt with the words HOT POCKET scrawled across my chest in red script. Oh, 'n' the six-inch Gucci heels—straight out of my sister Sonji's walk-in closet.

King ain't no fool. He knows quality when he peeps it. A five-star *bish*, boo. Thought you knew. I strutted up in that *beeeyotch* like I owned it. I served it!

Dropped it. Popped it. Twerked it. Swept the floor with it. Gave all the hot boys something to drool over. And the hatin'-azz chicks something else to add to their bucket lists: how to be me.

All I could do is give 'em that look that said *Go have several seats 'n' take notes!*

Anyway, King and I danced almost the whole night. Then chopped it up real lovely outside for almost an hour in the parking lot after the party was over. Before we finally exchanged numbers 'n' bounced our separate ways.

Now here we are.

And guess what? King can't kiss. He's all teeth, tongue,

'n' a buncha dang spit! No. Seriously. His lip game is capital h-o-r-r-i-d. Scraping his teeth against mine 'n' licking my mouth like it's a dog bowl is so not sexy! And usually for me, a whack-azz kisser is grounds for immediate, on-the-spot dismissal.

Poof!

See ya'self to the door!

But he's so dang fine. And somehow I've managed, along with the two blunts we've smoked, to let him melt away every ounce of my good dang sense, thinking—okay, *hoping*—that after a few practice runs he'd get it right.

Not. Epic fail!

And now I'm turned off 'n' royally disgusted.

He tries to kiss me again 'n' I jerk my head back just as his overly wet lips graze the side of my neck. I feel like I'm in the backseat with an overexcited Rottweiler the way this boy's tryna slobber me down.

Ewww.

Here's the thing with me. I flirt. I tease. And I might even do a lil lickin' 'n' kissin' if I get real hot 'n' frisky 'n' my ho-meter kicks up a notch. But be clear. I ain't givin' up the cookie to every boy with a hard-on.

No. You gotta earn this.

My name is not Trixie. And I am not giving out treats. No. But tonight, what I am givin' out is a bad case of blue balls to this fool right here; especially after laying my hand down in his lap and feeling what he's carrying in his blue American Eagle boxers. Ugh! This boy has two big potato sacs and no dang meat.

Blank stare.

See. I already know I'm dead wrong for even being in the backseat of this boy's 2008 Durango stretched out on black leather seats, letting him think I'ma let him tear it up. And the minute I slid in the front seat of his whip when he picked me up tonight, I knew I was making a mistake. I knew it was a bad idea. But *noooo*. I just needed to get out of the house and away from the likes of my mother.

So here I am.

The sexy sounds of R. Kelly flooding the space around us.

Weed smoke thick in the air.

Windows all steamy.

One perky boob out of my red lace bra, and this boy's rough hands squeezing 'n' kneading me like I'm a ball of pizza dough. Yeah, after talking to him on the phone I thought I wanted to give it to him in every position. But, womp, womp, womp…he is sooo not what I'm in the mood for.

He's breathing hard.

And I'm suffering; bored outta my mind.

"Damn, you got me turnt up, ma."

And you got me sick to my stomach!

"Ohh, okay, boo…" is all I say, rolling my eyes up in my head.

So what's a diva to do?

Give in 'n' go at it, watching him make crazy faces until I fake an orgasm? Close my eyes 'n' imagine it's Trey Songz's hands 'n' lips all over me?

No, no. No can do. Trey Songz is grown-man status, although it doesn't hurt to fantasize. Still, he's waaaay too old for me to even be thinking such dirty things.

So when in doubt, blame it on your cycle 'n' cramp it out. Trust. Tell him it's a crime scene in ya panties 'n' that'll stop him in his tracks. Or simply tell him no, thank you. If he's respectful, he'll pull up off 'a you, fix the situation in his pants, then shift gears.

I decide to go for the latter. After all, honesty is usually the best policy, right?

King starts grinding on me, deep 'n' hard.

Oh no... oh no... not dry humping me!

"Listen, boo," I say, tryna push him up off me. But he's already gone. Lost in a zone as he grabs my hips 'n' starts grunting 'n' pumping a mile a minute, like a dog in heat. And I have no one to blame but myself for allowing this mess to get this far. "King, stop! Get off me!"

It's too late.

He growls.

Then shudders.

Sweat drips from his face.

I blink.

King blinks.

Did this boy just make a baby in his own pants?

Yes. He. Did!

Ohhhhmigod! Yuck.

Ohhhkay. I am officially done! Dead to the bed! Flatlined! Sticky Drawz can now take me home. I blink several times, tryna wrap my mind around what just happened here as he finally lifts up off of me.

I eye him as he reaches for his shirt and slips it back over his head, then adjusts himself in his jeans. I try not to frown at this horn dog. But trust. I'm looking at him sideways 'n' all kinds of crazy.

For some reason, I feel dirty.

Violated.

I slip my boob back into my bra, slide my shirt back on over my head, then climb up into the front seat. Speechless.

He doesn't even try to sop up the mess he's made in his underwear with napkins, a towel, nothing. He simply climbs out of the truck, opens the driver-side door, then slides behind the wheel and drives off like everything's everything.

Alllllrighty then.

"Yo, why you all quiet over there?" he finally says, glancing over at me while we're stopped at a light. "You good?" He reaches over and places his hand on my thigh. His hand slides up farther than what he's earned.

I look over at him. *Are you effen kidding me?!* I grab his hand, gently remove it from out of my crotch. "Uh-huh," I say dryly. "Just dandy, boo. You good?"

"Yeah, yeah. No doubt."

His hand goes back up on the steering wheel, where it belongs.

I fake a tight smile, then turn my head toward the window and stare out into the night. *Yeah, I bet you are, with ya drawz all sticky 'n' stained with a bunch of man gravy!*

Ugh! How gross!

What a horrible way to end my dang weekend!

6

"Fiona! Heeey, girl…"

I pause in the middle of checking my messages, looking up from my cell 'n' scanning the crowded hallway. I spot Miesha—the only other *real* diva here amongst a sea of bottom-feeders 'n' wannabe divas—walking toward me, smiling. Like me, she lives for fashion 'n' stays dipped in all the hottest wears. She's a McPherson High transplant from Fashion High in Manhattan. And she's the only chick I really click with.

I mean, yes, I eat lunch with the cheerleaders 'n' I even hang out at the mall with 'em, but they're definitely not who I'd ever call real friends. No. All we will ever be is grins 'n' giggles. Nothing real. Trust.

Miesha, on the other hand, is *that* chick, too. Maybe not as fly as me, but she serves it up real close. There can only be one chick holding the number one spot—*me*. But Miesha is definitely a close runner-up. And I like that about her. And after she had to take it to our school's loudmouth mascot, Quandaleesha's, face—not once, but twice—in the beginning of the school year, ain't no one tryna see her with the hands.

Annnywaaay, after a few weeks of watching her toss her hair 'n' turn her nose up at everyone here, I decided it was time I stepped to her 'n' introduced myself 'n' welcomed her to McPherson High. I walked up on her at her locker 'n' greeted her. But girlfriend wasn't tryna have it. Ooh, you shoulda seen how she tried to give it to me, lookin' me up 'n' down like I was some scum beneath her cute lil heels. Chile, boom! Fiona can serve it back. Okay? Trust.

And I was looking too cute to even care, in my white stretch jeans 'n' white linen blouse with a white Gucci belt cinched around my ultra-tight waist. Mmph. And, yeah, I peeped how her eyes fluttered down at the slick pair of gladiator sandals I had on my feet that day.

Chickie peeped my work. But she still tried to play me to the left, tossing her sleek wrap, staring down at my hand as I extended it to her. Ooh, yes, *hunni*! Lil Miss Miesha was a mess. But that didn't stop a diva like me. I told her, "If you wanna be a snot, be one."

And just as I was about to spin on my heel, she came to her senses, *okay*. "Hey, wait. Thanks for the welcome. I didn't mean to come off rude."

Girl, bye! I tilted my head, narrowed my green eyes to slits, 'n' said, "Girl, please. Yes, you did." Then I started laughing 'n' so did she.

And we've been fly ever since.

Anyway, Miesha's been saying since the day I met her that she hates it here 'n' how she couldn't wait to go back to Brooklyn as soon as she turns eighteen.

Chile, *boom-boom*! I knew she wasn't going anywhere; especially not after she snagged one of the finest boys at McPherson. Antonio Lopez. Mmph. Yes, gawd! Six four with a rock-hard body 'n' a reputation for being a beast in the sheets. That boy has slung more meat than a butcher to the needy 'n' the greedy. Not that I'm one to gossip. But, *hunni*... that boy knows he's some kinda fine. And a real man-whore before he turned in his player's card for love. Ha! Ain't that something. Now ole cutie-boo doesn't even look at another chick—from what I can tell, that is. Mmph. Miss Thang either sucks the watermelon juice like a pro or she really put the whammy on him 'cause she got that boy hooked.

We hug 'n' give each other cheeky air-kisses.

As usual everything about her is stylishly fly, from the beaded knapsack I'm sure she's designed 'n' sewn, to her rhinestone-studded skinny jeans.

"Girrrrrl, you better work!" I say, stepping back 'n' wagging a finger at her. "I'm loooovin' the bag, boo."

"Ooh, you like?" She spins 'n' poses, modeling it for me. "I made it over the weekend."

See? I knew it. I can't hate. Miesha's exceptionally talented 'n' I know she's gonna go real far in the fashion world. Heck, she's already been accepted into Parsons The New School for Design, Pratt Institute, *and* FIT, okay? She better *werrrk!*

And here I am still trying to figure out what I wanna do with my life. Gettin' up outta my mother's house is definitely priority number one for me. I just need to focus 'n' get a plan in action. Ugh. Let me not give myself a headache thinking too hard about that. Moving on...

"*Like?* Girl, you servin' me with this bag. Ooh, you so messy! It's sooo cute!" She laughs as we start walking toward the stairs. "Where's your boo-daddy at?"

Her eyes light up as she smiles. "He texted me to say he overslept. So he probably won't even get here until after homeroom."

I waggle my eyebrows. "Ooh, nasty girl. Let me find out you rocked him into a coma last night. 'Cause I know you keepin' that boy flat on his back."

She laughs, waving me on. "Girl, bye. Not hardly. I spent the weekend in Brooklyn partying with my girls. You need to come chill with us the next time I go."

Now, I'm not one for slinging messy juice up on anyone, but Miesha's girls, with their tore-up weaves 'n' round-the-clock weed smoking 'n' drama are straight ratchet. *Hunni*, please. I know I'm from the hood, but thank God I'm not a hood rat. Those Brooklyn roaches live for the hood.

"Yeah, I just might," I say with as much enthusiasm as I can.

"You should." Miesha pulls out her phone, checking her messages, then drops it back down into her knapsack.

"Yo, what's goodie, Fiona, baby?" this boy Marcellus calls out with his tall, jet-black self. This boy's the antithesis of safe sex. There's no such thing, okay? He stays with a nasty drip.

"This honeypot," I say, patting the front of my goody-goody, "but you wouldn't know about that."

He laughs. "'Cause you stay frontin'."

"No, boo-boo. Because you stay down at the clinic."

Miesha laughs, shaking her head.

"Yo, that's effed up, yo. I ain't had an STD in over three weeks."

"Oooh, goodie," I say, clapping my hands. "Now spell condom."

"Yeah, a'ight, yo. I got ya condom alright."

"Boy, *boom*. Try rollin' it on that dirty stick then."

"Yo, you foul, yo."

"Uh-huh," I say over my shoulder, "'n' so is what's hangin' in ya drawz."

A few kids in earshot start clowning him, hard. He starts popping ish, calling me outta my name. But I ain't worried. It ain't ever easy being me.

"Girl, you a mess," Miesha says.

I toss my bouncy curls. "But I ain't ever messy, boo."

She keeps laughing. "Girl, okay. So what'd you do over the weekend?"

"Got molested," I say dramatically.

She stops in her tracks. "Ohmigod! *Whaaaat?* By who?"

I laugh, waving her on. "Girl, relax. Just some fine, horny college boy who kissed real wet 'n' sloppy 'n' used his tongue like a dishrag, humped my leg like a dog, then squirted his mayonnaise all in his drawz."

"Ohmigod! You have got to be kidding me!"

I twist my lips. "Mmph. I wish."

"*Illll!* How disgusting."

"And trust. I was disgusted 'n' real pissed."

"Ooh, I woulda been too through. I probably woulda laughed all in his face."

"Well, I didn't laugh in his face. But I was definitely lookin' at him all sideways 'n' crazy. Mmph."

"Ohh, I know you gave that boy the axe, too. *Chop!*"

"Well, uh, no. Not exactly. Not yet."

She shoots me an incredulous look. "Wait. You like him?"

I frown. "Girl, no. Not enough to ever make him my boo-daddy. But just enough to be something to do."

She glances over at me as we climb up the three flights of stairs toward our lockers. "So, what are you gonna do? Are you gonna chill with him again?"

I purse my lips thoughtfully. "I don't know. At first, I was like nope, never again. I mean, I know he'll never get a chance to tongue-wash my face again. And he's definitely *not* ever pokin' up in me with that toothpick of his. But now, after careful consideration, I'm thinkin' about introducin' his wet juicy lips to my cookie."

She cracks up laughing. "Ohmigod! Girl, I can't! Only you!" We stop at her locker first. She takes a few moments to stop laughing, wiping tears from her eyes. "Fiona, you're a hot mess, girl!"

I twist my lips. "Uh-huh. But I'm keepin' it a hunnid, boo. And you know I ain't ever messy."

She shakes her head, pulling open her locker then taking out books for her first three classes. She slams her locker door shut, then walks with me to the bank of lockers along the other side of the long hall so I can get my things out.

"Do you need a ride home after school?" Miesha asks, checking her phone for messages again.

I give her a look, opening my locker door. A folded piece of paper flutters to the floor. "Girl, you know I do," I say, squatting down and scooping it up. I grab my Spanish IV book, then shut my locker. "I'll be glad when my sister Sonji finally gets her new Lexus so she can give me her old one. Bummin' rides is so not cute. And you know I don't play the foot game. Me 'n' walkin' home ain't it."

Miesha chuckles 'n' shakes her head. "I know that's right. I wish I had four sisters who gave me anything I wanted. You're so lucky."

Boo, if you only knew…

Between you 'n' me, if it wasn't for my sisters, there's no telling who or what I'd be. Mmph. Probably some raggedy hot mess, like Miesha's girls in Brooklyn, real busted 'n' stank.

"Yeah, they my boos. Ohmygod. I love 'em to death."

"I know that's right." She points to the note in my hand. "What's that?"

I shrug, flipping the folded piece of paper over in my hand. "I have no clue." I glance at it, stopping in my tracks. *For your eyes only* is scrawled on the front of it.

WTH?

I open it. It's a poem.

OMG! No one has ever written me a poem before.

I Confess

I'ma keep it straight up, baby
I've been secretly crushin' on you hard for a
while
No matter how hard I try
I can't seem to get you outta my mind
Maybe it's ya smile
Or the sparkle in ya eyes
Or the way you move ya hips
Or the sexy way you lick ya lips

Or the way you say my name
All I know is
I dig ya style
There's something special about you, girl
That makes me wanna have you in my world
I ain't lookin' to spit game, baby
I want you
I need you
I gotta have you
More than you'll ever know.

"Ooooh, Fiona has a secret admirer," Miesha says in a singsong voice, laughing. "Fiona has a secret admirer."

"Girl, hush your lies," I say, folding the note back and tossing it into my bag, waving her on dismissively. "It's probably some psycho playing games. And you know Fiona ain't with the games, boo."

"Uh-huh. That's what you get for giving out all them free samples of that good-good. Now you have a potential stalker on your hands." She laughs.

"Ooh, don't do me, boo. Oh no, oh no. Lies 'n' fabrications. This juicy-juicy does make the boys go cuckoo, but I ain't signing up for the stalkers association. Oh no. Whoever it is better go stalk themselves on over to Thot-dotcom and catch the special on hookers 'n' hoes. Because Miss Fiona ain't on the list."

She keeps laughing.

I suck my teeth. "Boo-boo, I don't see nothing funny."

"Girl, relax," she says, shouldering her book bag.

"Yo, Fee," someone calls out in back of us as we snake our way through the crowded hallway.

I glance over my shoulder. It's Ceasar Mitchell, aka Lil

Cease—although there isn't one thing lil about this six-five, two-hundred-plus pound boy with his fine, sexy self, *trust*. But that's what they call him because he's named after his dad. Whatever. Cease stays having these lil McPherson High hot pockets tossing their panties at him. Ugh! Next to Miesha's boo, Antonio, Cease is second-in-command of the kingdom of whoredom. I think he's probably slept with as many girls as Antonio has; if not more.

I'm just glad he's never had any of my cute lil panty sets pasted up on his bedroom wall for wallpaper, or dangling from his ceiling fan. No ma'am, no sir.

"Ohgod," I mutter, rolling my eyes. "What does this hound want?"

"Who?" Miesha wants to know, glancing back. "Oh, Cease? Girl, be nice."

I smirk. "Mmph. I'm always nice."

"Yo, what's good, My?" he says as he's walking in step alongside us, wrapping his big muscled arm around me.

"Hey, Cease," Miesha says, smiling.

"Yo, what's good, Fee?"

"You're looking at it, boo," I say real sassy-like, tossing my hair, then pushing his arm off me. "Nature's goodness. Now how can I help you?"

"What you doing tonight?"

"Not you. Why?"

He laughs. "You cold, baby. But you know you still my boo."

"Yuck," I say.

Miesha laughs.

I roll my eyes.

"Yo, Fee, you need to stop playing with my emotions, for real for real," he says, feigning hurt.

"Boy, bye. And you need to stop playing with them nasty gizzards hanging in ya drawz, but you don't hear me talking."

He and Miesha crack up laughing.

"Girl, I can't with you."

"Yo, Fee, you shot out," he says, shaking his head. "That's why I effs with you, yo. I'ma catch y'all later, though."

"Bye, Cease," Miesha says, waving at him.

"Yeah, whatever," I say, eyeing him as he makes a bee-line into the boys' bathroom.

"Girl, you know you need to stop throwing Cease so much shade."

I swipe my bang from my face. "Girl, bye. I'm not thinking about him."

As soon as we round the corner, I spot loudmouth Quandaleesha. Not that I'm into being messy. But, chile, she's ratchet at its finest. And she's nuttier than a peanut patch. She's also Antonio's ex-boo. But I ain't one to gossip.

I glance at my watch. "Girl, we better step on it 'n' get to homeroom. You already know you can't be late. And Mr. Evans will flip his pacemaker if I step up in his homeroom late again. And trust. I have better things to do with my time than sittin' up in somebody's ole funky detention today."

"Later," she says, laughing as she steps into her own homeroom just as the bell rings.

"Ooh, *bish*," I hiss, racing down the hall. "I hate you."

7

Always keep a BWB—Boo With Benefits—on speed dial...

Miesha pulls out into the traffic, making her way across the other side of town to get to my house. As she drives I spot a group of boys coming out of a corner store 'n' immediately start salivating.

"Oooh, cutie alert! Blow the horn, girl!" I say, all excited as she drives by a group of sexy stud muffins walking down the Ave. "Oooh, yes. Three of 'em look like they could get it." I roll the passenger-side window down 'n' yell out, "Hey, boo-daddies. I see you."

They call out, holding their arms open like, "Yo, was-sup, baby..."

I stick my head back inside the car. "Girl, stop the whip. Pull over."

She presses down on the accelerator, rolling up my window with the press of a button, shutting down any hopes of snatching up a new boo-daddy. "Wrong answer, girl. I don't think so. I'm not checkin' for none of them boys."

"Umm, *hellooo*?" I snap a finger in her face. "I am. Just because you're all stuck on lover's island, doesn't mean you gotta try'n sink my ship. Let my boat float, boo."

"Well, you can float it on ya own time, girl. I'm tryna get home. It's bad enough I stayed behind waiting on *you* after school."

"Ooh, don't do it. I told you I couldn't be late to home-room. It isn't my fault that old sea monkey, Mr. Evans, has it out for me. That man lives to do me in. "

She laughs. "Well, that's what you get. You see I made it on time."

"Oh, whatever. The least you coulda done to help ease my detention woes was pull over so I could find solace in the arms of one of them sexy thug-daddies."

She glances over at me. "Not today. Not on my time."

I roll my eyes. "Party pooper."

"Whatever. Talk to the hand. You're too boy crazy."

I bat my lashes 'n' feign insult. "Who, *moi*?"

"Yes, *you*."

"I beg ya pardon. Never that! I'm *not* boy crazy. My boo juice doesn't splash for just any ole boy, hun."

She laughs. "If you say so."

"Ooh, ya messy behind's tryna serve me."

"Girl, bye. Think what you like. I'm tryna keep you from a buncha mess."

I give her a look. "Uh-huh. Sounds more like you tryna call me a ho on the low." I laugh. "And it ain't no secret, boo. I know I am."

She makes a left turn onto Martin Luther King Boule-vard, stopping at a light. I hear someone standing on the corner yelling out my name. I look. It's one of my ex-boos. Jerrell. Ooh, he's looking too damn fine for his own good. And mine. He isn't one of the tallest boys I rolled around 'n' got tangled up in the sheets with, but he sure was one of the sexiest. Deep, dark, delicious chocolate, mmph; need I say more? At five eleven, boo-daddy was (and still is) built like an African warrior. Chiseled outta soot. Dark like tar, but sweet like molasses. Mmm, yummy. And trust. What they say about the darker the berry the sweeter the juice, ain't no rumor, boo. And it ain't no lie, either.

Oh, then why aren't we still together?

Uhhh, *hellooo, hellooo…ding, ding, ding*! Because like with all the rest, I got bored with him. After about six weeks of feasting on his goodness, I dismissed him. Chile, cheese. He was tryna boo-bag me up 'n' I was not havin' it. What I look like, being wifed up? No, hun. Fiona Madison doesn't answer to no boy. And she doesn't commit to just one boy, either.

I toss him a lil wave. He flaps his tongue out at me. I lick my lips 'n' turn my head just as Miesha peels down the street. She swings a right onto Bergen.

"Fiona, girl," she says, glancing over at me. "I don't mean no harm, but you're too pretty to be messin' with all these boys out here. Don't you wanna settle down with one boy?"

I snap my neck in her direction, shifting in my seat. I look at her like she's crazy. *"Whaat?* Settle down? Who, *me?"*

She laughs. "Yeah, *you*. You know. Just chill with one boy, instead of having a buncha different boys all up in your face."

What? Girl, bye! Miss Chickie has let love soak her brain if she thinks I'ma ever be the settle-down type of chick.

Ha! Chill with one boy? Never that. I don't think so. Doesn't she know every diva should always have a rotation of cutie-boos at her beck 'n' call?

"Girl, *boom*! You have gone completely cuckoo-crazy. Why on earth would *I* wanna do some mess like that, huh? Boys are like playgrounds—no, no…like amusement parks. They can be fun 'n' tiring at times. And ohh so exciting the next. There's always something to hop up 'n' down on, bounce on, slide down on 'n' spin around on. It's like one big thrilling rollercoaster ride. You never know what you're gonna get or how the ride is gonna end until you strap up 'n' take it for a spin."

She turns down onto my street, shaking her head. "Ohmigod! Fiona, girl, you're a hot mess!" She starts laughing. "Only you would say some crazy ish like that. What about love, girl?"

I rapidly blink my eyes at her. Oh no, this messy *heffa* didn't just go there! Cursing me with that, that, that dirty *L*-word!

"*Love?* What about it?"

"Don't you want it?"

"No. I'm allergic to it."

She laughs. "Whatever. No. I'm serious. Don't you ever wish you had a boo you could call your own? Someone you can love 'n' know he's the same boy who loves you back?"

"Girl, please." I tsk. "There's no guarantee he's gonna love you back."

"Well, no. But you can't be afraid to take a risk, either. Sometimes you have to trust your heart. Look at me 'n' Antonio. I wasn't beat for him at first 'cause I knew he was a dog, but he kept pressin' me until I finally gave in, 'n' look at us now. Madly in love. And I trust him with all my heart."

"Ooh, Oprah, boo," I say sarcastically, rolling my eyes dramatically. "I didn't know you had it in you. Sign me up."

She rolls her eyes. "Yeah, yeah, yeah. Whatever. You don't know what you're missing out on, boo."

"Girl, let me stop. I do have it."

She gives me a confused look. "You have *what*?"

"Lots of love."

She stops her car in front of my house 'n' tilts her head. "Oh, really?"

I smirk. "Yes. I *love* turnin' boys out. It ain't no secret. I love sex, boo. Don't you? 'Cause I know you 'n' that boo-daddy of yours stays playin' Twister in the sheets."

She laughs. "Sex is not the most important thing with me and Antonio. Yes, I enjoy it with him. But it's not all we do. I love him for him. Not for what he does or doesn't do in bed. I enjoy his company."

I blink. "Dear gawd!" I clutch my chest. "*Boooorrrring*."

"Fiona, I think it's time you shut ya legs more 'n' open ya heart to love, boo."

"Girl, no." I shake my head. "Not interested. Love doesn't have a home here, boo. Lust is the only thing livin' in my heart."

She gives me a look that borders more on pity than appreciation for my truths. And I give it right back. Trust. There's nothing pitiful about *me* not wanting to be boo'd up with only one boy. If God didn't want me to indulge my desires, why would He tempt me, huh? Why would He dangle so many fine, mouthwatering cuties out in front of me, knowing my weakness, if He didn't want me to reach out 'n' sample 'em, huh?

I tell you why. Because He wants me to indulge. Because monogamy is about as played out as them dusty hood roaches on *Love & Hip Hop*, chasing behind that old nasty Joe Budden, okay? Ain't nobody got time for that. So, forbidden fruit or not, it is my mission, my divine diva purpose, to pluck more than one sweet, juicy, sexy boo-daddy from off the vine, gobble him up, then spit him out 'n' send him on his merry way. And, yes, boo. I stay doing it for the vine. Don't you?

"One nice boy is all you need, girl." She unlocks the car doors. "All that messin' with a buncha boys is real whack."

I wave her on, then grab my bag. "Umm, hello? Speak for ya'self. Why settle for one nice boy, when I can have two or three? No, thanks, hun. I'll leave all that stay-true-to-one-boo for you 'n' Tone."

She curls her lip up. "Mmph. Looks like you got company."

I look over toward the house, 'n' sure enough. There's Benji—one of my ex-BWBs—standing on my porch, uninvited 'n' unannounced. Now that's a no-no. Still, I can't help but lick my lips at the thought of seeing him stripped down to nothing but his boxers and Timbs.

Anyway, I'd been messing with Benji since like the beginning of the school year up until three weeks ago, when I decided to finally *chop* him. But every now 'n' then he still comes around. The thing with us, we had a special understanding. He didn't sweat me. I didn't sweat him. He wasn't my man. Just a boo-daddy with benefits. So he did what he did 'n' I did what I did. It cut down on all the drama. There was no cheating. No lying. And we both stayed very happy.

Well, that's until he no longer stayed on script 'n'

started tryna check for me like I was wifey. Stepping up to me at school tryna mark his territory. Getting all up in my face. Boy, bye! He mighta *thought* he was Ike, but I ain't Tina 'n' he ain't beatin' up this box. So, *boom*!

"Girl, please. That boy 'n' his love-stick are of no further use to me." I open the car door.

"Call me later," she says.

"Okay. Ummm, can I help you?" I say to Benji, shutting Miesha's car door.

"What's goodie, yo?" A smile eases over his fine, brown face.

I roll my eyes. "I don't know what's good with *you*. But I know what's not *goodie*. And that's *you* stalking my porch."

He chuckles. "Go 'head wit' that, yo. Ain't nobody stalkin' you."

"Uh-huh. Lies. But whatever! Why you here?"

"What you think, yo," he says, grinning again as I make my way up the stairs. Mmph. With his ole freak-nasty self. "I'm tryna chill."

I roll my eyes. "Define chill."

He sucks his teeth. "C'mon, yo. Don't front. You already know what it is."

"Uh, noooo. I know what it was. And I know what it isn't. If you wanted to chill with me, you shoulda brought ya butt to school 'n' chilled in class."

"Nah, I'm good. I wasn't beat today." He tries to pull me into him. He smells of weed 'n' alcohol.

I frown, pushing him back. "Are you frickin' kidding me right now? You're lit up."

"Nah. But I'm nice."

I sigh. A boy with no ambition, no motivation, no dang

drive—other than gettin' high 'n' gettin' his rocks off—is such a turnoff. I brush by him, opening the glass storm door.

He steps up in back of me. "Don't front, yo. You know we hot like fire together." His breath is hot on my neck.

I smirk. "Uh-huh. Hot fire or not, you ain't gettin' up in here, lil boo-daddy. So go have a seat. Ya heat 'n' hot flames ain't welcome here. So go take it over to some other ho's spot 'cause you ain't burnin' up no sheets over here. Not today." He tries to force his way in behind me as I slide my key in 'n' open the door.

He presses himself up into me. I bump him backward. "I know you straight up buggin', boy." He grabs me again. I push him off of me, again. "I'm not playin', Benji. The only thing I want is for you to go home. Or get maced down. Now, good day! Please 'n' thank you."

"Oh, word? It's like—"

I slam the door in his face, then press my back up against the door 'n' slide my way down to the floor. As sure as my name is Fiona, that boy's lucky I knocked him outta his rotation slot 'n' I'm done with him. Otherwise, I woulda wrapped my lips around him 'n' had me a taste of that lil boo-daddy juice. Trust.

8

Never let another chick steal your shine...

The one thing I hate more than a cheap pair of heels or a handbag with them frayed raggedy edges is a phony *bish*! And, trust. McPherson High's halls are flooded with the likes of 'em. Fakes. A buncha wannabe Barbies. All tryna be the next Nicki Minaj. Whoop, whoop! Chile, boom! Who let the clowns out! Epic fails!

Besides me, Miesha, 'n' a few of the cheerleaders, all these other chickies clucking around here in their *thot* wear 'n' lace fronts are straight-up fraudulent. Okay, well, not all of 'em. But most of 'em definitely are. And those are the ones that make the palms of my hands itch to slap 'em up. All they do is smile up in your face 'n' talk about you behind your back. Then when you step to 'em 'n' confront 'em, they wanna start hemming 'n' hawing 'n' backpedaling. Chile, boom!

But every now 'n' then I entertain their foolery. After all, I know how to serve up a dish of messy with the best of 'em. Bottom line for me is this: A real diva is her only competition. So *no* chick can do *me* better than I can do myself. No matter how hard she tries.

Trust.

"What, you can't speak?" this chick Alicia says, walking over to my locker as I'm slamming it shut. I look her up 'n' down. She's standing here holding a half-eaten Pop-Tart, wearing a pair of nondescript jeans with a cute lil black off-the-shoulder blouse 'n' a pair of red heels. Nine West, I think. But what I care? Not my feet. Not my worry.

She tosses her hair.

Two can play that. I flick mine. "Should you be eating that mess? Didn't you just get a ton of gut fat sliced outta you last summer?"

She rolls her eyes, sucking her teeth. "Don't worry about what I eat."

I shrug. "Your body." I flick my hair over my shoulder. "Now. How can I help you?"

"Don't get cute," she says, placing a hand up on her now size ten hips. *Now* being the operative word, because before her parents sent her away to some chunky girls' farm last summer, she was a thick, six-piece-'n'-a-biscuit, greasy-spoon, eat-a-whole-cake kinda chick. Size eighteen or twenty, I think. All I know is, she had like a sixty-inch waist 'n' was a real big beef patty. But now that she's serving up a few new curves 'n' a smaller waistline, she's really feelin' herself.

Now, I'm not gonna hate or even throw shade on the chick. Because that's not how I do mine. No, no. No, hun. No shade, ever. I give credit where credit's due. Alicia's real cute in the face. She has high cheekbones 'n' a kinda thin nose. She kinda looks...exotic. And her new 'n' improved body makes her fourth runner-up for the next Wish I Could Be You world pageant. Still, she ain't ready to go up against *moi*.

I blink. "Come again? Don't *get* cute? Ooh, hun, I *stay* cute. Would you like my autograph now or later, sweetie?"

She flicks a dismissive wave at me. "Girl, bye. Not."

I shake my head 'n' walk off, heading down the hall.

She falls into step alongside me, unwelcome. "What I wanna know is why you stood me up yesterday."

I shoot her an icy glare. "Excuse *you*? Sweetie, I know I didn't let you get the cookie last night, so why is you coming at me like you just blew my back out?"

"Tramp, bye. Miss me with that. You can't do a thing for me."

I give her a dismissive flick of the wrist. "Girl, have several seats. What do you want?"

She rolls her eyes. Tells me I was supposed to meet her down at the library so we could work on our English Lit project together. Uh, hel-*lo*? I didn't know I needed to hold her by the hand to get it done.

"Alicia, boo. Riddle me this, *hun*—'n' I'm only gonna ask you this one time: Did I eff with you when you had that double chin 'n' were rockin' thick glasses 'n' wobblin' your way down the halls the last three years?"

She frowns.

"Exactly," I say, not giving her a chance to respond. "I didn't do you then. So I'm not doing you *now*, sweetie, just 'cause you can finally squeeze ya'self into a pair of stretch leggings 'n' not look like a beached whale wrapped in Saran wrap. So if you think staying after school to work on some paper with you is gonna happen, you're sadly mistaken, hun. You do your portion. And…"

She bucks her eyes.

"Yo, what's good, Fiona?" P-Money—I mean, Pauley—says, walking by. *Hunnni*…listen. He's a real cutie-boo for a white boy. And he loves him some chocolate pie. Mmph. And he's hanging, too. Oh, how I know? Mmph. How you think? I sampled the vanilla stick. Let him swirl it all up in my chocolate love-cup last summer when I ran into him down on the Ave. one night. I sure did. Things got real hot 'n' heavy for like fifteen minutes, then it was over. Boy, bye. My engine was just gettin' revved up 'n' here this boy was already at the finish line. Sweating like he'd run a two-hundred-mile race. Mmph. Noooo, thank you!

"Heey, Pauley," I coo, checking him out. He's rocking the new KDs with a pair of baggy jeans. His red polo shirt is half tucked-in. And his long hair is done up in cornrows. Two weeks ago he wore his dirty-blond hair out in a huge 'fro.

Mmph. Can you say confused?

This boy can't decide if he wants to be the next Huey P. Newton or Snoop Dogg one minute or Malcolm X the next. Chile, boom! I can't with him.

"What's good, Alicia?" he says, keeping his shimmering blue eyes on me.

"You, boo," she says, grinning ear to ear. But she's too caught up in tryna be fabulous to see he isn't even checkin' for her like that. "You still have my number?"

He peels his gaze away from me, glancing at her. "Yeah, I got it. Why? You tryna chill?"

She smacks her lips. "Maybe."

I laugh.

Alicia shoots me a dirty look. "I know you not even tryna hate."

"*Hate?* No, hun. Never that."

"Then what the hell's so funny?"

I raise a brow. "First of all, check ya tone, boo. Second of all"—I ease up on Pauley 'n' loop an arm through his—"he ain't checkin' for you. Now, good day."

Pauley grins, then looks over at her. "Yo, me 'n' my baby out. I'll holla."

"Not today you won't," I say, tossing a look over at Alicia. She peers at me through narrow slits. I toss my hair. "Don't hate, boo."

"Eff you, tramp," she hisses, storming off in the other direction.

Pauley laughs. "Yo, why you do ole girl like that? You ice cold, babe."

I shrug. "I don't wanna talk about her."

He grins again, glancing at me. "Oh, word? What you wanna talk about? Me 'n' you?"

I frown. "C'mon again. Not," I say as we turn the corner toward my geometry class. "I hear you done bagged you up some ratchet-snatch."

He laughs. "Yo, you crazy, Fee. Word is bond. Where you hear that?"

"Don't worry, boo-boo. News travels. Besides, ya name's scribbled all over the girls' bathroom wall 'bout how you been motorboatin' Quanda's jugs."

He cracks up. "You wildin', yo. Hahahahaha. But, nah, nah. It ain't even like that. We just chillin'."

"Uh-huh. Code word for we sexin'."

He keeps laughing.

"You know I'm not one to gossip. But—" I stop, eyeing Quanda as she walks in our direction. "Ooh, here come ya boo now," I tease, leaning into him.

He laughs, shaking his head. "She ain't my *boo*. Just somethin' to do."

"Uh-huh. Good luck with that."

Quanda squints, her eyes darting from me to Pauley, then locking onto my arm looped through his. She stops deadsmack in front of us. Hand on hip, head cocked. "Umm, Pauley. You not even 'bout to play me, boy." She shoots me a look. "Umm. Do you mind gettin' up off my man?"

I look up at him, easing my arm free. "Ooh-ooh, no worries, hun. He's all yours." I start laughing. "Apparently somebody didn't get the memo. Pauley, I'll catch you later, boo."

He gives me a nod. "No doubt. Yo, what's good, Quanda? Why you steppin' up on me like that, like you tryna check a nucca? You know what it is, yo."

"I don't 'preciate you disrespectin' me, huggin' up on no trick."

I blink. Stop in my tracks. Turn to look at her. "Excuse *you*?"

"You heard me," she snaps. "Get ya own damn man 'n' stay the hell away from mine! You hoes stay tryna steal somebody else's boyfriend."

"Yo, hol' up, hol' up," Pauley says, putting his hands up. "Chill, Quanda. Now you doin' too much."

"Chill, hell, boy! You not gonna be playin' me."

I start laughing. "Ooh, sounds like somebody forgot to take her cuckoo meds this morning. Girl, bye. I'm not thinkin' about Pauley. And I'm definitely *not* thinking about *you*."

Quanda starts gettin' loud as usual, rolling her neck 'n' talking. Always on ten, always ready to bring the rah-rah, this chick loves attention. Loves to make a scene. She makes a buncha promises to beat my face in if I ever disrespect her again. Demands I keep my hands off of Pauley.

Now her lil performance becomes amusing to me. I crack up laughing. "Girl, *boom*! You a real live circus, boo. Go have several seats at the back of the bus, sweetie, 'cause you ain't ready for the front row. Trust. If I *wanted* Pauley, I would have him. Been there, done that. All you're doing, sweetie, is chasing behind what I've already had."

"All right, girls," Mrs. Sheldon—one of the AP English teachers—says, coming out of her classroom. "You girls break this nonsense up 'n' get to class before both of you find yourselves in detention."

Quanda sucks her teeth. "Oh, this ain't over."

"Girl, bye! Kiss my phatty, silly trick."

I step off just as the bell rings.

9

By seventh period I push into Mr. Nandi's African-American Studies class, exhausted 'n' so ready to get this class 'n' the rest of this day over with. And it doesn't help that my G-string keeps irritating the heck outta me. Oh, this is so, so not cute. I slide onto my chair in the back of the class, pulling out my notebook 'n' pen from my bag.

I glance up at the wall clock. The bell rang four minutes ago 'n' there's still no sign of Mr. Nandi. He's always late. Mostly because the old freak be all up in the staff lounge tryna sniff up in the French teacher Mrs. Duvet's drawz. She's married. He's married. And they both being messy. The whole school knows that she doesn't have a class seventh period, so he sneaks a few minutes right after his sixth period class to make goo-goo eyes at her. If you ask me—which you didn't—I think Mrs. Duvet gave his ole nasty butt some.

Ugh. How sickening.

"Yo, you ready for the test?" Travis Richardson says as he

slides into the seat next to me. He's one of my ex-boos. Dark chocolate, just like I like 'em. Okay, okay. He's not dark chocolate; try blueberry black. But whatever. Miesha has him in one of her classes. Algebra, I think. Anyway, she can't stand him. She calls him Crispy Critter. Yeah, he's exceptionally ugly in the face, but his body is ridiculous. Whew! Yes, lawd gawd, *hunni*! Seeing him standing in the middle of his bedroom in his wifebeater 'n' his boxers with a pair of Timbs on used to give me life. Yes, *hunni*! Muscles everywhere. But, honey-boo, trust. The minute he stepped outta them drawz. Womp, womp, womp. Chile, boom! Ring the alarm. Who stole the beef, boo? Just sinful. But whatever. I'm not messy so I'm not gonna go in on him like that. All we ever did was kiss 'n' grind 'n' I gave him a lil hand time, if you know what I mean. But whatever. That itty-bitty situation he's got going on in his lap is not my concern. Finding out more about this test is.

I peel my gaze from his big juicy lips 'n' look him in his eyes. "What test?"

He shakes his head, gettin' up from his seat. "Damn. I was tryna cheat off you. But I see you just as effed up as me. Wit' ya ugly azz."

I suck my teeth. "Boy, bye. Don't do me. Have you seen a mirror lately? Ugly is ya birthmark, boo. You wear it every day."

"Yeah, a'ight. I got ya ugly, all right."

I flick him a dismissive wave. "Yeah. You wish. It's painted on ya face."

"I got—"

"Okay, class," Mr. Nandi says, whisking through the door carrying a stack of papers. Silence quickly fills the air. Everyone knows Mr. Nandi can get real slick at the mouth, so no one says or does anything to get him turnt up. "My apologies for my tardiness. I was having copies made."

I purse my lips as he makes his way up to the front of the class. *Uh-huh. Sure you were.* He sets the stack of papers on his desk, then walks over to the chalkboard and starts writing.

"I need for everyone to clear off their desks. The only thing you should have out is either a pen or pencil. Nothing else. If you do, I will fail you." He turns to the class. "Is that understood?"

Everyone responds. Well, almost everyone. I'm still stuck on the fact that there's a test today. A test I do not recall being apprised of. Ooh, this is *so, so,* not good. Now I have to try to stage an escape so I don't wind up failing it. Getting an F is *not* an option. Oh no, boo. Fiona doesn't flunk, okay?

"Umm, Mister Nandi, sir?" I say all sweet 'n' whatnot, raising my hand.

He turns from the chalkboard 'n' looks at me. "Yes, Miss Madison." He tilts his head. If I were a wacko pervert who was into stalking senior citizens, I'd probably have a slight crush on him. He's tall 'n' blueberry dark with smooth, shiny skin. Not a wrinkle in sight for an old man. I'm not even gonna lie. But, um, he probably could get it, too, if I were like in my forties.

"How can I help you?" he says, smirking. "Let me guess. You didn't know there was a test today, so you're not prepared. Is that it, Miss Madison?"

I twirl the end of a curl, then toss my hair. "No. I'm prepared..." Lies. "I'm not feeling good, though." I lean forward, clutching my stomach. I grimace. "Uh. I really need a pass to the nurse's office."

He scans the classroom. "Who else needs a pass to the nurse's office because they're ill-prepared for today's test?" Everyone turns 'n' looks over at me.

I blink. *Oooh, he's tryna do me!*

"Well, I'll tell you what, Miss Madison." He walks over to his desk, pulls out a pink-slip pad, then starts writing. "If you need to make a mad dash for the nurse's office then go right ahead. But know this. You will still get an F. There will be no makeup tests. Do you understand?"

He tears off the hall pass then lays it on the edge of his desk.

I swallow. "Umm. That's okay. I'll wait until after I'm done."

"Smart girl. All right, class," he says, grabbing the stack of papers from off his desk. "Once the test is in front of you, you may begin. There are a total of ten questions, each worth ten points."

I say a silent prayer as he finally gets to my row 'n' places the test paper in front of me. The first question: How did the slave trade in Africa differ from the Atlantic slave trade?

I blink. Stare at the question for several minutes, then skip down to question number two: What was the Middle Passage?

Okay, okay. I know this one. I write in my answer, then move down to the next question: How did the American Revolution weaken slavery?

Yesss, *hunni*! I know this one as well. Now feeling more confident, I delve in, my brain clicking in overdrive to an-swer each question to ensure my grade is anything higher than a C.

Mmph. Old geezer tryna do me. Ha! I don't think so.

With twenty minutes left of class, I'm finished. I skim over all my answers. Well, the eight that I knew. The other two I just put what I thought made sense. Then I look up from my test 'n' see everyone else still bent over their papers. I roll my eyes at Travis, who's tryna sneak a peek on the low over at this chick Natalie's test. I'm not gonna be messy 'cause that's not how I do mine. But she isn't the brightest lightbulb in the socket, so I'm not even sure why he's straining his eyeballs over on her desk. Desperation brings out the worst in us, I suppose.

I glance at my answers one more time, then stand up 'n' walk to the front of the room, my hips swishin' 'n' swayin' every which way like nobody's business. Truth is, I'm shakin' 'n' poppin' these hips tryna get this annoying crack-floss situated. I make a mental note to never, ever wear these things to school again.

I plop my test paper on Mr. Nandi's desk.

He looks up from his magazine. "Ah, Miss Madison. Finished already?"

"Yup." I toss my hair.

He picks up the test 'n' glances at my answers. He eyes me, then reaches for the hall pass. "I guess you won't be needing this after all."

I blink. "Umm. Come again. Yes, sir, I still do. Please 'n' thank you."

He raises his brow 'n' eyes me all kinda crazy before he hands me the hall pass. I turn 'n' hurriedly head back to my desk to gather my things. Of course, Travis says something real slick under his breath as I walk by his desk. I pop him upside his pickle head.

"Ow."

"Miss Madison!" Mr. Nandi scolds. "I will not have violence in my classroom. Do I make myself clear?"

I roll my eyes.

"Miss Madison, do you hear me speaking to you?"

"I heard you," I snap, snatching up my handbag.

"Good. Now hear this: You'll have two days' detention starting tomorrow."

"*Whaaat?* Are you *frickin'* kidding me, right now? He's the one who said he wanted to eat my cookie out!" I smack Travis upside his head again.

"Now let's make it three days. And if you keep it up you'll find yourself spending the rest of the week in in-school suspension." Travis laughs. "Mister Richardson, I wouldn't be too quick to laugh if I were you because if I catch your eyes wandering over onto anyone else's test paper again, I'm going to fail you."

I stomp off, swinging open the classroom door. I shut the door, mindful not to slam it. I'm pissed. Not stupid, okay?

"Yo, what's good, Fiona?" Benji says as he's coming out of a classroom across the hall at the same time as me. He licks his lips, then grins. "Damn, this must be my lucky moment. I was just 'bout to hit the bathroom to handle this situation in my pants, but here you are."

I roll my eyes. "No. Your lucky moment will be when you graduate from high school." I keep walking. "But don't let me stop you from handlin' that situation in ya drawz."

He hurries over 'n' falls into step beside me. "Yeah, a'ight. Whatever, yo. Where you on ya way to?"

"Why?"

"Let's go sneak in the girls' bathroom."

I shoot him a nasty look. "Boy, bye. Your ten-minute joyrides into heaven are over, boo."

He laughs. "You know you still want this beef jerky."

"Lies, lies, 'n' more lies. Think what you like, boo-boo."

He moves in closer to me 'n' lightly nudges my shoulder with his as we round the corner for the stairs. As soon as we get into the stairwell, he's up on me, pulling me into him. His hand moves all over me. He covers my lips with a kiss.

"Stop!" I say, tryna push him off me. But he doesn't let go of me. He keeps pressing himself into me, tryna feel up on my boobs. So now I gotta turn it up a notch. "What the hell?! I said stop, Benji! Get off me!"

Whap! I slap his face. Then knee him in his groin. He lunges over, grabbing his crotch.

"Ow, ow, ow!"

"See, I told you to get off me." I slap him again. "No means no. Asshole!"

I storm off down the stairs. I don't know if I'm more pissed at the fact that he really tried to do me in the stairwell, or that I almost broke a fingernail.

All I know is, I need a Pepsi 'n' a cigarette!

10

Always keep 'em guessing...

"Yo, for real for real, that was some real foul ish I pulled on you earlier," Benji says over the phone. His voice is low 'n' he sounds apologetic. But I'm not letting him off the hook. One thing I don't *ever* do is let some boy disrespect me 'n' think it's all good. Oh, nooo, honey-boo. Not cute! I'll take it straight to his head, face, throat, and/or them lil man-nuggets hanging between his legs.

Don't do me!

"I was dead wrong, yo."

"So why'd you do it then?" I unbuckle my jeans, then slide them down over my hips 'n' step outta them. "After I told you to get off 'a me?"

"I don't know."

"Lies 'n' fabrications," I say, stepping outta this annoying thong, then tossing it in the trash. Ugh. I slip into a pair of boxer shorts one of my BWBs left here one night after a hot night of bed bouncing. Chile, mmph! But I don't ever kiss 'n' tell, so movin' along. He accidentally overslept 'n' had to be hurried outta here through the window when I heard my mother downstairs. But he left his drawz hanging on the doorknob in all the haste. But whatever.

He had to get up outta here, free-ballin' 'n' all. Ruthie-Ann was not about to catch me in bed with some boy. Oh no-no-no, honey-boo. I'm too classy for that. Okay, okay... all right already. I'm too slick for that. At least I like to think I am.

I pull my AP English reading assignment—*The Bluest Eye* by Toni Morrison—from out of my bag, then sit cross-legged in the center of my bed, holding my cell up to my ear. We're having a discussion on this book in class on Thursday 'n' I am nowhere near finished. But I will be. So far, from what I've read, it's such a depressing story. And, *hunni*, trust. *Depression* 'n' *Fiona* do not fit in the same sentence. Ain't nobody got time to be feeling sorry for themselves or some character in a book. Chile, *boom*!

"Well," I say, tossing the novel over onto the side of my bed 'n' glancing over at the time on my laptop: 8:34 P.M. "I'm still waiting for you to tell me why you did what you did." I decide I'm giving this boy five more minutes of my time, then it's a wrap. I've already given him enough of my precious time. He's lucky I don't have him stomped out for tryna do me today.

I yawn.

"On some real, yo. Thinkin' 'bout you, then seein' you. You got me goin' through it, yo. I mean. I had you on the brain all day, rememberin' all the lil freaky ish we used to do when we used to chill 'n'..." He sighs. "I was buggin', yo. I was on rock all day. Then when I saw you comin' outta class at the same time as me, I don't know. I wanted you, nah'mean. But I was dead wrong, a'ight?"

I twist my lips up. "Uh-huh. What, was you on that molly trip?"

"Yo, you wildin'. Hell no. I don't eff wit' that ish, yo. Straight bud 'n' that Fireball when I wanna get my drink on. You already know."

Yeah. I know. Your horny behind is a pothead 'n' a future drunk.

"Mmph. So thinkin' about this goody-goody got you actin' all nutty, is that what you saying? Got you tryna snatch a chick's drawz off, huh?"

He laughs.

"Boy, I am *not* laughing."

"Nah, nah. I know you dead-azz, Fee. It's just how you said it, that's all."

I grunt. "Well, it doesn't make a difference how I say it. No means *no*. Next time you're gonna get more than a knee to your man jewels, boo. Next time I'ma claw 'em out with my nails, then sling 'em out into traffic. Don't get it twisted. So the next time a girl says stop or get off her, get the hell off."

"You right, yo. My bad. I just miss chillin' wit' you."

"Well, you sure have a crazy way of showin' it. We coulda still been chillin' if *you* didn't mess it up tryna make me wifey. You know I told you I wasn't wifey material, so why you even tried to take me there is beyond craziness."

He blows a breath out into the phone. "True, true."

"Are you smoking?"

"Yeah. A mild."

I shake my head. Between you 'n' me, Benji coulda

been upgraded to "main boo-daddy" status had he played it cool 'cause, *hunni*, he knew/knows how to ride these curves. And his engine stays revved up. Trust. Every time we were together it was a turn-out-the-lights-'n'-light-a-candle-then-tear-the-sheets-up kinda night.

"Keep it a hunnid, yo. You miss chillin'?"

Ooh, I miss the sex.

"Nope."

He laughs. "Yeah, a'ight. Front if you want."

"Then why you ask?"

"Maybe I wanna hear it." He lowers his voice. "Yo, let's Skype. I wanna show you somethin'."

Now it's my turn to laugh. "Bwahahahaha. Boy, bye! I ain't Skypin' with you. You can't show me anything I haven't already seen. You better go light a blunt 'n' have several seats."

"Yo, I'm about to spark up in a minute. What you gettin' into tonight?"

"My sheets."

"Alone?"

"Not with you," I say, picking up my comb from off my vanity. I start running it through my hair.

He laughs. "Ouch. That hurt."

"Whatever. Are you coming to school tomorrow? Or do you plan on spending your day drinking 'n' smoking the day away?"

I ask him this, unsure as to why I even care. It's his life, not mine. I guess a part of me still kinda likes him. Okay, okay. I do. But not enough. Anyway, he needs a whole lot more than a nice body 'n' a good sex game to keep a diva like me interested. And, even more, he needs to be focused in school. Please. What I look like, spending my time or my life with some boy who can't even graduate from high school? Oh no, hun. I don't do dropouts or chronic truants.

"Nah, nah," he says, exhaling into the phone. "I'ma pro-lly chill. I got some moves to make later tonight, so it depends."

I frown. "Benji, are you hustlin' now?"

Silence.

"Listen," I say quickly. Somehow feeling the need to let him off the hook. "Forget I even asked. Okay?"

Finally he takes a deep breath. "Nah. It's all good. I'm doin' me, a'ight?"

"But why? The streets are hot 'n' you know the po-po stay running up on ninjas. They baggin' everybody. This is your last year in school. Why would you wanna risk messing everything up like that, huh?"

"Yeah. I hear you. But school ain't really doin' it for me right now, babe. A muhfuggah tryna stack them ends, nah'mean? I gotta do what I gotta do. The struggle is real, yo. I'm tryna eat, feel me?"

This conversation is over. Okay? Heck, what more can I say? He ain't my boo-daddy. And he'll never be someone I'd spend the rest of my life with. So if missing school to be in the streets to be some low-level dealer is what he aspires to be, who am I to knock him? No judgment, honey-boo. Trust.

"Then go eat, boo-boo."

11

Say hi to the haters...

"Yo, what's good, sexy?" Brent Selder says, walking over toward my locker. It's like four minutes 'til the third period bell rings. And here he stands.

Sexy? Boo, I know I'm sexy. Still...

Brent has never, *ever*, called me that. Not that I need him to, 'cause trust. Fiona doesn't need a boy to confirm what she already knows. I was born sexy. Okay? Anyway, Brent's one of the star players on the lacrosse team 'n' one of the finest, sexiest boys alive. Okay? Yesss, *hunni*. He can get it. All day. Every day! With his Indian-looking self.

Now hold up. I know some of you are rolling your eyes up in ya heads sayin', *Please. Who* can't *get it?* Don't do me, honey-boo. I'ma tell you like I tell everyone else: Sex is good for the soul, hun. Trust. Besides, I keep tellin' you I don't have sex with everyone. Only boys I really like. Or if I'm extra bored 'n' don't have anything better to do. Anyway...

I eye Brent real slow 'n' sexy-like, batting my long lashes. He's in a pair of gym shorts 'n' a sweaty McPherson tank, looking all delish 'n' whatnot. Boo, I ain't even gonna front. If I was a messy kinda chick, he could get the cookie unwrapped. Yes, gawd! Ooh, I know he'd make some pretty babies with all that wavy hair 'n' beautiful skin. Not that I'm thinking about gettin' knocked up by him or any other boy. This is all hypothetically speaking. You know. *If* I did give him the cookie raw, 'n' *if* I wanted to push out his babies. Uh, I mean, baby. 'Cause I'm only letting one stretch out this bangin' body. Fiona isn't doing the kitten thing, okay? Popping out four 'n' five babies. I think not!

And I'm not tryna be like my mother, havin' babies mad young. Chile, please. She was pregnant at fifteen 'n' had my sister Leona when she was sixteen. Then she popped out my sister Kara when she was eighteen. Then my sister Sonji at twenty-one. Then Karina when she was twenty-four. Then nine years later came her mishap. Me. Some hot 'n' heavy one-night stand in the backseat of my daddy's pickup truck. Mmph. And she *thinks* I wanna end up like that. No, honey-boo. I think not!

I glance down at Brent's legs. Deargawd! They're beautiful. Mmph. I have to fight the urge to reach down 'n' swipe a hand up over his thick, heart-shaped calves, then up his brown, hairy, muscular thigh. Oooh, I just wanna forget where I am 'n' have my way with him.

I shut my locker 'n' pop my lips. "It's about time you got ya mind right, lil boo-daddy, 'n' recognize sexy when you see it. It took you long enough."

He grins, walking alongside of me. "Nah. I always knew you were sexy."

I stop in my tracks. Run a hand up my hip, then toss my

hair. "Well, of course I *am*. I'm drippin' with sexiness, hun. Glad you know."

He laughs, shaking his head. "Fiona, you mad funny. But seriously, how you?"

"Fine 'n' fabulous, boo. Can't you see?"

He laughs some more. "Oh, I see you."

"Uh-huh. So why all of a sudden you steppin' to me?"

He smiles. "I'm sayin'. I've been kinda checkin' for you for a minute, but I didn't really know how to step to you."

I twist my lips. "Uh-huh. Last I checked you were still goo-goo, ga-ga over Miesha."

The beginning of the school year all the hot boys were tryna get at Miesha 'cause she was the new chick on the campus. Fresh meat. And Brent was one of the many boys tryna make a move on her. But Antonio snatched her up 'n' shut all that down real quick.

"Nah, nah. She wasn't checkin' for me like that. She's wit' who she's supposed to be wit'. So it's all wavy, baby. We just mad cool."

I eye him. "What, so you think I'm gonna be second runner-up to Miesha?"

"Nah. It's not even like that. On some real, I didn't really think you were beat for me."

Ooh, I'm so, so beat for you, boo-daddy! You have no idea.

I smirk, slinging my massive Michael Kors bag up over my shoulder. "Boy, bye. I'm still *not* beat for you."

He laughs. "Yeah, a'ight. What you doing after school? You wanna chill 'n' go grab something to eat?"

I blink twice. "*Chill*, like in a *date*?"

"Nah. Not unless you want it to be."

"Uh-huh. Well, I'ma have'ta pass. My sister's picking me

up after school." He wants to know what time I'll be home. I tell him late. He wants to know about tomorrow. I tell him maybe; if I'm feeling generous.

He laughs. "Oh, word? It's like that?"

I grin. "Maybe."

I notice this big wide-back chick Samantha in my peripheral vision—elbowing Quanda and pointing over at Brent 'n' me. Of course I'm not one to entertain dumbness, so I act like I don't peep it.

"Heeey, Brent, baby," Sam says all deep 'n' husky, sounding like she tosses back whiskey 'n' smokes a pack of Marlboros a day. She's such a big-hand man-girl. All done up with a buncha clown paint on her face 'n' drawn-on eyebrows. Where they doin' that at? Using Magic Marker to draw on eyebrows? Mmph. Only the circus, honey-boo. Only the daggone circus.

All I can say is, *Send in the clowns*.

"What's up, Sam?" Brent says to her, thrusting his chin up at her.

"You, boo. It's all you."

He smiles. Quanda speaks to him. He speaks back. I act like she's invisible.

Samantha says, "So whose man you tryna steal now, FeFe?"

Quanda laughs.

I cringe. I hate that name *FeFe*. It sounds so, so nasty. Like feces, or something horny inmates use in prison with Vaseline 'n' spit to do they nasty business in. Ugh. This beast is really tryna do me. But I'll never give her the satisfaction of knowing that she gets under my skin calling me that. Oh no, hun. That's not what a diva does.

I eye her. She's in a pair of tight jeans 'n' a white blouse with a pair of wedge heels on her big feet, looking like the next top flop from off of *RuPaul's Drag Race*. But I ain't one to be messy.

So my lips are sealed.

I simply laugh in her face.

12

"So how was school?" my sister Leona asks the minute I slide into her Benz 'n' buckle my seat belt. When I get old like her, I wanna be just like her. Fierce. Young heads stay checkin' for her, but she ain't havin' it. I don't blame her, though. She has a master's degree in marketing from NYU, owns a fabulous crib with tons 'n' tons of closet space packed with designer clothes 'n' heels 'n' handbags for days. And she has a fab job working in the city for American Express, making loads of money. She gets to travel all over the world, so I can understand why she wouldn't be interested in havin' a young boo-daddy on her arm.

But if you ask me, girlie needs to drop down 'n' get her freak on. I mean, she needs some serious sheet action. All work 'n' no play is soooo not it. For the life of me, I can't understand why she doesn't have her a lil boo-daddy. It's not like she's disturbingly ugly or something, so I don't understand what the problem is. She claims she doesn't

have a man because she doesn't have time for one 'n' that
she refuses to settle.

Is that what they callin' it? *Settle?* Chile, boom! Her
manless drought is soo not cute. But, uh, um, so you settle for cobwebs all up in ya honeypot instead? Girl, bye!
Go out 'n' get you some!

I flip down the mirror 'n' recheck my lip gloss, sighing.
"My day was *borrrring*. New day, same old mess. But I did
almost have to beat this hood rat down for steppin' to me
over some boy a few days ago."

She looks over at me. "Please tell me you didn't."

"I said *almost*. You know fighting is not my thing unless
I'm provoked to take it there. Besides, who got time to be
breaking up fingernails? Not me."

"Good," she says, pulling off. "It's your senior year and
the last thing you need is to get yourself suspended for
foolishness. You know what happened the last time you
got into a fight."

Yeah. Don't I.

She's talking about the fight I had three years ago when
I stabbed this girl in her forehead with a fork because she
kept yappin' her jaws. I told the chick to fall back. To take
it down several notches. But she kept tryna bring the rah-
rah. She wanted to show out in front of her lil crew, so I
slammed a fork into her forehead, then beat her down.
Yeah, I had to get locked up for it. And, yeah, she had to
get rushed to the hospital. Oh well. But I tell you what. I
bet you she keeps it moving anytime she sees me now.
Every time she looks at herself in the mirror she sees my
four-prong stamp. Bottom line, don't eff with me 'n' I
won't have to take it to your head!

I grunt. "Mmph. I'm not thinking about that trick. But if she steps to me like that again, I might have to do them ten days, 'cause I'ma beat the skin off her. Senior year or not, she stays tryna get it turnt up. I can't stand her."

"What do I always tell you, Fiona?"

I sigh. "I know, I know. Pick 'n' choose my battles."

"Exactly."

She goes into mom mode. Tells me how it's not ladylike to be cussing 'n' fighting, especially over a boy. I quickly enlighten her on my diva rule: Read 'em for filth. *Snap, snap!* Never, ever, look for trouble. But if trouble comes strutting your way, give 'em a tongue-lashing before a beat-down. Please. I ain't got no time to be breaking a nail or twisting an ankle in my heels. Going with the hands should always be a diva's last resort. Well, um, that's un-less a trick puts her hands on you *first*, then it's showtime.

She chuckles. "I don't know what I'm going to do with you, girl. You're so much like Sonji. That chile was always suspended for fighting some girl when she was in school. It's a wonder she even had enough credits to graduate."

Sonji lives in New Haven, Connecticut, with her hus-band, Rondell. Her 'n' I aren't as close as I am with Leona or my sister Kara. I think I'm probably the closest to those two, more so than with Sonji 'n' Karina, because they were the ones who spent the most time with me. Usually, wherever one of them went, I went with her.

"Well, I can't wait to graduate. Trust. I'm so over high school."

"Don't rush it. Savor it for as long as you can. Trust. It'll be over before you know it."

"*Hunni*, four months 'n' counting. I can't wait."

"Well, wait until you get out into the real world, sweetie. You're going to wish you could have stayed in school longer. You'll be tryna rewind the clock. Don't rush it."

"Chile, *boom*! I can't wait until I'm eighteen 'n' grown. I'm outta here."

"And where are you off to? Have you even given any thought to what you want to do once you graduate, since you're so anxious to be out on your own?"

I shrug. "I don't know. I thought maybe I could come stay with you."

She peels her eyes from off the road. "Oh, really? And do what?"

I toss my hair. "Shop 'n' be fabulous, of course."

She shakes her head, laughing. "Girl, get those grandiose delusions out of your head. You have a lot to learn."

I turn toward her. Poke my lips out. "So, you're saying I can't come stay with you?"

"No. I'm not saying that. I'm saying it's time you start giving some thought to your future. And moving in with me can*not* be your post–high school life plan. Have you even taken the SATs?"

Ohgod, is she serious? Not this again.

"Yesss. I did. I took them a couple of months ago. But I'm going to take them again, just to see if I can improve my score." Truth is, I'm okay with my SAT scores: 1100. I'll take it. Now what I'm going to do with them is a whole other story.

I'm not sure I wanna go to college. I wanna travel to exotic places 'n' be able to wine 'n' dine in fancy restaurants. I wanna rock lots of ice 'n' rock a fly whip, like my sisters. I think I'ma have to snatch me a baller 'n' marry rich.

"Good. Get your college degree, then land a great job and you can have the kind of life you've always dreamed of."

Uh, ohhkay. "Girl, hush. I already have a fabulous life, *hun*. I'm young. Gorgeous. Smart. And I get all of my sisters' wardrobes. What more could a girl ask for?"

She chuckles. "And let's not forget being spoiled rotten. And while we're at it, let me add conceited to the mix."

"Hahaha. You wish. Never that. Okay, maybe a lil spoiled, though."

She shoots me a look. "A *little*? Really?"

I laugh. "Okay, okay. A lot. But it's mostly your fault."

She laughs with me. "Yeah, yeah. I know. I'm guilty as charged."

I look over at my sister 'n' smile. I love her so, so much. I swear. I don't know if she realizes how much I look up to her. She's like everything I want to be. Fly 'n' paid!

"Mom said you and her got into it the other night," she says, broaching the subject ever so lightly. Ugh. She knows I hate talking about our mother. Well, I don't mind talking *about* her; just not talking about something she's told one of my sisters about *me*, which is usually some level of exaggerated BS.

"No," I say, shifting in my seat. I reach for the controls on the side 'n' adjust my seat. "We didn't get into anything. She slick-talked 'n' I checked. Game over."

"She says you told her to kiss the back of your—"

"Omigod! Lies 'n' fabrications! I told her to go have several seats. I didn't *tell* her to kiss anything. I *thought* it." I give her a run-through of what really popped off.

"It was still disrespectful, Fee." I shrug. Tell her respect is given when it's gotten 'n' I'm not respecting her until she respects me. She shakes her head. "Well, who is this boy she said you ran up out of the house to be with?"

"Some lil boo-thing I chilled with. Nothing serious. The boy couldn't even kiss."

She glances over at me. "Fiona, you're a beautiful girl. You know everything shouldn't always be about sex."

I frown. "Who said anything about *sex*? I said he couldn't kiss." She gives me a look like *Okay, and?* "Trust. I didn't have sex with him if *that's* what you're thinkin'. He had sex with himself." She frowns, giving me a confused look. I give her a dismissive wave. "Long, sad story. Anywho... for the record, I don't sleep with *every* boy I chill with." *Only some of 'em. Okay, okay... most of 'em. Still... I'm a selective ho.*

She sighs. "I just want you to be careful. Mom's worried you're going to end up pregnant, or worse—contract some kind of STD."

"Ohmigod. She is so over herself. Why is that lady all up in my honey hole? What she needs to do is go out 'n' get her some. Maybe she wouldn't be so miserable. Jeezus. Trust. I don't do *nothin'* raw. Period. Ain't nobody tryna get pregnant. I'm a handbag 'n' heels girl, boo. Diaper bags 'n' strollers are so not it."

She sighs, shaking her head. "Fiona, you know I love you, honeybun, but sometimes your mouth is real extra and you know it. I know Mom can be a little rough..."

"A lil? Uhh, you *think*?"

She chuckles. "Okay, a lot. But that's still our mom. And you have to know when to pick and choose your battles."

"Omigod, Lee!" I cross my arms in front of me, feigning insult. "You don't know what I have to put up with. I try iggin' her. I try bitin' my tongue. But her mouth is reckless. That lady has always treated me like crap. And you know it."

"*Stupid little girl.*"

She shakes her head. "I know Mom hasn't always been exactly nice to you..."

"Ooh, you don't say?"

"*I can't stand yo' high-yella azz!*"

"*You make me sick...*"

"*I shoulda never had you...*"

My own sisters saw her hatred toward me, which is why they always tried to protect me from her beatings 'n' erratic tirades the best they could. But then one day, everything just stopped. Her yelling. Her name-calling. Her beatings.

Maybe it's because I went to school 'n' told Miss Neilson—my seventh grade social studies teacher—who told the prinicipal, who then called New Jersey's Division of Youth and Family Services on her. Maybe it's because DYFS threatened to bring charges against her butt the next time she put her hands on me, beating me with brooms 'n' hairbrushes. Mmph. Or maybe it's because I pulled a knife on her 'n' was ready to slice her in her sleep. All I know is, it stopped. And I know it didn't stop 'cause she knew what she was doing was wrong, or that she felt bad, or that she loved me.

Leona takes her eyes off the road, reaching over 'n' grabbing my hand. "And you know I'm so sorry you had to go through all that."

I shrug. "It's a little too late to do anything about it now. The damage's already done. She's ruined me."

She gives me a pained look, squeezing my hand. She tries to tell me that I'm not damaged or ruined. That I shouldn't ever think like that. That I'm far from ugly. That I'm beautiful 'n' talented 'n' bright 'n' loved. Blah, blah, blah.

Yeah, okay. That's how I feel sometimes. Ruined. Damaged. Ugly. Thanks to my mother. I swallow, turning my head toward the window. I'm done talking. I swipe a lone tear lingering in my eye. Ugh! That woman's not even here 'n' somehow—once again—she's managed to spoil my dang mood.

13

"Hello."

"Fiona?"

"Uhhh, yeah. Who's this?"

"What's up? It's Brent."

"Oh, okay."

"I wanted to make sure you didn't give me the wrong number."

"Oh no, hun. I'm too grown for that. I ain't wasting my time givin' out no wrong numbers, boo. If I'm not beat, I just say it. Who got time for them kinda tricks?"

"Yeah. That's what I like about you, Fee. You different. Always have been."

"Well, I'm glad you called," I tell him, not sure how much of it's truth. I mean, yeah, I've flirted with this cutie-boo 'n' I've even lusted for him on the low for a minute. But all Brent's ever been is a fantasy boo. Someone I have shamelessy laid in bed thinking about in the wee hours of the night with my wandering hands 'n' eyes closed 'n', well, uh…you fill in the blanks.

"I'm glad I hit you up, too."

I smirk. "It took you long enough."

I'd given Brent my number right after seventh period today when I ran into him in the hall 'n' he asked me for it. So I'm not surprised that he's calling me seven-and-a-half hours later. Sure, he coulda played it like he really wasn't beat 'n' let a few days go by or even the rest of the week. But he didn't. And he wouldn't have. I'm sure lil daddy couldn't resist holding out any longer than he's already done. Mmph. I've known him since freshman year, so the fact that it's taken him 'til senior year to finally get up the nerve to step to me says he's a bit slow, or shy, or maybe even…special.

Ooh, bless his lil heart.

But I'm not gonna hold that against him. Oh no. But I got something I'ma hold him against. Yes gawd, *hunni*. Trust. Miss Fiona has been wanting her a lil taste of Brent since the moment I laid my green eyes on him in freshman gym 'n' saw him 'n' all'a his goodness in a pair of gym shorts. But I never stepped to him 'cause: one, I had too many other boo-daddy distractions; and two, I'm many things, but thirsty ain't ever gonna be one'a them, so sweatin' a boy is a no-no.

Boys sweat *me*.

"Oh, a'ight. That's wassup."

"Oooh, you have a sexy phone voice," I say, sliding my tongue over my teeth.

I'm lying on my stomach with my feet in the air, flipping through a magazine while posted up on Facebook going through friend requests. So far I've accepted seventy-five outta ninety-three. I smirk when I see that Cease has sent me another request. This is like friend request number five or six. Why he's so pressed to be up on my page is beyond me. But, like all the other times, I don't accept him for any other reason than not wanting him up on my page.

Brent laughs. "Oh, for real? Thanks. You have a nice voice, too. I always wondered what you sounded like."

"Well, now you do. So what I sound like?"

"Sexy."

"Of course I do, boo. Sexy's my middle name. I thought you knew."

"I do, I do."

"Uh-huh. Glad you do."

"True, true. I'm sayin' though...what's up with you?"

I shut my magazine 'n' toss it over onto the floor. "Nothin'. What's good in your world, boo?"

"Chillin'. Hopin' I didn't catch you at a bad time."

Ooh, catch me, boo. Come save me from this boredom!

"No, not hardly." I glance over at the clock. It's a little after nine P.M. Leona dropped me off home around six thirty after an afternoon of pampering then an early dinner at a nearby restaurant. So here I am. Home alone 'n' practically bored outta my skull, knowing dang well I should probably be doing homework instead of wondering what kinda underwear he wears. Boxers? Or boxer briefs? Omigod, if he wears those lil tighty-whitey punk panties, I'ma drop to the floor 'n' die.

"So what you gonna be doing later on tonight, like in an hour?"

Hopefully ripping your clothes off, boo. I smack my lips together. "Nothing. Why, you wanna come over 'n' keep me company?"

"You want me to?"

Ooh, do I?

"I want you to do *what*ever you want, *Brrrent*." I lower my voice. "Tell Fiona want you want, lil daddy, 'n' tonight just might become ya lucky night."

"Oh, word? It's like that?"

"I'm a grown woman, boo. Trust. It's like however I want it to be."

"Daaayum. You talkin' that talk."

"And I can walk that walk too, lil daddy. Trust. Fiona don't play no games, boo. Come through 'n' you gonna learn tonight."

I can hear the excitement ringing in his voice; the sweet promise of a hot, sweaty night, as he tells me he's been wanting to get with me for a minute. Ooh, this lil boo-daddy has no idea what kinda delicious, dirty trouble he's about to get into messing with me.

I roll over on my back, crossing my right leg over my left knee. "So why you wanna chill with me, huh? You wanna know if the rumors are true? That Fiona's a beast in the sheets?" I don't give him a chance to answer before I say, "Trust. They ain't no rumors, boo. So before you even try'n step up in the furnace, you better be ready to handle the heat."

He starts breathing kinda heavy in my ear. I laugh to myself at the thought of him on the other end of the phone, drooling while tryna ease the excitement creeping up in his lap. I start talking all low 'n' freaky in his ear, teasing him.

"*Daaaaayum*. You don't even know what you done started. I need that like ASAP."

I start grinning. "You know where I live?"

"Over on Wilkerson, right?"

"Yeah." I give him the address. Tell him to come through in about thirty minutes.

"A'ight, bet. I'ma hit you when I'm on my way."

"And you better not even come up over here with no musty balls or wearin' no Spider-Man or SpongeBob drawz, either."

He cracks up laughing. "Nah, nah. Wrong dude. I stay clean. And my boxers always on point."

"Mmph. We'll see."

"You already know."

We talk a few minutes more before disconnecting. I toss my phone over on the bed, then scramble around my room, pulling out a black lace cami set 'n' my scented candles. Yes, *hunni*, trust. It's gonna be a Durex night he'll never forget.

Ooh, I'm so glad I had my feet done today. I'ma stuff these toes all in his mouth.

14

The next morning, I strut into the school building without a care in the world, humming Britney Spears's "Work B**ch." I just love that song. I swing my hips, working it in a pair of designer jeans that are practically poured on over my curves, with a cute lil black tee that has a big red cherry painted in the middle of my chest. The words POP MY are scrawled across the cherry in black cursive. Ooh, you can't tell me I'm not servin' it. *You better work, bish!* My heels click against the tile as I make my way down the hall.

"Yo, what's goodie, Fee?" Kent calls out as I walk by.

"You, boo," I say, winking at him.

"Yo, what's good, Fee?" Luke wants to know. "You comin' to my party next weekend? It's gonna be live, yo. Got them drinks on deck."

"Ooh no, thanks. I'm not even tryna see you pissy drunk in ya boxers again."

He laughs. "Yo, chill, chill."

"No. You need to chill on the drinkin', boo. You're one pint away from a rehab stay."

He laughs. "Nah, nah. Never that. I'm on my grown-man ish. I holds mine, baby."

I smirk. "Uh-huh. And that's why there's flicks of you on ya knees prayin' to the porcelain gods all up on Instagram. Yeah, you holdin' it all right, boo. Right around the toilet bowl."

I keep stepping, hair bouncing every which way as I walk.

"Daaayum, baby, let me get some'a that thick shake..." I glance over my shoulder. It's Marcellus with his nasty self, grabbing his crotch. "I gotta whole box of condoms just for you."

"Hold ya breath, boo. This shake ain't for you. The only thing you can get is a hall pass to the clinic."

He laughs. "Damn, you cold."

I wave him on. "Uh-huh. Cold as ice, baby."

Up ahead, Keyshaun stops talking to two of his boys when he spots me 'n' says, "Yo, what's poppin', Fiona, baby?"

"You 'n' all'a dem baby *muhvers*, boo. I hear you got some other dumbo knocked up."

He laughs. "Nah, nah. My mans 'n' 'em ran up in that. I was strapped."

He gives his boys pounds.

I roll my eyes. "Well, you need to be strapped to a gurney 'n' castrated."

"Ouch!"

His boys laugh.

"Oh, a'ight, a'ight... I see you, Fee," Benji calls out as I continue down the hall. "Let me get up in them jeans with you."

"Benji, *boom*! Not today, lovey."

"Damn, Fee, baby," Christian aka Crusty Drawz says, practically drooling as I walk by him posted up at his locker. "When you gonna let me hit that?"

"Middle finger up," I snap, tossing my right arm 'n' middle finger up in the air at him. "Never that."

"I'm sayin'...you can get it all night for free, word is bond, yo."

"And you can get ya face slapped."

He laughs. But he knows I'll do his face real dirty if he presses me. So he kindly stays in his lane. "Fiona, you my peoples, yo. You know I'm only effen wit' you."

"Uh-huh."

I peep Cease scoopin' LuAnna up in his arms, giving her a hug. She's all grins 'n' giggles, like she's all stuck on silly. He lets her go when he spots me, but I act like I don't see him 'n' turn the corner. Then of course I hear some hatin' trick say something slick, tryna disguise her voice. "Tramp on deck." I don't peep who says it at first until I spot Quanda 'n' Samantha eyeballin' me.

"Ooh, don't do it, booga-bears," I say, wagging a finger over at them. "You bully-azz hoes don't want it. Not today, hun. Sam, where's ya drunk-azz mammy, boo? I heard she was down on the Ave. picking through the trash again for ya dinner."

"*Bish!*" she snaps. "Where's ya damn mammy? Least mine wants me."

"Yeah, only when she's drunk," I snap back. I stop in my tracks when she says something slick about my father. He's dead. And he's off limits to talk about. Go in on Cruella all day, but keep my father out ya mouth. "Ooh,

don't do it, Miss Piggy-Wiggy. You know you don't want it.
You don't even wanna play the daddy game, boo."

"No, *you* don't want it, ho."

I laugh, sliding my hand down into my bag, feeling for
my travel companion—Miss Swiss Army. *Let this bitch say
something else slick 'n' crazy 'n' I'ma take this blade
straight to her face.*

I toss my hair. "Leap, booga-bear."

"No, you leap," she shoots back.

I laugh, giving her the finger, then stepping off. "Talk to
the phatty."

I climb the stairs to the fourth floor, then make my way
toward the bank of lockers. I blink, blink again, as I approach my locker. Brent is standing there, grinning at me
as I approach.

Oh, he has got to be kiddin' me...

"Hey," he says. "I was hoping to see you before homeroom."

I give him a confused look, then glance around to see
who else is in earshot. "For what?"

"About last night. I—"

"Oh no, oh no," I say, cutting him off. "We are not even
about to do this here."

He looks over my shoulder down the hall, then back at
me. "Nah, it's nothing serious." He lowers his voice to almost a whisper. "It's just that I kinda wanna keep what
happened between us on the low. Feel me?"

I laugh, opening my locker. A note falls to the floor.
"Listen, boo." I reach down 'n' pick up the note, stuffing it
in my back pocket. I eye him. "I gave you a lil taste of
heaven 'cause that's what I wanted to do. But trust. I don't
kiss 'n' tell."

I go back to rummaging through my locker for my books for the first three periods.

"Yeah, I know you don't. Me either."

I peer around my locker door 'n' look at him. "Well, I wouldn't care if you did or didn't. All I know is, I'm not saying anything. What we did is nothing newsworthy, so no worries, boo. Trust." I slam my locker shut. "It's like it never happened."

Between me 'n' you, the night ended in less than twenty minutes. I'm not messy so I'm not gonna put him all up on blast like that. But let's just say, boo-boo couldn't handle the heat.

He gives me a dumb look.

Bless his lil heart.

I reach up 'n' kiss him on the cheek, then spin on my heel, heading down the hall toward homeroom. It's not until I am sitting in my second period class that I remember the note I have tucked in my back pocket. I pull it out, then slowly open it. It's another poem. I frown, flipping the paper over looking for any clue, any sign as to who coulda slid this into my locker. Just like with the other poem. There is none.

At first I think it might be from Brent since he was in fact standing at my locker when I walked up to it this morning. But then I quickly shake the craziness of that outta my head. I start reading:

<u>I Got My Eye On You</u>

I got my eye on you, pretty baby
I'm inspired by your smile
intrigued by your style

I wanna breathe u in
taste your skin
I wanna swim in your love
you are all I think about
all I desire
makin' you mine is at the top of my list
I imagine the taste of your lips
I fantasize about our first kiss
I wanna love you down
but for now, baby
I'ma keep diggin' you from afar
just know…
I got my eye on you

I blink. Omigod. I read it again, then silently pray that whoever is leaving me these poems isn't some cuckoo stalker. The last thing Miss Fiona needs is a nutcase riding her heels. Oh no, boo. Chickie don't play that. I quickly fold the note, then slide it down into my bag.

15

"Girrrrrrl," Miesha says, setting her tray down in front of me 'n' pulling out a chair. She takes a seat. "Omigod, I got some juicy scoop for you. Wait. Why didn't you text me back last night?"

I look up at her. "What text? I didn't get any texts from you."

She tilts her head. "Uh-huh. Wrong answer. Try again."

"No, for real." I pull out my phone 'n' scroll through it. "Oops." Sure enough, there's a text from her: GIRL I GOT SUM SCOOP 4 U! CALL ME

"My bad," I say apologetically. "I don't know how I missed that."

"Well, you did. But, whatever. Annnnywho...guess who's checkin' for you, *hard*, girl?"

I frown. "Oh boy. Should I even care?"

"Yesss, hun, you should."

I groan. "Who is it now? And if you tell me it's some boy

in the Glee Club with a thong fetish, or that cute Middle Eastern boy, Ahmad, with the hairy back, I'ma scream."

She cracks up laughing. "Eww. No, girl." She waves me on. "I'm not even tryna see you with no boy wearing a rug on his back. I wouldn't do you like that. Although it would be hilarious to see you combing his back."

I can't help but laugh myself. "Ugh. Girl, the only thing I'd do with that boy's back is run a lawn mower over it. I can't do nothin' else with that. He needs a good wax 'n' a new back." She keeps laughing. "No. I'm dead serious, Miesha. I don't need any more news about some freak of nature wantin' a slice of my cherry pie. The bakery shop is closed. I'm not doin' any more American horror stories."

"Girl, I can't." She laughs. "Trust me. I wouldn't do you like that. This is major."

I tilt my head. "Okay, I'll bite. Who? Brent?"

"*Brent?* Girl, no. Why'd you think it was him?"

I shrug. "He came up to me yesterday 'n' asked me if I wanted to chill 'n' grab a bite to eat." I decide not to tell her that the only thing that got eaten last night was, well, um...*me*, of course. Or that he can't hold his excitement in for long before he starts howling out like some wolf. Oh no, hun. Fiona isn't even about to do him like that. So since I ain't one to gossip or kiss 'n' tell, we gonna keep movin' on.

"Ooh, interesting. Well, he is real cute. But Brent's too nice for you, Fiona. You're like a man-eater. You'd eat that boy up alive. I don't think he's ready for that kinda heartbreak, girl."

Girl, if you only knew. That boy ain't ready for much of anything.

I feign insult. "Omigod, I wouldn't do *him* like that. He's too fine." *And has a tongue like an erupting volcano.*

She laughs. "Lies! Oh yes, you would."

I suck my teeth. "Whatever. Well, if it's not Brent, who is it then?"

She takes a sip of her drink, raspberry iced tea in a glass bottle. She pulls a napkin from off her tray 'n' dabs her mouth with it. "Cease, girl."

I blink, blink again. "*Cease?* Girl, bye!"

"No. I'm serious. That boy's big on you, boo."

I raise a brow. "And where'd you hear this craziness from?"

"It's not craziness. Trust." She leans in, lowers her voice. I have to strain to hear her over the lunchroom chatter. "You can't say anything. But Tone told me last night that he keeps beatin' him in the head about you. Girl, that boy's sweatin' you on the low. Why you think he stays grinning in your face?" She toots her lips. "Mmph. I think he wants to ask you out."

I roll my eyes. Please, all Ceasar wants is to finally get him a lil taste of heaven before we graduate in a few months. Not gonna happen. Mmph. Fine or not, I'm soo not interested.

"No, thanks. I'm not thinking about that boy like that."

"Girl, why not? Tell me you don't think he's fine."

"Yeah, he's fine all right, 'n' real nasty."

She laughs. "Girl, don't front. Nasty's right up your alley."

I smirk. "Ooh, you know me so well, boo. But Cease can't do nothing for me that I can't get from some other lil boo-daddy. Trust."

"Girl, stop. So you're sayin' if he stepped to you on some *let's chill* type ish, you wouldn't? Or what if he asked you to prom? You'd turn him down?"

I gaze across the lunch tables, just in time to spot him laughing it up with Antonio 'n' Luke—another one of his boys on the basketball team—as they walk into the cafeteria. He looks over in our direction. He's wearing a pair of shades, but I know his eyes are on me. I can feel 'em.

I look away. Bring my attention back to Miesha. "Yup. I sure would."

She chuckles, plucking a grape from her fruit salad. "Yeah, right. Lies you tell. You know you'd jump all over that."

"No, I wouldn't. Cease tried to hook up with me freshman year 'n' it didn't work out then, so I know it's not gonna happen now."

"Why not?"

"Because..."

"*Because* what?"

"Uhh, because I caught him kissing this ugly, pie-faced girl with big horse teeth."

"Girl, bye. That was three years ago. People change."

"Uh-huh. Not dogs like him. I was humiliated, to say the least, that he'd choose that horse head over"—I run my hands over my body—"this."

"And I'm sure he's been kicking himself ever since."

"Well, he should be. Still, I don't believe in second chances, boo."

She shakes her head. "You act like you scared he might turn you out or something."

I suck my teeth, flicking a dismissive wave at her. "Turn

me out? Ha! Never that, boo. Nasty or not, I'm not looking to get down 'n' dirty with Cease; that's all. Besides, isn't he supposedly messing with flat-back?"

"Who?"

I suck my teeth. "You know, Chantel."

She shrugs. "Oh. Uh-uh. Not that I know of." She laughs. "Omigod, you so wrong for callin' her that, though. Flat-back? Really?"

"Well, that's what she is. All boobs 'n' no booty. Girl, you know I ain't messy, but, uh, I get so sick of seein' her pants all sucked up in her crack. She needs her azz beat for comin' outta the house tryna rock tight jeans. That girl has a nasty case of suction. Isn't that some kinda disease?"

Miesha cracks up laughing. "Omigod, you know you not right for that."

"Mmph. But am I wrong? Anyway, didn't Tone mess with her, too?"

She twists her face up. "Mess with who? Chantel? Girl, boom. Who 'n' what Antonio did before me is *not* my concern. Trust. But no. She played head doctor, once. That's about it."

"Ole jizz guzzler," I say, turning my nose up. "Nasty dome gobbler. I heard she stayed with her face pressed down in some boy's crotch."

"Umm," she says, twirling a finger at me. "You know, that's what they say about you, too."

My eyes pop open. "Ooh, lies 'n' falsifications, girl! *Boom, boom!* Don't do me. I don't know where you heard that mess from, but take it back to the lab, boo. I'm many things. Trust. But a lollipop licker ain't ever been one of 'em. My mouth doesn't go anywhere south."

She starts laughing. "Girl, you know you be *drankin'* that watermelon."

I laugh, waving her on. "Oh, okay, Beeeeyoncé. Think what you want. But Fiona ain't putting her mouth on nothin', boo. And she ain't down on her knees slurpin' seeds all willy nilly. Trust."

She cracks up laughing.

I pick at my tuna salad, scooping a forkful into my mouth. I spot ole messy Quanda at one of the tables across the room 'n' roll my eyes.

"What?" Miesha asks, looking in the direction of my glare. "Oh." She keeps laughing, shaking her head. "What that chick do now?"

"Girl, that trick tried to do me the other day 'cause she saw me walkin' down the hall hugged up with Pauley."

She shakes her head. "What, she tried to go with the hands?"

"Yeah, right. Picture that. Ooh, I wish she woulda tried it. Please, boo. Please do. All talk. Trust."

Miesha asks what Pauley said when all this was going down with Quanda.

"Not one damn thing. That punk stood there lookin' all goofy 'n' ish."

"Mmph. I knew he was soft as cotton."

"Yeah, but he's hard as brick 'n' steel in all the right places," I say, thinking back to our night of naked Twister down in his basement. I shudder. "What a waste."

She sucks her teeth. "Umm, you do know that there's more to a boy than his sex, right?"

"Ohhhhh-emmmmmm-geeeee! Now you sound like my sister Leona."

"Well, it's true."

I give her a blank look. "Like what? Do tell."

But before she can explain to me what more a boy has to offer other than sex, Antonio 'n' Cease are headed our way. "Ooh, here they come now," she says all excited 'n' whatnot, like I'm supposed to be all grins 'n' giggles about one of the school's biggest man-whores tryna check for me.

No ma'am, no sir. Not interested. I stand up.

"Wait. Where you going?" she wants to know. I tell her to the computer lab to finish typing an English paper. "Ooh, lies! Don't even try it. Since when you start going to the computer lab?"

"Since today."

She starts laughing as Antonio 'n' Cease walk over.

"Hey, Tone," I say.

"Wassup, Fee? How you?"

"I'm good." I eye him as he leans in 'n' kisses Miesha on the lips.

"How's my sexy babe doin'?"

She blushes. "Better now."

I roll my eyes.

"Yo, what's goodie, My?" Cease says to her. She speaks back. Tells him nothing much. He turns his attention to me. "Oh, so you not speakin'?"

I flick him a wave. "Hey, Cease."

"Oh, so it's like that?" he says, eyeing me. "Why you act like you ain't see me earlier? You just gonna play me to the left like that when all I'm tryna do is give you my heart?"

"Boy, bye. You play too much."

"Nah, I'm serious. Be my valentine."

I suck my teeth. "Valentine's Day was last month, fool."

"Nah, baby. E'eryday's V-Day when you're around."

"And the answer is still no."

Miesha gives me the eye.

"Oh, word? That's how you doin' it?" He spreads open his arms. "A brotha can't get no love? I mean, damn. Can I at least get a hug, then?"

Before I can tell him hell no, he grabs me up in a big hug, grinning all crazy. "Damn, you smell good, girl."

Mmph. Of course I do, boo. Thought you knew.

He sniffs me. "Whew. You got me goin' through it, yo. I wanna lick ya neck."

Miesha giggles.

Antonio laughs. "Yo, Cease, man. You wildin', yo."

I roll my eyes. "Whatever, Cease. Where's ya lil girl-friend?"

"*Girlfriend?* Nah. I don't have one of those, *yet*. But maybe if you act right I'll make *you* my girl."

I step outta his embrace. "Boy, bye! Not interested." I glance over at Miesha 'n' Antonio as I'm grabbing my tray. "All right, lovebirds, peace out. I'm outta here."

"Oh, word? A'ight then," Antonio says, eyeing Cease.

"You need a ride after school?" Miesha wants to know, easing her arm from around her boo-daddy's neck. I tell her no. Tell her my sister Sonji is picking me up 'n' taking me to the mall to go shopping right after school.

I try not to look over at Cease, but I can feel the heat of his gaze on me. I pop my lips 'n' toss my hair. *Get ya look on, boo!*

"Ooh, I so hate you right now," Miesha says. "Weren't you just out with your other sister, like yesterday, shop-ping?"

I laugh. "No. We only went to the spa to get facials 'n' mani-pedis. And that was two days ago."

"So. I'm still jelly."

Antonio pulls Miesha into his arms 'n' kisses her on the side of her head. "You ain't gotta be jelly, babe. You know ya daddy got you. I'ma take you to get ya feet done on Saturday, a'ight."

She grins. "*And* my hands?"

He laughs. "No doubt." He takes her hand in his 'n' turns it over, then kisses her palm. "Yo, my baby got them soft hands." Miesha giggles.

Ugh. These two are sickeningly in love with each other.

"Yo, let me see them pretty toes, Fee," Cease says, licking his lips. He's seated at the table, plucking a sweet potato fry from off Miesha's half-eaten tray of food. "You know I gotta foot fetish, right?"

I smirk. "How cute."

"I'm sayin', though"—he lowers his voice—"when we gonna chill? Me 'n' you?"

I roll my eyes. "Never, boo." I toss up two fingers. "Deuces. I'm out."

"Yo, Fiona?" Cease calls out.

I glance over my shoulder. "Yesss?"

"C'mere for a sec."

I suck my teeth 'n' stalk back over to him, popping my hips real hard 'n' fast, making sure everything shakes for all to see.

"What is it?"

"Let me get some sugar, yo."

I frown. "What, a *kiss*?"

He grins.

"Are you serious? Right here?"

"Yeah. Right here. I dare you."

Miesha 'n' Antonio look on, both with silly grins on their faces.

"Okay," I say. Cease puckers up those sexy lips of his. I lick my lips real slow 'n' sexy-like for him. Then lean in as if I'm about to take him up on it. But instead I take my fingers 'n' pluck his lips, just enough to sting.

"Oww! See, you playin', right?"

"Bye, Cease." I shake my head, shoulder my bag, spin on my heel, 'n' head off to class, way before the bell rings, with my booty bouncing 'n' a sly grin plastered on my face.

16

"Fiona!"

I quickly slide the earbuds to my iPod into my ears 'n' ig her.

"Fiona!"

I start singing all loud 'n' off-key to an Ariana Grande song.

"Fiona!" She bangs her hand on the foot of my bed.

I snap my fingers, continuing to sing "The Way." Pretend to be oblivious to her presence.

She stands in front of me. Hand on hip. Face extra tight. "Fiona! You hear me talking to you, girl!"

I suck my teeth, looking up from my notebook at her, pulling an earbud out. "What?"

"Don't *what* me. Why aren't those dishes done?"

I give her a blank stare. Really? Is she frickin' kidding me?

I take a deep breath. "I'll do them in a minute. Why are you even here?"

"I'm getting ready to leave for work. Don't leave up

outta this house, either. You think I don't know what you be doing when I'm not here."

I huff. "And what is it you *think* I'm doing, huh?"

She glares at me. "Don't try me, girl. You either got some boy running in 'n' outta here, or you sneaking up outta here all hours of the night. And just because I haven't said anything, don't think I don't know about that boy you had climbing up outta your bedroom window two months ago."

I blink. *How'd she know about that?* Then it dawns on me that Miss Pitney next door musta had her ole nosy butt all up in my business. Ole messy heffa! She stays minding somebody else's business. She swears she's the Neighborhood Watch.

I frown. "Tell your spies to get it right. I don't *sneak* out. I walk out through the front door, then walk right back in the same way. I'm not climbing outta windows or tiptoein' out the door 'n' duckin' down in trees to get in *or* out."

"Well, I don't want you sneaking no damn boys in or outta here either. It's not right."

"That was one time," I say nonchalantly. Like get over it. No big deal. But what I really wanna say is, *Why you care? Maybe you should try gettin' you some.*

"And who was that boy you had leaving up outta here the other night?"

I frown. "A friend."

She twists her lips. "Uh-huh. Well, it's still downright disrespectful."

I take a deep breath. "Okay, whatever you say."

"Yeah. I know it's whatever I say. All this trampin' you doin' needs to stop."

I give her a blank stare. "Not to be rude. But, um, can I help you? I'm tryna study."

She plants both of her hands up on her hips. Her jaw set tight. Her nose flares. I can tell she's counting in her head. I ease up just in case she's thinking about jumping on me.

"Fiona. No boys in this house, you understand? And I want those dishes done. I shouldn't have to keep tellin' you the same thing over 'n' over again."

Then stop doing it! Now get the heck outta my room!

I huff. "Okay, dang. I heard you. No boys. Do the dishes. Bye."

She lunges at me 'n' swings an arm. But I'm too quick for the big girl. I jump up off the bed outta her reach.

"I'm sick of you, girl! I can't wait to toss ya slick-mouth azz outta here the minute you turn eighteen. You not gonna keep disrespectin' me like you do, girl."

"Good day, ma'am," I say, flicking a dismissive wave at her. "Please 'n' thank you." She keeps talking all sideways 'n' crazy 'bout how she's gonna end up knocking my teeth down my throat. But I'm not really hearing her. I keep saying, "Good day, ma'am. Please 'n' thank you. Good day, ma'am. Please 'n' thank you."

I know y'all think I'm disrespectful to her. But I don't care! You have no idea what she's put me through over the years. So what you see is the best I can do. I don't wanna relive the past, so I'm not tryna go there 'n' bring it up.

She stares me down.

I stare right back at her. Tilt my head.

But I know today's stare-down won't be long 'cause she has to leave for work, like now.

"Did you cook?" I ask, knowing the answer already. No.

She narrows her gaze. "No, I didn't cook. What I look like, slavin' over a damn stove for some disrespecting girl who already thinks she's grown? You know how to cook. You wanna eat, then get in there 'n' cook it ya damn self."

I fold my arms. "I need money to order something."

She smirks. "Oh, really? Ha! Like ya fresh mouth always tells me: Girl, bye. Miss me with that. You better eat what's down in that refrigerator or you just don't eat."

With that said, she's out the door, her hips 'n' big booty angrily bouncin' 'n' shakin' with each step. My door slams shut.

I suck my teeth, fishing through my handbag. *Lady, boom! I didn't need ya lil change anyway. I stay with my own coins, boo. Boom! I just wanted to see what you were gonna say.*

I snatch up my cell 'n' call Travis's big-head self. He picks up on the third ring. "Yo, waddup?"

"Bring me something to eat, boo-daddy."

He laughs. "Oh, word? Now a nucca ya *boo-daddy*, huh?"

"Oh, boy, stop. You know you always gonna be my lil boo-daddy."

Lies!

"Yeah, a'ight. That's what ya mouth says. But I couldn't get no love the other day, right?"

"Boy, bye. Are you gonna feed me or what?"

"What I'ma get, huh?"

How 'bout ya face slapped?

I roll my eyes up in my head so hard I almost make myself dizzy. "What you want, boo?"

I can practically see him lickin' his lips 'n' grinnin' through the phone. "You already know."

I purse my lips. "I want a chicken cheesesteak with fries. And I want it nice 'n' hot."

"Yeah, a'ight. And I want that thang-thang or that mouth nice 'n' hot, too."

Yeah, ohhhhkay. Not!

"Okay. I got you, boo-daaaady. What time you gonna get here?" He tells me in about two hours. Maybe less. That he's watching his lil brother until his moms gets back from the store. Like I really need to know all that. Just bring me my dang food. I shake my head. I already know his two hours or less really means like in four hours. I could be dead from starvation by then. I don't think so. "Okay. I'll see you when you get here."

"Yeah, a'ight. Wear that lil sexy see-through jump-off I like. The red one."

Boy, bye!

"Okay, boo-daddy." I disconnect. And dial up King.

"Wassup, baby? How you?"

"I'm good," I coo into the phone, lying on my stomach. I bend my legs up 'n' cross my ankles, twirling a lock of my hair. "I been thinkin' about you."

"Oh, word? That's wasssup."

Yeah. I've been thinking about you bringing me some food.

I moan. "Mm-hmm. I can't stop thinkin' about you. Do you have classes tonight?"

"Nah. Why, wasssup? You tryna chill?"

Not really. Not with you 'n' all that spit you got goin' on. "You already know I am."

"That's wasssup, babe. I been thinkin' about you, too."

Uh-huh. I bet you have.

"Can you bring me something to eat when you come?"

"Yeah. I got you. What you want?"

Ooh, I know you do, boo. Bless ya lil slobberin' soul. I tell him Chinese—garlic shrimp 'n' steamed broccoli with brown rice—from the spot downtown.

"A'ight. I'll be over in like an hour."

I smile. Then end the call. *Boom!* This diva will never go hungry. But if either one of them fools think I'ma serve 'em up a dish of this warm goodness, they have another think coming. I don't trick for Meals on Wheels, honey-boo.

No, ma'am.

17

"Yo, that was real foul how you played me last night," Travis says the next morning, walking up to me in the hallway as I'm standing here talking to this dang girl Alicia about our English assignment. "But you got that off, yo."

I tell Alicia I'll catch her in class.

She rolls her eyes. "And you do know this project is due next week, *right*?"

I blink. "Yeah, and?"

"You know what?" She throws her hands up. "I can't. If we fail, we fail."

"Boo-boo. Be clear. Fiona doesn't fail. So you can miss me with that."

"Yeah, whatever." She spins off 'n' I bring my attention to Travis. He's standing here showing off his muscled chest in a tight-fitting Hollister T-shirt. I glance down at the half-sleeve tattoo on his right arm, then meet his gaze.

"Now what were you sayin', lil daddy?"

"Nah, don't *lil daddy* me, yo. That stunt you pulled was mad foul, yo."

"Boy, bye. Get over it or move along."

He's still hot at the fact that I opened the door last night when he showed up all late 'n' crazy at like almost midnight. Oh noo, boo-boo. You not even about to make Miss Fiona sit 'n' wait on you. A diva sits 'n' waits on no one. Not even some boy who's bringing you a hot meal. No, ma'am. She always has a plan A, B, 'n' C.

So when he finally decided to show up, I snatched the bag of food outta his hand, then slammed the door in his stank face. Midnight? Really? When I called ya black behind at like four o'clock. And you show up ringing my door at *midnight*? Twelve hours wrong! Oh no, boo-boo. The carriage has already turned back into a pumpkin 'n' this Cinderella is already being entertained 'n' fed by someone else.

I laugh. "Well, at least I came to the door in that red nightie you like. And I texted you a thank-you, didn't I?"

He sucks his teeth. "Yeah, whatever, yo. You owe me nine dollars."

I wave him on. "Let me know how you make out with that."

"Whatever, man. But it's all good. You probably needed it more than me."

I stop in my tracks. Neck cocked, one hand slung up on my hip, the other sliding down into my bag, yanking out my wallet. "Oh no, don't get it effed up, boo. Fiona doesn't need a boy for jack. Trust. You want ya lil change back? Here"—I toss him a ten-dollar bill—"have at it. One thing I'm not is some charity case."

He pushes it away. "Nah, you good."

"Uh-huh. I know I am."

"You stay playin' for real though."

I grin, snatching my money back 'n' stuffing it back down into my bag before he changes his mind. I sidle up alongside him, wrapping an arm around his waist. "You know I love you, boo."

"Whatever, man. I ain't beat." He laughs. "All you love is playin' games, yo."

"Ooh, lies, lies, 'n' more lies." I inch up on my tiptoes 'n' give him a quick kiss on the cheek. "Thanks for the food, boo. I'ma eat it when I get home from school today."

He pushes me off him. "Get off me, yo. I ain't effen wit' you, Fee. You play too much."

"Ohh, I'm not playin', yet." I inch up again 'n' whisper something real nasty in his ear. He tries to act like he isn't beat, but he starts grinning 'n' licking his lips.

"Yeah, a'ight. When?"

"Now," I tell him. "I'ma go in the bathroom 'n' take 'em off for you. So you can have something to think about throughout the day."

The nasty dog starts drooling. I tell you. Boys. I wish some boy would tell me he's gonna take his drawz off for me to sniff; I'd slap his dang face off. But this lil horny hound is all excited about getting my panties. Mmph.

I start walking down the hall. "I'll have 'em for you when I get outta next period."

"Nah. I want 'em now."

I laugh. "Boy, you stoooopid."

"Nah, I'm dead-azz."

"Whatever." I huff, brushing my bangs outta my left eye.

"Come on." He follows me to the girls' bathroom 'n' waits outside by the doors. A few seconds later I return from the bathroom with my pink lace panties neatly folded, then hand 'em to him. Now he's all grins 'n' giggles. Just that quick he's forgotten about how he got played last night. Silly fool.

I make it to my next class two minutes after the bell rings.

"Glad you're able to join us, Miss Madison," Mrs. Sheldon, aka Mrs. Haterade, starts in the second I waltz through the door. This lady stays tryna turn up. I can't stand her. She's such a…ooh, she's lucky I don't call old ladies the B-word. 'Cause that's exactly what I'd call her. And if you ask me, I think she has some kinda complex toward the real pretty girls. Yup. I sure do 'cause she's just as sweet as molasses to the lot lizards 'n' chicks that look like baboons. But let it be a fly chick like me 'n' she stays tryin' it.

Lady, go have several seats! Don't be jelly 'cause I'm young 'n' beautiful. Hate ya'self, boo.

But I'm not messy. So I'm gonna keep it cute 'n' move along. I open my mouth to explain my reason—well, okay, my lie—as to why I'm late. But she shuts it down. "Save it. Take your seat."

I roll my eyes. *Don't do me, boo.* I take the nearest seat next to Alicia—not that I really wanna sit next to her— dropping my bag onto the floor beside me. I peep her looking at me outta the corner of my eye.

I turn to her. "Can I help you?"

"You're such a snotty bitch," she hisses.

"And you're still a ox stuffed in a thick girl's body, but

you don't hear me calling you names, now do you? Good day, ma'am." I shift in my seat.

Mrs. Sheldon clears her throat, shooting daggers over in my direction. "Excuse me, ladies. Am I missing something? This is an AP English class, is it not?"

Alicia says, "Yes."

I just stare at her.

"And you are *both* seniors, correct?"

"Yes," Alicia says again.

"Miss Madison, please feel free to chime in."

I twist my lips. "Mm-hmm."

"Great. Now I trust the two of you have been getting along and working diligently on your project to present next week."

Alicia shifts in her seat 'n' of course the messy *bish* tries to toss me under the dang train, bus, 'n' garbage truck all in the same sitting. "Well, I don't know what *she's* doing." She tosses a look over at me. "But I'm doing *my* part," she says, flicking her hair over her shoulder.

I toss my hair back. "Good day, boo. And how does that have anything to do with today's lesson, ma'am?" I ask.

A few kids in back of me jeer her on. "Ooh, she tryna play you, Missus S."

She narrows her eyes at me.

I shrug. "No, shade. I'm just tryna understand the relevance of the question since last I checked I *thought* we were supposed to be discussing"—I pull out my book—"this. *The Bluest Eye* by Toni Morrison, which, by the way, wore my nerves down. Ooh, don't do me like that again. No, ma'am."

She blinks. "Excuse me? Please elaborate."

"The book is extremely depressing."

"And why is that?" she wants to know, tilting her head.

I sigh. "Not that I wanna be center stage today, but..."

Someone says, "Yeah, right."

A few kids chuckle.

I throw my left hand up, then middle finger up. "Ooh, don't do me." And of course, Mrs. Haterade tries to give it to me, like I'm the one causing problems. "Annnnyway," I continue, igging her. "The whole time I was reading this mess I felt like I was in the middle of a horrible nightmare. First of all, she hates herself to the point where she thinks havin' blue eyes 'n' blond hair is gonna make her more beautiful. It's like she was obsessed with it. I mean, dang. She shoulda just embraced her ugliness 'n' kept it movin'."

"That's a bit harsh," Mrs. Sheldon says, frowning.

"Omigod!" Alicia snaps. "Are you frickin' serious? That girl—"

"Her name is Pecola," Mrs. Haterade interjects.

"Okay. Pecola," Alicia says, "was treated like shi...uh, crap. If someone is always ridiculed 'n' made to feel worthless, like she was, how you expect her to like what or who she is? She's spit on, teased. Then her own father, with his nasty self, rapes her, and ends up knockin' her up. Pecola's whole life was bleak. Her father tried to burn down their house. He drinks. Her own mother doesn't really show her any love 'n' all they do is beat each other down. Her parents fight. I mean, c'mon. Her whole life was effed up."

"Girl, relax," I say dismissively. "You takin' up for the chick like she's a long lost cousin. It's *only* a book 'n' it's *my* opinion. Get over it."

"And now I'm giving you facts. Almost everyone around her mistreated or abused her. So, *you* get over it."

I shoot her an icy glare. "And like I *saaaid*, in my opinion, the book was *borrring* and too dang depressing. And Fiona has no time for tragedy 'n' heartache. Period."

"Okay, girls," Mrs. Haterade says. "Settle down. Let's not turn this into a verbal sparring match. Yes, it's true. The book is very sad and haunting. But it's a deep and inspiring one as well."

I grunt. "Mmph. I can't tell. The only thing it inspired me to do was shut it."

I blink back the burning sensation that's building up in the back part of my eyeballs. I feel like I am about to burst out in tears at any moment. I didn't realize talking about this dang book would have me feeling all types of crazy. Snippets of my own damn life being tossed in my dang face. Not that my father was a drunk. Or ever tried to rape me or burn down our house. But I know what it's like to be ridiculed 'n' made to feel like you're nothing by your own mother. That was most of my life. And it had nothing to do with being dark-skinned 'n' ugly. Or having brown eyes or blue eyes, or wanting to be white.

I have green eyes 'n' blond hair. And I'm very light-skinned. Almost white, at first glance. But guess what? That ish doesn't mean jack. Growing up, I still felt worthless. Still felt like I didn't belong. And, even now, sometimes I still do. But I'm not about to admit it here. Oh, no ma'am, no sir. Not in front of these clowns. That's my dirty lil secret. Trust. I didn't need to read about feeling ugly 'n' being treated like crap in some miserable book. I can look in the mirror if I wanna be reminded of misery.

I take several deep breaths, then push out, "Well, someone shoulda sent her silly butt the memo that having blue
eyes like Shirley Temple doesn't make you more loveable.
And being white or light doesn't guarantee your parents
are gonna love you more, or respect you more. And it definitely doesn't mean you're gonna be accepted by anyone."

Someone in back of me says, "On the real, what Pecola
went through is no different than what my lil thirteen-year-
old cousin went through last summer when her moms's
boyfriend raped her. Dude kept on rapin' her 'n' her
moms was walkin' around actin' like she didn't see or
know what was poppin' off. No different from Pecola's
moms, if you ask me. My cuz ended up pregnant 'n' with
gonorrhea at the same time. And my aunt blames her for
that mofo...oh, my bad, Missus S. But she blames my cuz
for what happened."

The classroom starts to rumble.

"Omigod!"

"Oh, that's effed up!"

"I hope his butt's in jail."

"Mister Croix, I'm sorry to hear about your cousin,"
Mrs. Haterade says. "And you're right, her story is no different from what we hear today. Truth is, Pecola's story, although fictional, is the reality for so many of us. There are
hundreds and thousands of Pecolas in the world. And just
like in this book, for many of them, there are no happy
endings."

I choke back tears. My stomach starts to twist in knots
'n' I can feel my breakfast bubblin' up inside of me 'n' I
can tell I am gonna be sick. Like right now. I can taste it in
the back of my throat.

Oh no, oh no. These fools will not see me break down. Not today. Oh no, honey-boo. I snatch up my things 'n' bolt for the door with Mrs. Haterade calling after me, but I don't make it to the bathroom in time before I am hunched over in the middle of the hallway, tossing up my guts along with every nasty word my mother has ever said to me.

18

*"**I**'m so damn sick of you, lil girl!"*
"I swear, I'm sorry I ever had you...!"

"You think I wanna be tied down to some lil snotty, fresh-mouthed kid?"

"You're gonna end up worthless like the rest of them hot-in-the-azz little girls in the streets you tryna be like...!"

"I'm not raising whores up in here...!"

I open my eyes. Blink several times to adjust to the darkness. My head is pounding. I'm breathing heavy. And judging by my covers being off the bed 'n' my pillows all over the place, I musta been tossing 'n' turning in my sleep again.

Another nightmare. This time I was being chased by a pack of rabid dogs 'n' my mother was leading the pack, wielding some type of black leather whip, talking all reckless. She sicced these wild mangy dogs on me 'n' had me running for my life.

I'm not sure exactly what the dogs in my dream mean

since we've never owned any. But what I do know, what I always remember, is the mean, evil way my mother is always glaring at me.

"*Fiona, don't let what she says get to you*," Leona would whisper to me as she hugged 'n' rocked me until I'd fall asleep or simply be too cried out to shed another tear. "*You're beautiful. Don't ever forget that. Okay?*"

And, yeah, I would nod like I believed her, but deep inside I didn't feel it. How could I? I mean, really. My own mother thought I was some ugly misfit who ruined her life.

But I know better now. Still, it hurts sometimes when I think too long about it, which is why I do everything I can to *not* think about it, or remember any of it.

I don't like her. And, honestly, I don't think I ever will.

Oooh, boo, pull ya'self together. You too fly to be lookin' 'n' feelin' all crazy.

I swipe tears from my face, then reach over 'n' grab my cell from off the nightstand to check the time: 1:13 A.M. *Omigod, I can't believe I slept through* Scandal. I don't even bother checking the six messages I have. I climb outta bed, dragging myself to the bathroom. I flush, wash my hands, then a few minutes later I step out 'n' head down the hall toward my mother's bedroom to see if she's home. Why I even bother when I know she's not is beyond me. Her door's closed. I press my ear up against it, then slowly turn the knob, opening it.

Empty.

Just like I knew it would be.

Why you care?

She'd rather be at work instead of being here, or being a mother, any-damn-way, so get over it.

Oh, trust. I'm over it.

Lies.

Mmph. Well, lies or not. The truth is, sometimes it gets lonely being up in this big ole house alone. Not that I want some annoying lil sister pestering me 'n' working my last nerve tryna suck up all'a my attention, or bugging me about borrowing my things, or worse—going through my ish without permission.

Oh no, hun. Trust. Ain't nobody got time for that. I'm not that kinda bored. Still. It'd be nice to have someone here, sometimes. Uh, hold up. Let me rephrase that. It would be nice to know there's someone here who gets me, someone who I like. Not some ole grump who just wants to eat, sleep, work, 'n' slick-talk me every chance she gets. Like, jeezus, get yo' life, lady. Anywaaaay...

I shut her door, head downstairs to get something to drink, then ease my way back up to my room, grabbing the remote 'n' turning on the TV. I climb back up in bed, flipping through channels. Then decide to go on Facebook 'n' page stalk until I finally drift back to sleep.

I don't snap my eyes open again until, until... seven o'clock. "Aah!" I shriek, bolting up in bed. "Omigod! I'm gonna be frickin' late. No, no, no!"

I plop back against my pillows, struggling with the idea of getting up 'n' getting dressed. *God, why can't today be Saturday?* I swear. I live for the weekends. *Girl, snatch back these covers 'n' get yo' life! You have no time for lying around acting all pitiful 'n' feeling sorry for ya'self. No no, honey-boo, get ya'self together!*

I stretch 'n' groan, then begrudgingly hop outta bed, feeling no more rested than I did when I awoke in the middle of the night. I feel real groggy 'n' extremely cranky.

And I know waaay before my soft feet hit the floor that today's not gonna be a good day, for me or for anyone who dares to try me.

I curse myself for oversleeping as I race around my room like a wild woman, yanking a black bra 'n' panty set from outta my dresser drawer, then snatching a cute pair of jeans off a hanger along with a sexy lil red wrap blouse. *Ooh, I hate rushing.* I turn on my stereo 'n' let my boo Ariana Grande do me right as I sing along to one of her latest songs, heading for the shower.

Forty minutes later, I strut into the kitchen 'n' stop in my tracks. *She's* home. Mmph. I cut an eye over at her. She has a cup of coffee in one hand 'n' the *Jersey Journal* in the other. She has her face pressed all into the newspaper, mumbling 'n' shaking her head about some old man getting punched up by three men over on Duncan 'n' Mallory Avenues.

I have no interest, so I pretend to not hear her. I don't even wanna be in the same room with her right now. But I am too hungry to turn back around. I shuffle on over to the refrigerator 'n' pull out a container of vanilla Greek yogurt 'n' a bowl of sliced strawberries. I pour some yogurt over the fruit, then seal the container, placing it back into the fridge.

"Oh, so there must be something wrong with your mouth, huh? You too cute to speak, right?"

Oh, here we go with the BS already. I frown. "Um, hello. I don't see you sippin' through a straw, so that tells me your jaw's not broke. So what's wrong with you speaking to *me*?"

"What?" She slams the paper down on the table. "Lil girl, I think you keep forgetting who the parent is up in here. You're gonna walk up in here, go inside *my* refriger-ator 'n' eat food *I* buy 'n' *not* open your mouth 'n' say one word to me, like you don't see me sitting here? You have it all backwards. You're the *child*. I'm the *adult*. When you walk into a room, *you* open your mouth 'n' *you* speak. I don't give a damn if I saw you or not, with your disre-spectful azz. I'll be glad when you get the hell up outta my house."

I shoot her a dirty look. "Trust. The feeling's mutual. Please don't even sit there 'n' act like you've rolled out the red carpet 'n' welcomed me with open arms. You didn't want me here the moment they sliced me outta ya stom-ach. So boom! I'm sick of you actin' like it's my fault you had ya lil nervous breakdown or that you're three scoops from damn crazy. I didn't ruin ya life, boo. *You* did. It's not my fault ya husband ran off 'n' left you for some other woman." I tsk. "I see why he left you…"

"Whaaaat?!" She glares at me. "Keep it up, Fiona. Okay? Keep testing me. I'm this close"—she snaps her fingers—"from hoppin' on ya tail. I don't know what you were doing all night that you couldn't get up for school on time, but I'm not signing no notes."

I shoot her another dirty look, pulling out a stool 'n' sit-ting at the counter, as far away from her as possible. "I didn't ask you for one, either. Did I?"

"Well, I'm telling you."

"Mmph. Well, thanks for the notification. You coulda at least made sure I was up."

She grunts. "For *what*? Making sure you get up for school is not my concern. You grown, remember?"

"But you just *said* you were the parent here, *remem-ber*? Make up ya mind."

"Don't try me, lil girl. Now hurry up 'n' get the hell up outta here."

Oh no, hun. She is not about to do me.

I take a deep breath. Count to ten slowly in my head, then backwards. I can hear Leona in my head saying, *"Pick 'n' choose your battles."*

But little does this lady know I'm in no mood for her. Oh no. I'm so not. I'm getting sick of picking my battles. She keeps pickin' 'n' itchin' for a fight. And I'm about ready to give her one 'cause I wanna get bloody on the battlefield. Still. I'm tryna bite my tongue 'n' keep it cute. For now.

"Umm, why are you even home?"

She grunts, iggin' my question. "Mmph. And what was wrong with you yesterday?"

Uhh, duh. "I was sick." I don't even look at her when I say it. Just keep flitting about the kitchen. But I can feel her stare burning into me.

"*Sick* with what?"

Sick with memories of you!

"All know is, I don't know what kinda mess you're tryna pull, but all that throwing up you were doing yesterday in school had better be because you had food poisoning."

I am breathing heavily. I shut my eyes tight. So tight that I think I'm going to mash my eyeballs in. Right at this very moment, believe it or not, I am desperate for some kind of control. Anything to keep me from servin' her. But she's tried it. One. Time. Too. Dang. Many.

And I'm done.

"Trust, I'm not pregnant. Nor am I stupid enough to wanna be." I pop my eyes open 'n' make a face at her. She threatens to get up 'n' slap me. I threaten to call the po-po 'n' have her dragged up outta here in silver wristlets if she even tries it. She calls me a whore. Tells me that's about all I'm ever gonna be. Umm, really?

You think?

Wrong answer, boo.

I laugh sarcastically. "You know what, I'll be whatever you want me to be. What you think about me can't hurt me no more than it already has. So, boom. But what we both know is, it takes a whore to know one."

Next thing I know her coffee cup is being hurled across the kitchen at me 'n' she's jumping to her feet, like she's ready to toss it up. I slam my spoon into the half-empty bowl 'n' push myself away from the stool, which falls to the floor with a loud crash. Then let her have it. For. *Filth*.

19

Never kiss 'n' tell. Always keep 'em guessing...
I shut my locker, then jump. Cease is standing here. And, yes, he's startled me. "Ohmigod! Boy, are you crazy? What are you doing sneakin' up on me like that?"

"My bad." He smiles. "I didn't mean to spook you."

Shoot. I forgot my Latin book. I huff, reopening my locker. "Well, you did. I mean..." I force myself to pause 'n' take a deep breath. "How can I help you?"

"I heard you were throwin' up everywhere the other day, so I wanted to see if you a'ight."

I smirk. "Yeah, right."

"Nah, nah. I'm dead-azz. You good?"

"Oh, I'm always good, trust."

"Well, I'm tryna find out..."

"Heeeeeey, Cease," this Spanish chick Maribel says, sticking out her boobs like she's tryna offer 'em up on a platter to him. That's really about all she has going for herself. I'd like to see how far those watermelon jugs get her in life. By the time she's twenty they'll be dragging down to the ground from all the boys she's had hanging on 'em. But I'm not messy, so I'ma leave it at that.

"Yo, what's good, Maribel?" he says, giving her a head nod.

She cuts her eyes over at me. I toss my hair. Make her invisible.

"*Nada*, papi."

"Oh, a'ight."

She's still standing here.

"I think you better go sign her autograph," I say, smirking.

She rolls her eyes at me.

He looks over at her. "Yo, I'ma holla at you, a'ight?"

"Yeah, make sure you do, papi." She shoots me a dirty look before finally catching the hint 'n' bouncing. Silly trick.

"Ooh, *papi*," I tease, running a hand over his chiseled chest. "She's gonna ride ya enchilada. Giddy up, giddy up, boo."

He grins, leaning against the lockers. "Yeah, a'ight. How 'bout you ride it?"

"I'll pass. I don't do Mexican."

He laughs. "Yeah, a'ight. How 'bout a soul pole?"

I frown. "Not interested."

"Yo, what's goodie, Cease, man?" his boy Justin says as he walks by. With his fine self. "We still hittin' the gym after school?"

"No doubt, son." They bump shoulders, giving each other dap.

I eye Justin on the low. Mmph. McPherson High got some real cutie-boos on the basketball team. Trust. I'm not even gonna lie. Justin could get it. With his nerdy-looking self. Still. He's super cute. Real tall, like I like 'em, 'n' he has really nice skin.

"What's good, Fiona?"

"You, boo-daddy," I coo.

He laughs. "Oh, word?"

I lick my lips. "Uh-huh. You already know." Yeah, I'm flirting shamelessly, knowing Cease is checking for me. So what?

"You stay flirtin'." He looks over at Cease. "Yo, man, I'ma get at you later. I'll catch you at lunch."

"A'ight, bet." They give each other a pound, then Justin walks off. Cease brings his attention back to me. "Why you be playin' me, yo?"

I smirk. "What are you talkin' about, boy? Ain't nobody playin' you."

Okay, yeah, he's cute. No, scratch that. *Fiiine.* And yeah, he has mad swag. So what? Am I supposed to now all of a sudden fall at his big feet 'n' worship him because he's tryna get at me?

No, hun. Not over here. I'm not one of his groupies.

"Yeah, a'ight," he says, eyeing me. "All school year you've been playin' me to the left. You know what you be doin', yo. How you gonna flirt wit' my mans 'n' I'm standin' right here, yo?"

I shrug. "I'm single. He's single. What's the big deal?"

"Yeah, a'ight. Whatever. And what was that stunt you pulled the other day at lunch, huh?"

I feign ignorance. "What *stunt*?" I bat my lashes. "Oh, when you wanted me to kiss you? Boy, bye. I don't know where your lips been."

"Let me show you where they've been. Or where I want 'em to be." He smirks that sexy smirk that makes him so effen fine 'n' almost irresistible. Almost.

"Not."

"I'm sayin', though. I'm tryna make you mine."

"Lies 'n' fabrications. The only thing you tryna do is make me late for class."

"Stop, yo. I'm feelin' you, Fee. You already know what it is. I've been diggin' you for a minute, but…"

I run a hand through my hair 'n' purse my lips. "Why?"

He gives me a perplexed look. "Huh?"

"I asked you why. Why now, Cease?"

"C'mon, Fee. You know I've been big on you since freshman year, yo."

"Uh-huh. And that's why I caught you with your tongue stuffed down in some mare's mouth, 'cause you were so *big* on me. Right? Boy, bye. Lies 'n' fabrications."

"Mare? Girl, whatchu talkin' 'bout? You ain't ever seen me kissin' up on no horse."

I roll my eyes, stuffing my book into my bag. I peer around my locker at him. "Boy, don't play dumb. And don't give me that selective amnesia crap you boys stay tryna act like you have. You know *who* 'n' *what* I'm talkin' about. Freshman year. Fifth period. Behind the gym bleachers. Big head. Big face. Big teeth."

Realization registers in his eyes. "Ohhhh. *That*. *Her*." He laughs.

I don't.

"Damn. You still on that, yo? I tol' you then she was a dare. You know I wouldn't a done you like that for real, for real. That chick was mad ugly."

"Uh-huh. That's what ya mouth says. But your lips were sayin'—or should I say, *doin'*—something else. You chose Horse Face over *me*. That was a no-no, boo."

"C'mon, Fee. It wasn't even like that. I wasn't checkin' for that girl like that."

I slam my locker shut. "Yeah, well you *claimed* you were *checkin'* for me back then, but then I catch you holed up behind the bleachers. You were too busy *checkin'* that chick's tonsils with your tongue for me to believe that lie. Ha! You weren't checkin' for her. You got me once, you won't get me twice."

Okay, let me hip you right fast. See. I'm not even fazed about what Cease did with that horse-face chick freshman year. I had only been so-called messing with him for like three days. So it wasn't even all that serious. Trust. I wasn't spilling no tears over him, or over what he did. Be clear. Fiona Madison doesn't play the backseat to no boy unless we back there to get it poppin'. But play the backseat to some other chick? Not. Still. He had no business doing it.

Dare or not, I don't think so.

Anyway, the girl doesn't even go to this school anymore. Shoot. I can't even think of her name. All I see is her gigantic face, those big gums of hers, 'n' her huge white teeth that reminded me of piano keys every time I looked in her mouth.

And, yeah, I heard a few days after I caught them tonguin' it up that the whole thing was supposedly some dare, or stupid-boy bet to see who could get with her first.

I guess he won.

And nope...I wasn't all broken up about it, either. I simply tapped him on his big wide shoulder, then reached up 'n' slapped his face when he turned to look over his shoulder at me. He tried to explain. Tried to apologize. But I wasn't hearing it. It was over. And by the end of seventh period, I had moved on. Yup. I had me a new boo— his boy, Luke.

He shakes his head. "Nah, yo. You got me all wrong. I'm a grown man now, baby. I ain't on them lil kiddie games like that anymore. I've paid for my sins long enough, Fee. Don't you think it's time for you to forgive a bruh? Can I live, yo?"

"Sure you can," I say, walking off 'n' glancing over my shoulder. "You can *live* with the fact that you coulda had all'a this goodness. Now watch it shake."

I bite the inside of my lip to keep from laughing as I throw an extra bounce in my step, for emphasis.

Pow! How you like me now? I throw a hand up in the air at him, popping my hips down the hall, smirking.

He laughs. "Awww, man. You killin' me, yo."

20

"So what are you gonna do about Cease?" Miesha wants to know, pulling out her phone 'n' checking her messages. It's our lunch period 'n' she and I are sitting together as we usually do unless I'm gracing the cheerleaders' table, or she's either called over to sit with her boo 'n' his jock buddies at their table, or the lil lovey-dovey duo take it out to his or her car for a lil private time.

I frown, pulling a red velvet cupcake from one of my favorite bakeries in Harlem outta a small Tupperware container. "Uh, what do you mean, what am I gonna do?" I slide my tongue over the creamy whipped frosting. "Nothing."

She stares at me. "Ugh! Omigod, what a freak."

I shrug, smacking my lips 'n' licking more frosting before taking a bite into the moist mini-cake. I moan. "Ooh, this is so delish. I know I'ma have to call one'a my lil boo-daddies over tonight so I can burn these calories off."

She shakes her head 'n' starts texting, her fingers clicking the keypad a mile a second before she finally looks up at me. "Antonio is always somewhere doing too much."

I roll my eyes. "Oh, please. And what is Mister Wonderful doing now?"

"Ooh, save the sarcasm, heifer." She wags a finger at me. "We are not about to get off topic. Now what do you mean, you're not gonna do *nothing*? Girl, are you serious?"

I bat my lashes. "Boo, I'm as serious as a one-day shoe sale."

"Umm, let's see here." She purses her lips 'n' taps a finger up to her chin as if she's in deep thought. "So, you're gonna potentially let a good guy slip right through ya fingers, is that what you're telling me?"

"Chile, boom! Not interested."

"Omigod! You're such a liar."

"I am not."

"Now you're really lying."

I laugh. "Okay. I am. Maybe. But I'm not really gonna say if I'm interested or not."

She gives me a look.

"Okay, okay. Just a little interested."

She claps her hands together. "Ooh, I knew it. And, *hunni*, curiosity always kills the cat."

I put a finger up. "Uh-uh. Pump the brakes, honey-boo. That doesn't mean I'm *curious* enough to do anything about it."

She gives me a confused look. "Um, and why not?"

"Because I'm not checkin' for him like that."

Chickie immediately starts going in about settling down 'n' having a boo of my own, blah, blah, blah. Like really? Is she serious right now? Chile, boom! Ain't nobody got time

for that. Like I said before, why would I settle for one boo-
thang when I can have two or three or four?

"Girl, I keep telling you it's time you open ya heart 'n'
let a lil love in."

I press my lips 'n' tap my heeled foot against the floor,
repeating my mantra: Never, ever, get too attached to a
boy. All that letting a boy be your life is a no-no. And trust.
Fiona Madison has no time for that.

I take another bite of my cupcake. Slowly chewing 'n'
thinking, wondering if I should tell her that I've never really
had a boyfriend, not like a boyfriend-girlfriend type of
thing; or that I've never, ever, been in love before. Okay,
lies, lies, 'n' more lies.

I have loved. Bubbles. And, *hunni*, it was love at first
sight. He was so cute. Jet black 'n' sweet. I swear. He was
my everything.

My lil boo gave me life!

Then my heart got ripped outta my chest when he died.

And I haven't been the same since. Chile, boom! It was
horrible. I musta cried practically every day for almost a
week before I was finally able to get over it.

Ish happens, right?

Still. It hurt. And I know I'll never, ever, find another
fantail goldfish that'll be as special to me as Bubbles was.

But aside from him being the love of my life, nope.
Well, okay, I've since fallen for Gucci 'n' Jimmy Choo 'n'
Louis 'n' Marc Jacobs—who, by the way, has a really, really
cute handbag I'd just die to have. But as far as falling for a
living, breathing being? Nope. I've never been in love with
a boy before. The whole idea of it makes me nauseous.
No, seriously. It makes me really, really sick.

I unscrew the cap off of my bottled FIJI Water 'n' take a sip.

"You do realize you could be throwin' away the chance to lose your V-card to one of the hottest guys, besides my boo, at this school?"

I suck my teeth. "Ooh, shots fired!"

She laughs. "What, boo? You're not a virgin?"

I roll my eyes 'n' laugh in spite of myself.

"Speaking of ya future, boo," Miesha says in a singsong voice as she stares straight ahead. "There he goes now."

I follow her gaze, all the way across the cafeteria to where Cease is standing with Luke, all buffed 'n' sexy 'n' knowing he's fine in his loose-fitting jeans 'n' Affliction tee that wraps around his bulging muscles.

Ooh, I can't stand it.

I swallow. Then wave her on. "Girl, bye. Like I said, I'm not thinking about that boy."

"So let me get this straight: You're really not gonna try to get with him?" She peers at me through narrow slits, her curious eyes taking me in as if she's waiting for me to confess to some hidden fascination with that boy. Please. I don't think so. I mean, yeah, okay...I said he was fine. *And?*

So am I now supposed to roll out the red carpets, summon in the trumpeters, then bow at his deliciously big feet?

Chile, *boom*! I think not.

Fiona Madison will *not* be featuring Ceasar. No, ma'am. But that doesn't mean I can't look. Just not touching, that's all.

"Nope. Not interested," I say, feeling my pulse quicken as he looks over in our direction.

I eye him as he 'n' Luke give a few of the football play-ers dap 'n' shoulder bumps. Miesha teases me about tryna eyeball him on the low. I give her the finger 'n' she laughs.

I shift in my seat when they finally make it over to our table. He 'n' Luke speak to the both of us. We speak back. Luke pulls out a chair 'n' takes a seat next to Miesha.

"Yo, so what's good for the weekend?" Cease asks no one in particular as he pulls out a chair 'n' sits beside me.

Miesha shrugs. "I don't know. It's whatever Antonio wants to do."

Cease smirks. "Awww, look at that. My boy got you trained well."

She raises a brow. "*Bloop, bloop*. Wrong answer, boo. I trained *him*. Get it right."

He laughs. "Oh, a'ight. Right, right. My bad." He looks over at me. "So what's good wit' you? What you got planned?"

I shake my head. "Studying, that's about it. My life is over for the weekend."

Cease scoots his chair closer to me, draping his arm over the back of my chair.

"Nah, you gotta think positive."

"I am thinking *positive*. I'm positively sure I'm going to do horrible on this test if I don't get my mind together. And trust. Fiona doesn't do horrible well."

"Don't sweat it, babe," he says with a grin. "Dumb blondes are mad sexy, yo."

Miesha 'n' Luke both find what he's said funny.

I don't. I punch him in the arm.

"Ha, ha, ha. Real funny."

He rubs his arm, tryna rub the sting out. "Damn, babe, you got a nasty right punch."

I roll my eyes. "And I have an even nastier left hook. So don't do me, boy."

"Oh, daaaaaamn, son," Luke says, laughing. "Sounds like she tryna call you out."

"Looks that way to me," Miesha teases. "Cease, rough her up."

Cease leans back in his seat. Folds his arms up over his head. "Nah, it's all good. I ain't tryna rough up this pretty lil thing, yet," he says all sly.

I buck my eyes open. "Uh, not ever."

He smiles. "Yeah, a'ight. I welcome a challenge." His gaze 'n' the way he's licking his lips is kinda unnerving me. And Fiona doesn't get unnerved. Not by some boy. But here I am, shifting in my seat. I cross my legs.

"And I'd love to do you. But you frontin' like you scared."

"Awwww, sookie-sookie." Luke starts making sex faces. And I can't help but laugh at his silly butt.

"Nah. Fiona ain't ready for all this over here," Cease carries on, jokingly. Well, at least that's how I'm taking it 'cause this boy has no idea what I'm ready for. I peep what he's doing. He thinks he's gonna reel me into some kinda mind game. No, boo-boo. Not gonna happen. I'm too swift for that.

Miesha points a finger over at me, smirking. "Whatchu gonna do, boo?"

I suck my teeth, waving her on. "Chile, cheese. Not a thing. I'm not thinkin' about Cease."

"It's all good, babe. But I stay thinkin' about you."

I swallow. "Boy, whatever. You stay playing."

"Nah, that nucca ain't playin', yo," Luke volunteers,

adding his two cents like somebody's asked him for it. Like somebody gives a damn. "He's dead-azz."

Cease looks at me. Then winks.

I quickly look away.

It's like one minute I am breathing, my heart is beating, 'n' then the next: _____.

Flatline.

Dead to the bed!

Nailed to the bottom of the sea!

This boy has come over here 'n' has straight hijacked my whole groove.

21

"**M**om told me the two of you got into it last week and what you said to her," my sister Sonji says on the phone. "I can't believe how disrespectful you were." I roll my eyes. That lady stays tattling on me, like my sisters are gonna check me. Chile, boom.

Check me, boo?

Who, you?

Not.

"Yeah. Well, I'm sick of her," I say dismissively. "She's always comin' at me crazy 'n' I'm done with it."

"She's still our mother, Fee," she says like I need reminding of that dreadful fact. "And the way you spoke to her was crazy."

"How you know? Were you there? Did you hear how she was coming outta her neck all crazy at me? No."

"You're right. I wasn't there. But you know I know your mouth. And—"

"And you know hers. How many times did she slick-talk you?"

"No matter what Mom may have done or said to us, none of us would have spoken to her the way you do."

"Omigod, Sonji! Really? You're gonna come at me like you tryna advocate for her like she's some victim? Chile, boom." I suck my teeth. "You have your lil fancy life with ya hubby 'n' kids in Connecticut, while I'm stuck here with this miserable witch. Not once have you offered to let me live with you, so don't do me, boo."

"Wait a minute. I'm not *doing* you, so take it down several notches, hun. And I'm not advocating for Mom. I'm simply saying that what you said to her I think bothered her. If you really wanted to move up here you'd be welcomed with open arms. And you know it."

I frown. "Well, maybe. Still. You're not here with her. I am. And good if she's bothered by something I said to her. It's about time."

She sighs in my ear. "Fiona, I know you're angry with her. And, no, maybe she hasn't been the perfect parent…"

"Oh, you think? I don't know why you 'n' Leona always wanna take up for her…"

"I'm not taking up for her," she says defensively. "I'm—"

I cut her off. "Making excuses for her like you always do. I know she's our mother. I don't need to be reminded of that tragedy. But that doesn't mean I'm gonna ever respect her when she has never respected me. No, thank you. Not gonna happen. Not with Fiona, boo. No, ma'am."

"That still doesn't give you the right to think it's okay to tell her to go jump in front of a truck, Fiona. That was way out of line, even for you."

I blink. "No. That's *not* what I told her. What I *saaaid*

was, if she's so miserable with her life 'n' with me in it, then she should just go toss herself over a bridge 'cause I'm not about to slice my wrists over her. No, ma'am."

Okay, maybe I shouldn'ta said that to her. But you know what? Oh well. Once it came out, along with everything else that flew outta my mouth, there was no stopping it or taking it back. And trust. I gave it to her good 'n' gotdang dirty.

Not once have I ever cursed out my mother—even though there are many times when I wanted to. Still, I don't cross that line. And I probably never will. But do I serve her attitude? Yup. Lots of it. Do I let her know what I think about her? Yup. Every time she tries to do me, I do her back. Period. So why Sonji is on my line acting like I've committed some cardinal sin is beyond me. Yeah, I know all about how kids should honor their parents. Yeah, yeah, yeah, yada, yada, yada. And they should when they are being treated right; otherwise no, ma'am. There's no honor in a mother always frickin' ridiculing me. So, boom! I'm not subscribing to that channel of BS. So my sisters 'n' whoever else can miss me with that.

"And calling her a *whore*," Sonji says tightly. "That was really uncalled for, Fee. And you know it."

"Omigod! Lies, lies, 'n' more lies, Sonji. She called *me* one. And all I said was, it took one to know one. Boom, there it is. If she didn't want the heat, then she shouldn'ta turned up the fire."

She sighs. "You are still responsible for what comes out of your mouth, Fee."

"Oh, and she's not? Puhleeeeease." She tells me I need to apologize. I tell her absolutely not. That I meant every dang thing I said to her. From her peeling her panties down 'n' sleeping with another woman's husband 'n' sex-ing him in the backseat of his car; to her gettin' knocked up, then expecting him to leave his wife for her. Oh no, hun. I let her know: Don't hate me 'cause life didn't go ya way.

I let her know that I wasn't the one who put her in the cuckoo ward for thirty days 'cause she suffered from post-partum depression right after I was born. No, hun. That is not my soundtrack to play. It's hers. And I'm not the one who walked out on her 'n' left her with four daughters to raise on her own before she got knocked up with me. No, sweetie. Don't take ya misery out on me.

I let her know that, too. And I also let her know that it wasn't my fault she didn't get the man but got stuck with a baby instead. Maybe my father did love her. But not enough to leave the wife 'n' family he already had over in Bayonne. I called her a trifling homewrecker 'n' a hater.

And guess what? She couldn't handle the truth. So you know what she did? She slapped me. *Whap!* Right across my face. But no worries, trust.

I didn't blink. Didn't splash a tear. Didn't even hit her back, or call the police on her, like I wanted to.

I ate it.

Just like I've eaten every-dang-thing else she's dished out to me.

Okay, okay. I *know* my mouth can be a lil extra 'n' my attitude a lil stank. But I don't bring it unless you bring it to me first. Then she had the nerve to say I'm grounded for the weekend. Ha! Picture that. Who, me? Not. What I look like, sitting up in this house on a weekend, no less. Yeah, okay, boo. Hold ya breath 'n' let me see how you make out with that. My name is Fiona. Not Boo-Boo the Fool. Trust.

"You should still apologize," Sonji insists. I blink, pulling my cell from my ear 'n' looking at it like there's a set of jagged teeth on it before placing it back to my ear. Oooh, I wanna really give it to her, but I can't, won't. Like I said before, Leona 'n' Kara are more like mothers than my sisters. If it weren't for them, I'd probably be somewhere popping pills like they were Skittles 'n' tossing 'em back with caps of NyQuil. Or worse. So, no matter what, I keep it cute 'n' bite down on my tongue. And trust. It hurts like hell. But I'm chomping down on it 'cause I know meddling in my damn business 'n' tryna play mediator is what my sisters do, 'n' they mean well. Still. I said what I felt 'n' what I meant to my mother 'n' I don't think I should have to apologize to *her* or anyone else for *my* feelings.

"Wrong answer, boo. I'm not doin' that."

"Why not? It's the right thing to do," she counters. "There's still a thing of respecting adults even if you don't agree with them. Sometimes you gotta—"

"I know, I know. Know when to keep ya mouth shut, yada, yada, yada. Sorry. I'm not subscribin' to that channel. A closed mouth doesn't get fed or heard. And two things I'm not about to do. Starve or stay quiet."

"Sometimes doing what's right," Sonji continues, "doesn't always feel right."

"Oh, really? For who? Like I told mommy dearest when she disrespected me 'n' we started goin' at it: I didn't ask to be born. But I'm here. That was her choice, not mine. So I shouldn't have to live my life feeling like I'm the mistake just 'cause some hot-drawz chick gave it up raw. She chose to have a buncha kids. Not me. But she takin' it out on me like I'm the one who held her down 'n' forced her to get her hump on."

Boom! And I meant every word of that. And that's why she laid hands on me. Mmph. The truth hurts. Oh well. Her tryna slap my face off was worth everything I said to her.

I'm seventeen 'n' even I have enough sense to know having some mofo's baby ain't gonna get him to stay with you, or even want you after you done let him use you up. No, boo. I'm not claiming that as my fault. And I ain't pulling out no violins to play you no sob song. It is what it is.

And sorry, *hun*, I'm not tolerating disrespect. Not even from my own mother. I've put up with it long enough. And I'm sick of it. So love me, hate me, or slap me up, I don't give a damn. 'Cause the truth is this: I'm effen done holding back. That lady needs to know how badly she hurt me.

"Come here, lil white girl..."

Like really? *White girl?* Are you kidding me? When she was busy letting a *white* man smash? Really?

Who does that? Calls their kids all kinda nasty names?

I swipe tears from my face. Then shake my head, just as another call is ringing through. It's Miesha. I tell Sonji to hold on. Put on my happy face, then click over. "Hey, girl."

"What are you doin' later tonight?"

I swallow back my emotions 'n' tell her my sister Leona is picking me up for dinner around six, but after that not a damn thang.

"Ooh, good. I feel like bowling tonight. You down?"

"Bowling? Oh no, boo. Let me know how you make out with that. You not even about to get me into a pair of them ugly shoes."

She laughs. "Oh, c'mon. Don't be so dang corny. Live a little. It'll be fun."

"Mmph. Not interested. But look, I have my sister Sonji on the other line so I'ma have to hit you back."

"Make sure you do. Bowling. Tonight, girlie. Me 'n' you. So don't get cute, boogah."

"Ooh, you tried it. I stay cute. Trust."

She laughs. "And you still ugly, boo."

"Ooh, *bish*, bite me." We both laugh, exchange a few more words before I tell her I'll call her back. I click back over to Sonji. "Sorry about that," I say apologetically. "Now where were we?"

"We were about to go over your apology to Mom," she says matter-of-factly, like I'm really about to sign up for that lie.

"Ooh, not. But good try." We go back 'n' forth about why she thinks I should apologize 'n' it goes in one ear 'n' out the other. But I'm standing my ground, boo. And one thing about Fiona Madison: Once her mind is made up, there's nothing you gonna say or do to get her to change it. So Sonji can go have several seats with the apology crap.

It's not gonna happen.

I power on my laptop, then log into my Facebook page 'n' update my status: FEELIN' FRUSTRATED. ☹ BISHES KILL ME. THEY CAN SAY WHATEVER DA HELL THEY WANT, BUT GET ALL CAUGHT UP IN THEY FEELINGS WHEN YOU SERVE IT BACK TO EM. CHILE, BOOM! #DONTEFFWIFFME! #TAKEITSTRAIGHT2YAHEAD!

Three other calls ring through while I'm on the phone with Sonji—King, Travis, 'n' Benji. I don't bother clicking over, though.

"I'll give you that Louie I know you love so much," she says, tryna bribe me. My knees buckle. Ooh, she's playing dirty. She knows how bad I want that bag. "I'll even throw in the red Michael Kors tote."

Ooh, this bish playin' real dirty.

I feel myself getting sick. Now I gotta make a decision between pride 'n' purses. I roll my eyes 'n' suck my teeth. "Y'all always do this ish."

She laughs. "But we love you more."

"Uh-huh. Y'all stay bribin' me to be nice to that lady, though."

"Hey, we do whatever we have to do to help you 'n' Mommy coexist."

I sigh. "Yeah, okay."

"Is it working?"

I grunt. "Ugh! I hate you! Throw in a pair of heels 'n' we good!"

22

I'm not psychic, but I can always read a boy's nasty thoughts by staring into his lusty eyes. And this boy right here—the way he's slithering his serpent tongue over his thick, chapped lips—is thinking, *Damn, mami, I wanna slide up in them guts 'n' bury my face in between them beautiful boobs*... Oh, he's thinking some other things too, but I'm too much of a class act to repeat such filth. I'll just clench my booty cheeks 'n' keep it cute.

I glance around the area 'n' take in the sights. Pitiful. There's not one cutie-boo in sight. And I can already tell it's gonna be a depressing night.

"Yo, you fine as *fuqq*, ma," he starts, leaning into me. His warm breath tickles the inside of my ear. *Ohhhh-kaaaay... tell me something I don't already know.*

I bring my gaze back on him, taking a step back 'n' tossing my hair, then batting my lashes. *You think...?* Well, of course he does. But he doesn't need to know that I know that he does. Oh no. A diva knows how to stay cute. Play coy. Be demure. Umm, you do know what demure is, right?

Any*whooo*...

Where the heck is Miesha? I'm waiting for her here at Hudson Lanes. And of course she is *nooo*where to be seen. Why I even agreed to meet her to go bowling is beyond me. We coulda hung out at the mall 'n' shopped, then caught a cute lil flick or something. But, nooo, she chooses bowling 'n' expects me to wear those hideous flats. I mean shoes. Then toss a bowling ball down a lane. Something I haven't done in, like, forever. An activity that could potentially break a dang nail.

I glance at my watch. It's almost a quarter after nine. I knew when she told me to meet her here at nine o'clock I shoulda had my sister drop me off thirty minutes fashionably late, like I normally do. But, nope. The one time I'm on time, she decides to be late. Several guys walk by, snapping their necks to either check me out or get my attention. It's mad packed up in this spot. But I'm not seeing many cutie-boos up in here so I already know it's gonna be one long, *borrring* night.

"You mad sexy, too."

I shift my handbag from one hand to the other, leaning a foot back on one heel. "Thanks." *Click-clack, click-clack*. I start popping my gum all loud 'n' belligerent. A sign that I'm soo not beat for the okey-doke.

Shark Teeth is eyeing me like he's fresh outta lockup. All hungry 'n' ready to sink the jagged edges of his grill into me. Bless his lil heart. He has gotta know I have no intentions of letting him take a bite outta my sweet, juicy fruit. He can't even breathe on it! No ma'am, no sir!

One, he's too old—twenty; two, his teeth are big 'n' yellow; and three, he's too ugly. Zoo status ugly. Like wrap his face with gauze, then stuff his head in a Hefty trash bag type ugly. So no, thank you. Still. That doesn't mean I have to be mean 'n' nasty 'n' remind him of how ugly he is. Being messy is so not cute. He should already know he's ugly. Then again...maybe he doesn't. Some guys have been misled 'n' lied to their whole lives. Poor ting-tings.

I blink. Try not to make any oogly-faces. But the truth is, looking at this man-boy is hurting my eyes. Like really. Ooh, he has the kinda face only a mother could love. 'Cause, baaaaaby...not Miss Fiona!

"You have some beautiful eyes, too" he adds, holding my gaze. "I bet you hear that all the time."

For the love of God! And you need a breath mint. And major dental work. Ooh, his teeth look like big chicken nuggets. Looks like he's been chewing on rocks. But who am I to judge? I'm not messy like that.

I giggle. "Yeah. Sometimes." *Jeezus, get Sharkie away from me. Please 'n' thank you!* I smile. "Sooo, what, you wanna follow me on Instagram now?"

He laughs. "Nah, nah. But if you got Facebook, let me get ya info. So we can stay in touch. Maybe we can link up. You know, catch a bite to eat, or hit up a movie."

Um, I think not!

"I'm sayin'...how old are you?"

I blink. *Oh—my—god, why his lips look all cracked 'n' ashy? Them soup coolers too dang big to be lookin' all crazy!*

"Too young for you," I say, tilting my head. Heck. I'm grown. Real grown. But not *that* grown, tryna mess with some guy over nineteen wit' ashy lips 'n' a tore-up grill. No, hun. Save that ish for them ratchet chicks.

"Nah, nah. As long as you like sixteen, seventeen, we good. I like 'em young." He licks his over-stretched lips. "The younger the better. And you just right."

Eww. What a creep!

He licks his lips again. "So where you from?"

A land called Nunyadamnbusiness.

"Um, where *you* from?" I ask, igging the question.

Click-clack, click-clack...

"Bayonne."

Click-clack, click-clack. "Oh, okay." I glance around the bowling alley. *Where the heck is Miesha?*

I fish through my bag 'n' pull out my cell, sending her a text. HOOKER! WTH? WHERE R U?

"So who you here wit'?"

My phone buzzes. I pretend I don't hear him talking to me.

"Ya man?"

It's Miesha. I open her text message: OMW N NOW

I frown. "No, boo. I don't have one of those."

He grins. "Oh, a'ight. Ya girl?"

"Sorry, boo-boo. I don't swing that way, either." Well, umm, I do. I mean I have, but that's none of his business. Ole nasty freak. "So, annnyway...who *you* here with?"

He glances over my shoulder, then looks back at me. "My BM."

Ooh, this ninja's real sloppy 'n' disrespectful! He's out here with his baby mother, all up in my face, tryna get his ole nasty stick wet. Triflin'-azz! No-good dog! I let him have it real nice, then kindly tell him to step outta my face. Ain't no way I wanna be arguing with some booga-chick over the likes of some swamp creature. Chile, boom! I'm not tryna go to jail for beatin' down some ho with one'a them bowling pins for even thinking I want this rusty-dusty creep.

"It's all good, though. She knows how I get down."

I frown, then start popping my gum real loud 'n' crazy. *Click-clack, clickety-clack-clack!* "Oh really? And how is that? Not that I'm really interested."

This ninja has the audacity to part his crusty crumb-lickers 'n' say he has nine kids 'n' five baby mothers. "And you so fine, I might make you baby mother number six."

Hand on hip, face twisted, neck rolling, I give it to him real good. "Whoop, whoop. Blow the whistle. Who let the clown out? You better go hop back in ya box 'cause this fly chick over here is *not* interested in nothin' you dishin' out. You better go get those teeth together. I don't do raggedy grills, boo. No, sir. Good day."

"Daayuuumn, it's like that? Yeah, I know my teeth effed up. But I got a big—"

"Talk to the hand, boo-boo. I'm out." I spin off on him, popping my hips through the crowd, running smack into Miesha, Tone, *aaaand* Cease.

Cease?

What the heck is he doing here?

"Yo, what's goodie, Fiona?" Tone says, wrapping an arm around Miesha.

"Oh, nothin'. Standing here mad long waitin' on ya girl, lookin' all crazy tryna beat off the predators."

He laughs.

"Aah, what's good, Fee," Cease says, grinning.

I toss a hand up at him. Keep it real easy. "Hey."

"Can I get a hug, yo?"

"Uh, I guess." I step into his embrace. "I didn't know you were gonna be here." I shoot a look over at Miesha. She gives me some ole sheepish look. But I give her a dirty look that says *Tramp, I'ma claw ya eyes out*.

This heifer coulda told me Cease was gonna be tagging along.

23

"Sooo, who's ready to bowl?" Miesha says, rubbing her hands together.

"Yo, you know I'm ready," Antonio says.

Cease glances at me. "And you know I *stay* ready. What about you, babe?"

I tilt my head. "Trust. I'm always ready."

Lies 'n' fabrications. The only thing I'm ready to do is hit the door. But oh well. I'm here. He's here. So I might as well make the best of it. It's really no biggie. But trust. I can't wait to get Miss Miesha together when I get her alone. She thinks she's so dang slick.

"Okay, so it'll be me 'n' Fiona against you 'n' Cease," Miesha says, dodging my daggers. "Losers pay for our food. Okay?"

"Bet," Tone says.

"Yo, hol' up, fam," Cease says, shaking his head. "Who said y'all gonna win?"

Miesha puts a hand up on her hip. Then finger snaps. "Oh, trust, boo-boo. We about to do this."

Cease laughs, giving Tone dap. "Yo, tell 'em, son. We 'bout to run this."

"Boy, bye! Me 'n' my girl, we got this. We rock. We rule. We gonna run ya pockets. Ain't that right, Fee?"

I blink. Ooh, why is she poppin' ish? Ummm, does this chick not know I'm the queen of gutter balls? Well, I guess not. But she's gonna learn today.

She must peep the blank look on my face. She raises a brow. "*Bish*, you can bowl, right?"

"Uh-huh, straight down the gutter."

Miesha's face cracks. "Oh, just frickin' priceless! Let's go get our damn shoes so we can hurry up 'n' lose!"

Cease 'n' Tone crack up laughing, following her over to the counter. I drag along in back of them.

"Oh, it's on now," Cease teases. "Yo, y'all 'bout to get got."

"Word is bond," Tone cosigns. "I hope y'all got ya paper up 'cause you got two hungry ninjas on deck."

Cease looks over at me 'n' winks.

I roll my eyes, sucking my teeth. *Boy, boom! I'm not even tryna feed ya ole big, thick-necked, biscuit-eating butt.*

Miesha wags a finger at me. "I see you, girl."

I feign ignorance. "You see what?"

"Ooh, don't do it, boo. Wipe the drool from ya lips. Tryna act like you ain't checkin' for Cease. Girl, bye. I see you checkin' him on the low-low when he goes up to bowl." She cracks up laughing. "You ain't slick, boo."

I roll my eyes 'n' suck my teeth. "Girl, bye. I'm not hardly checkin' for that boy like that."

"Ooh, lies, lies, 'n' more lies!"

I laugh with her, crossing my legs. Truth is, I have been eyeing him on the low-low. Heck, he's cute. He has a nice body. And okay, okay. He has a really nice butt. Shoot me for looking. I'm a girl. That's what we do. Look. Besides, it's not like there are any other boys worth looking at here tonight. And I'm not even about to sit here 'n' be staring at Antonio Lopez. Although, yes, he is *fiiiine* 'n' real eye candy, but that's Miesha's man. And I don't believe in being messy. No, ma'am.

"Okay, busted. But you see all them muscles, girl?"

She shakes her head, laughing. "Nope. I only have eyes for my boo."

"Girl, bye. You can still look."

She giggles. "Well, I ain't lookin' hard, trust. But, yeah, I peeped 'em. How can you not? Now tell me you didn't like our double date."

I cough. "*Double date?* Girlie, this ain't no damn double nothing. All *this* is, is a situation that you created."

She waves me on. "Girl, bye. Call it what you want. You can thank me in the morning." She chuckles.

"Girl, please. Middle finger up."

"Uh-huh. Lies, lies, 'n' more lies! I peeped how the two of you been tossing glances at each other all night. You know he's feelin' you, girl. And it's obvious you feelin' him, too."

I fold my arms across my chest 'n' toot my lips. "I don't know what you talkin' about, boo."

She laughs some more.

I see Antonio walking over to us with Miesha's food order. Nooo, we didn't win. But after I was finally able to get the hang of it, me 'n' Miesha spanked 'em silly. Three games later. Ha! Okay, okay, so what if my legs flew out in front of me, twice, 'n' I landed on my butt. Or that I bowled backwards most of the game. Or that my feet are real sweaty in these funky bowling flats, uh, shoes. Or that Miesha 'n' them have done nothing but laugh at me most of the night. Fact is, we still got a win.

Yeah, Antonio 'n' Cease beat us, bad, the first two frames. But they *still* paid for our food. Mmph. What I look like, tryna spend my coins on some boy. Not! They were probably gonna pay anyway. But just in case they weren't. Let it be known, Fiona Madison ain't the one.

"Yo, what y'all over here gigglin' 'bout?" Antonio wants to know, handing Miesha her food.

"Ohhh, nothing," she says, smirking as she reaches for her food. "Thanks, babe."

"You know I got you, boo." He leans in 'n' kisses her. *Ugh! These two are sickening!* "So who y'all laughin' at?"

She shakes her head. "Just girl stuff." I peep her cutting her eye real quick over at Cease as he walks over, then back over at Tone, signaling to him that we were talking about Cease.

Tone nods. "Ohh, right, right. I got you." He grins as Cease hands me my food.

"Thanks," I say.

"No doubt," he says, taking a seat next to me. All I can do is roll my eyes at Tone 'n' Miesha. They laugh.

"Yo, what's so funny?"

I suck my teeth. "Don't pay them two any mind. You know they all drunk in love."

"That's right," Antonio says, smiling. "This here's my heart. Ain't that right, baby?"

"Yup," Miesha says. Then she leans in 'n' kisses her man

on the lips. Awww. Not! I mean. Trust. I'm not hating on my girl 'n' her boo. But, geesh. All that lovey-dovey mess is waaay over-the-top.

Cease, with his clown self, tries to lean over 'n' kiss me 'n' I smack him on the lips with my fork. "Uh-uh, boo-daddy. You better keep them big juicy lips right on over there."

Antonio 'n' Miesha burst out laughing. And me 'n' Cease join in. Then for the rest of the night the four of us sit 'n' eat 'n' bug out, then bowl another round. This time with Antonio 'n' Miesha as partners. So surprise, surprise. That leaves me with Cease. And a few times his ole slick butt calls himself tryna show me how to hold the ball. Chile, cheese. All this boy wants to do is press up on me. I know what time it is. But I let him get his feel on. All in the name of winning the game.

And guess what?

I get my first strike!

"Yes! Yes! Yes!" I scream excitedly. I'm so caught up in seeing all those pins topple over that I don't even realize that I've jumped into Cease's arms until I come to my senses 'n' realize my feet are dangling in the air. *Ooh, boo-daddy!* "Boy, put me down."

"You know you wanna be in my arms, girl," he teases, slowly letting me down. Frankly, I don't see the need for a comeback. I push back from him 'n' I toss my hair, sashaying on over back to my seat. I just got a strike. You can't tell me ish, boo!

By the end of the tenth frame, I end up bowling a ninety-eight. Yippee! Oh, don't do me. Yeah, it's low, but it's better than my last two scores. Fifties. Mmph. So not cute! But thanks to Cease's five strikes 'n' multiple pairs, we beat

Miesha 'n' Tone real right. And that's all I care about. Winning, boo!

It's a little after midnight when we finally pack it in. And I'm not even gonna front, boo. It was cute. Bowling. Okay, and the four of us hanging out. Still, Miesha was dead wrong tryna fix me up with Cease on the low like that.

"I'm sayin' though," Cease says, walking with me to Miesha's car. He 'n' I are kinda strolling a few feet behind Miesha 'n' her boo-daddy. "We should link up tomorrow. I can come scoop you 'n' we can go somewhere 'n' chill."

I stop in my tracks, raising a brow. "Uh, and why would I wanna do that?"

"Uh, how 'bout 'cause you had a good time. Or maybe 'cause you feelin' me."

I toss him a dismissive wave, walking off. "Lies! I'm not even about to go anywhere alone with you, boy. Psst. I don't know you like that. You could be some psycho who preys on young cutie-boos."

"Yeah, a'ight." He walks alongside of me. "Keep it a hunnid. Tell me you didn't have fun tonight."

I shrug. "It was okay."

He reaches for my arm, stopping me. "I wanna take you out. No pressure. Just me 'n' you. Think about it, a'ight?"

I grin, opening the passenger-side door, then sliding in. "Maybe."

He laughs. "Yeah, a'ight. Front if you want. Ain't no maybe, baby."

"Boy, boom. Middle finger up. You better try again."

I shut the door in his face.

24

Serve 'em grace 'n' face. Politeness with a smile goes a long way...

Early Monday morning, just as I'm swinging open the front door to walk up the block to Miss Moosey's to grab me a honey bun 'n' some Life Savers gummies before Miesha gets here to pick me up, I run smack dead into Cruella. Of all the dang people I wanna see first thing in the morning, *she* is *not* one of them. Trust. Her evil spirit is suffocating.

I take a deep breath. *Uh, excuuuuse you...*

I haven't really seen her since our verbal throw-down last week when we tore the kitchen up. And, trust, I'm still lookin' at her extra sideways for throwing her coffee cup at me. But whatever! She did that. However, since then she's stayed outta my way. And I've happily stayed outta hers. Hey, it works for me. And obviously it works for her, too.

She scowls. "I hope there are no dishes in my sink."

I blink. *Well, maybe if you had the dang dishwasher fixed, there wouldn't need to be any in your sink.* "Um, and good mornin' to you, too," I say snidely. "Have a nice day."

She grunts. "I asked you if you did the dishes."

I sigh. "Oh, that was a question? My bad." I bat my lashes 'n' toss my hair.

Her raggedy tote bag hits the floor with a *thud* as she steps outta her bright white Nikes. I stare at her. She looks exhausted. She has bags under her eyes 'n' her edges have seen better days. Chickie needs a treatment bad.

God, she looks so haggard 'n' run-down. If she would just slide a lil gloss up on them lips 'n' fluff that dang hair up, maybe she'd get herself a lil boo-daddy to knock the dust up off 'a that ole dried up snatch-patch.

"Girl, what in the world you just standin' here looking at me for? Is that kitchen cleaned?"

"Ohmigod! What is with you 'n' the dang dishes all the time? Is this some kinda fetish? 'Cause if it is, it's so not cute."

"I want you in this house right after school."

Screech! What the what? Hold the heck up...chickie's already tryna get it turnt up. It's too early for this.

"Excuse you? Since when you start givin' *me* a time when I come home?"

She throws a hand up on her wide hip. "Since I told you that you were on punishment 'n' you left up outta this house over the weekend anyway."

Of course I did.

"Hahaha. Try again, hun." I strut toward the door, reaching for the screen door handle. I stop in my tracks, turn to her. *Apologize to Mommy. It's the right thing to do.* "Look.

I'm sorry if you still feel some kinda way about how I served you."

"How you *served* me? You had better go on 'n' get outta my face before *you* get served up in here again."

I suck my teeth. "Anyway, I apologize for comin' at you all crazy like that. But, trust, I will never apologize to you or *anyone* else for saying how I feel."

She narrows her eyes. "Fiona, your sisters have never spoken to me the way you do, 'n' if they even tried it I woulda knocked every last tooth outta their heads. But you…"

"News feed update, boo. I'm not Leona 'n' them. And last I heard, you *wanted* them. *Not* me. You didn't call them names, or treat them like crap. And if you did give it to 'em, they kept their mouths shut 'n' took it. Well, sorry. I'm not that chick."

She shakes her head. "I'm tired. I'm tired of looking at you. I'm tired of dealing with you. I'm tired of having to be responsible for you. You're disrespectful. You're hateful. And I have no use for you 'n' that filthy mouth of yours."

"And so are you!" I snap, giving her a disgusted look. We stare each other down. I narrow my glare. "You just don't get it, do you? I am the way I am 'cause of *you*. You made me this way. And if you haven't noticed, the *only* person I'm hateful 'n' disrespectful to is *you*."

"I'm still your goddamn mother!" she argues. "And the least you could do is respect me!"

Oh, cry me a dirty river. Here she goes again with that word. *Respect*. I grunt, glancing at my watch, annoyed that she's tryna disrupt my morning flow with her foolery. "*Respect* you? Ha! That's an oxymoron if I've ever heard one. How do you expect me to respect *you* when all you've ever done is remind me of how much you wish you'd never had me, huh?"

"Lil girl, you got the game all screwed up! You respect *me* not 'cause you want to. But 'cause *I* gave birth to *you*. Because *I* keep a roof over ya damn ungrateful-azz head! Because *I* continue to allow you to eat 'n' sleep in comfort! Because *I* haven't snatched you by the neck 'n' choked out your last damn breath. That's why *you* respect *me*!" She jams a finger into her chest. "Your mother! Now get outta my damn face! I want you in this house by three o'clock! Not a minute after. And I will be up in here to see that you are!"

Mmph. This chick sounds like she needs another stay at the cuckoo farm if she even thinks I'm subscribing to the nuttiness she's talking.

I raise a brow. "Good luck with that."

"Try me, lil girl." She threatens to shut down my phone 'n' Internet service if I'm not walking through this door at said time.

My nose flares. I will not be blackmailed, bribed, or threatened by her or anyone else. "Oh no, oh no," I say, shifting my bag from one arm to the other. "We are not about to do this. Not today, boo. I have too much on my mental for what you sayin'. Check for me later with the threats. Not when I'm on my way out the door to start my school day. Who in the heck needs that kinda stress on them? Where they do that at?"

"You heard what I said, lil girl."

"My name *is* Fiona," I say, swinging open the door just as Miesha's car pulls up in front of the house. "*Not* lil girl. And the last I checked, being a mother didn't come with a trophy or a money-back guarantee. I'll see you when I see you."

I politely shut the door in her face, pullin' out my buzzing Sidekick, my backup phone. The one Cruella doesn't even know about. Lady, boom. Shut me down if you want. As long as I got T-Mobile on the low-low, I stay ready.

"Hey, girlie," Miesha says as I slide into the passenger seat, shutting the door.

"Hey. Just—one—second," I say, tapping away with my thumbs. It's King wanting to know if I wanna chill tonight. I can't even remember why I gave him this number instead of my other number. But, whatever. I tell him yeah—after eleven though. "Okay, done." I toss my Sidekick back into my bag, then fasten my seat belt. "Heeeeey, honey-boo. Heeey, sugah-foot."

She laughs. "Girl, you silly. So, why you have your face all tight comin' outta ya house?"

I suck my teeth, dramatically rolling my eyes. "What else? Cruella."

She looks over at me, confused. "Who?"

"My dang mother."

She laughs. "Ohmigod. I can't believe that's what you call her."

Even though I really haven't given Miesha all the dirt on how messy my mother is/was, she knows enough to know we don't get along. That's all I've ever been comfortable sharing with her, or anyone else. The rest of my miserable life, living with that lady, I keep to myself. The last thing I want is pity. Oh no, hun. Fiona ain't looking for no Hallmark moments. No, thanks.

I give Miesha a dismissive glance. "Trust, it's one of the nicer names I have for her. I swear that lady's crazy."

"Welcome to the club. You know I know all about crazy."

I nod knowingly. Even though Miesha decided to stay in Jersey 'n' live with her aunt so she could finish school with her boo, Tone, her mom decided to move back to Brooklyn with her dad. And from what Miesha's told me, her dad likes to feed the needy 'n' greedy his man-pole. But her mom keeps putting up with his cheating. Leaving him one minute, then taking him back the next. If you ask me, that's just too much craziness going on.

"Well, it's really gettin' on my last nerve," I say, pulling out my cosmetic case, removing a tube of pink cotton candy lip gloss. "That lady stays tryna do me. I swear I think her mission in life is to ruin me." I flip down the visor, then glide a coat of gloss over my lips. I pop my lips. "She better get her life." I toss the lip gloss back into my compact then stuff it down into my bag, venting. "I swear, she better be glad it's open-toe season 'n' Fiona ain't tryna have her pretty feet stuffed inside a pair of blue bobos; otherwise I'd turn it up on—"

"Girl, what the hell?"

"Going to jail, boo. If I didn't love my freedom 'n' havin' cutie-boos at my fingertips, I'd be doin' a bid by now. Trust. 'Cause most days my mother really makes me wanna take it there."

"Stop. Just bring it back," Miesha says as she drives down the Ave., holding one hand up while gripping the steering wheel with the other. "Enough of the drama with ya mama. Give me the dirt, girl. All of it. Scoop by scoop, boo. Don't hold nothin' back."

I give her a confused look. "What are *you* talking about?"

She shoots me a look, shaking her head. "Uh-uh, don't do it, boo. Hel-*lo*? You. Cease. Sunday."

I frown, twisting in my seat. "Whoop, whoop! Blow the whistle. There was no me. Cease. Or Sunday."

"Girl, I don't know why you frontin'. You know you like him."

I pucker my lips. "Sorry to disappoint you, boo, but Cease can't do nothin' for me; except maybe massage my feet 'n' nibble on these toes. That's it. Trust."

She laughs. "What a freak."

"Uh-huh. But I ain't messy."

"Yeah, okay. You need to stop playin' 'n' snatch that boy up before somebody else does."

I shrug. "They can have 'im. Cease is nice 'n' all. And we both know he's fine. But..." I pop my lips. "I already know if I gave 'im some of this good-good he'd end up strung."

"Girl, you a mess." She chuckles, shaking her head.

"Mm-hmm. But I ain't lyin'. The world already has enough fiends out here; no need for me to add another one to the census count."

She laughs. "Yeah, okay. Front if you want. You scared to chill with him 'cause you know that six-five hunk'll pro-lly be the one turnin' *you* inside out."

I laugh. "*Mitch*, please. Never that. I'm a beast in the sheets. Trust. That boy ain't ready."

Brows raised, smirking, Miesha looks at me. "So he didn't call? Text? Skype? Or hit you up on Facebook?"

"Nope. He doesn't have my number, anyway. And we're not Facebook friends. And I'm definitely not about to Skype with some boy who ain't one of my boo-daddies. So there you have it."

"Uh-huh. For now," she says, pulling into the lot. She shuts off the engine.

I gasp, opening the door 'n' climbing outta the car. "And what is that s'posed to mean? *For now?*"

She grabs her things, slamming her door shut, then arming the alarm. "You keep tryna convince ya'self not to like him 'n' let me know how you make out."

25

"W. E. B. Du Bois wanted people of color to blend in and become one with whites, but he also rationalized the need for Blacks to maintain a separate institution within black communities. Whereas, Booker T. Washington was considered more practical." Mr. Nandi pauses. And *hunni*, trust. I find myself struggling to stay awake in class. Well, okay...lies. I can't concentrate.

One word: *Cease*.

There, I said it.

And, noooo. I'm not gonna get all stalkerish on him. Chile, boom! It's not that serious. I'm not about that life. Trust. Still. I can't help *not* thinking about last Saturday night at the bowling alley. And, yeah, I know I really wasn't beat to be swinging a ball down an alley. But, mmph. It ended up being a good time. And I ain't even gonna front 'n' act like I wasn't cheesin' all hard inside when Cease stood behind me 'n' pressed himself into me, tryna show me how to handle a bowling ball. Ooh, he was so cute. Mmph.

Girl, get your drool together 'n' stop the foolery!

Girl, I'm just sayin'...

Chickie, boom! All that salivatin' over a boy is so not cute.

Yeah, but...

Mmph. I'm not gonna act like I forgot how I'd gotten all hyped when I got my first, and *only*, strike of the night, 'n' leapt into his arms. And how he kinda spun me around, all hyped with me. Oooh, he's so big 'n' strong 'n' too dang sexy for his own damn good. Mmph.

But I'm not even about to sweat no boy. Oh no, boo. That's not what Fiona does. This diva keeps it moving.

Then why am I sitting here wondering why I didn't see him during fourth period lunch? Well, okay. Not that I was looking for him, really. I mean, I happened to glance around the cafeteria a few times 'n' look over at the jock table for him, like once or twice. But that's it. And, of course, I wasn't even about to ask Miesha if she'd seen him. Psst. Please. I'm not even about to look thirsty.

Oh no, hun.

It's a good thing I'm not one'a them weak-minded, thirsty chicks, like Quanda or some other dumb-dumbs I know; otherwise I'd probably be standing outside of his classroom before the bell rings, waiting for him to walk out. Or I'd be clicking my heels three times tryna find my way to his bed. I mean, to his house.

Ooh, cuckoo-cuckoo. That is sooo nutty.

But *baaaaby*, trust. I know some silly girls who stay doing that crazy ish. Boys, too! But Fiona isn't tryna hop a ride on the cuckoo train with the rest of the half-nutty nut-nuts on campus.

Uh-huh, picture that! Me falling for some boy!

Ha! What a joke!

Divas don't fall, boo. They stand strong.

"Miss Madison...?"

I blink, looking up into the face of Mr. Nandi, who is hovering over my desk.

"Huh?"

"Word to the wise, young lady," he scolds as he glares at me, tapping my desk 'n' eyeing me. "Daydreaming will have you *failing* this class."

I blink again. Then frown. "Ooh, see, you doin' too much, Mister Nandi," I say, waving him on. "Fiona Madison doesn't fail. Oh no, hun. Trust."

"Well, does *she* take notes, *hun*? Because all I've seen since the beginning of the period is her staring into space looking starry-eyed."

A few kids giggle.

Ooh. He tried it!

I suck my teeth. Then shift in my seat. I fight to keep my eyes from rolling. *Ooh, he's lucky I'm not doin' senior citizens today. I'd drag him by his dentures.* "I'm paying attention. Trust."

"Then I *trust*," he says, raising a brow, "you'll ace next week's quiz. Now how about you tell me what year Du Bois was born and during which president's term?"

I give Mr. Nandi the stink eye. He stays tryna be messy! But I'm not even about to let him do me. Not today, boo. I toot my lips up. "He was born in eighteen sixty-eight. The same time President Andrew Johnson was in office."

Boom!
Take that!
Mr. Nandi smirks, swiping his chalk-dusted hands across the back of his jeans. "That is correct." He eyes me one last time, then shuffles his way back to the chalkboard, where he writes 'n' speaks with his back to us.

"Okay, folks, next week's quiz *will* be on the social and economic philosophies of Booker T. Washington, W. E. B Du Bois, and Marcus Garvey. So my advice"—he glances over his shoulder—"ladies and gentlemen: Take notes. And *pay* attention."

This nobody chick in back of me with the orange-colored hair 'n' gapped teeth taps me on the shoulder. I crane my neck, giving her a girl-have-you-lost-your-mind-touching-me look.

She frowns back. "Look. Don't shoot the messenger." She hands me a folded note.

I give her a confused look. She nods her head over to the left, shooting a quick glance over toward David, sitting four seats over from her. He winks at me, licking his lips.

Ugh. I roll my eyes, turning around in my seat. I open the note: *yo. U wanna come thru 2 nite?*

Boy, boom! I don't think so. Been there, done that!

I glance over my shoulder at him, giving him my answer. Middle finger up, hell no. I wish I would get back on his leash 'n' let him drag me around in some dog collar after he beat his ex-boo's face in. No, ma'am. I ain't signing up for no bedspring bouncing with some happy-handed boy.

Fiona's not that chick. Trust. I sling the note back at him across the room.

He laughs. "You know you want it."

"Boy, lies! I *had* it," I correct, snapping a finger. "And *you* didn't know what to do with it."

Mr. Nandi snaps his neck over his shoulder 'n' lands his glare directly at me like I'm the one causing problems up in here. "Miss Madison..."

I roll my eyes.

"Harriet Tubman, Sojourner Truth, A. J. Cooper, M. C. Terrell, Ida B. Wells, and M. W. Stewart all have what in common?"

See. He stays trying me. And I am so over him. But no worries, trust. A diva is always prepared. *Never let 'em see you sweat.* "Well, aside from being strong women who spoke their minds 'n' didn't take no mess," I say, twisting my lips up at him, "they were human rights activists."

"That is—"

The bell rings, cutting him off as everyone hops up from their seats 'n' bolts for the door.

"Oh, Miss Madison?"

Dear God! What now?

I stop dead in my tracks.

"Yesss?" I turn around slowly, barely breathing as I study Mr. Nandi, tryna figure out what the heck he could possibly want with *me*. Does he not know that I left my compact home this morning 'n' I need to pop a lil gloss up on these lips 'n' fluff my hair a bit before next period? That I'm tryna get to the bathroom to do a spot check to makes sure my hair 'n' face are still in place?

I swear. Some of these teachers are just so dang inconsiderate. They have no regard for my time.

"Is everything all right?"

I blink. "Of course it is. Everything's fabulous. Why wouldn't it be?"

"You seemed a bit distracted today, that's all."

"Oh, trust. Fiona has it together. Always."

He eyes me. "Well, I hope she does. It's too close to the end of the school year for her to start slipping. As much as I enjoy having you and your magnetic personality in my class, Miss Madison, I will not hesitate to fail you." He tilts his head. "Do you understand me?"

Fail me?

Ooh, he's tryin' me.

I meet his gaze. "No worries, Mister Nandi. Trust. Fiona is not doing red Fs slashed across the top of any of her tests. I got this."

Mr. Nandi takes me in, shaking his head. I know I'm too much for him. Mmph. "Make sure you do. You have two minutes before the next bell. I suggest you get going."

Whaaat?

He can't be serious. I need to make a pit stop in front of a mirror.

"Umm, what about a pass so I can go to my locker?"

"You still have time to make it."

I blink. "Ooh, see you tryna be messy," I say, placing a hand up on my hip. "You know there's no way in—"

He cuts me off. "Miss Madison, standing here won't get you there any faster. I suggest you make a mad dash for it. That's unless you wish to spend the afternoon in detention. I'm hosting."

I don't give him a chance to say anything else. I hurry up outta his classroom as if my life depends on it. Well, it does. Detention is hell on a diva's social life.

I zigzag my way through the maze of students still cluttering the halls, trying to avoid bumping into anyone, so intent on getting to my next class while digging in my bag to make sure that I at least have my notes with me for my next class.

I can't believe him! Hatin' on me 'cause I'm beautiful. Ole stank—

"What the *fu*—"

"Damn, sexy, where's the fire?"

Cease.

"Oh, hey," I say coolly, tryna keep the surprise outta my voice.

Where the heck you been all day?

"What's good?"

"Nothing much. Tryna get to class before I'm late."

"Oh, a'ight. I feel you," he says, walking alongside of me.

"Where you headed?"

"Weight room."

I swallow 'n' try not to breathe him in. Or cut my eye at him on the sly. Or think about him in his workout gear, pumping weights 'n' getting all hot 'n' sweaty.

"Oh, okay."

The bell rings.

Damn.

"Yo, you think about what I asked?"

"Boy, bye! Ain't nobody been thinkin' 'bout *you*."

He laughs. "See. There you go. That's not even what I asked you."

Oops.

He rounds the corner with me. "I meant no, I haven't given it any thought. I'm not interested."

"Yeah, a'ight. Look. On some real ish, Fee. I need to holla at you 'bout somethin'." He pulls out his cell. "Let me get ya digits so I can hit you up later."

I suck my teeth. "Boy, please. What you need my number for? Tell me now. I'm already late."

"Nah, yo. I gotta get to the gym. I'ma hit you up tonight, a'ight?"

I twist my lips, reluctantly taking his phone as he hands it to me. "Mm-hmm." I punch in my number, then hand him back his cell. "And don't be tryna breathe all in my ear talkin' no nasty ish, either."

He starts laughing, sliding his phone back down in his front pocket. "Yeah, right. You know you want it."

I give him the middle finger, walking into class almost four minutes late.

Looks like I know whose face I'll be looking into this afternoon!

26

My ringing phone wakes me up from outta a deep, delicious sleep. I was chillin' on Rodeo Drive in Beverly Hills on a shopping spree with my boo Trey Songz. Ooh, my boo-daddy was doing me right, goshdangit, letting me run his wallet real lovely. I was modeling a real cute off-the-shoulder silk jersey dress with a pair of six-inch red-bottoms as he sang "Playin' Hard" while I strutted my hotness, swayin' my hips.

Ugh!

Now I won't know how it all ends.

I knew I shoulda turned my ringer off.

I reach over 'n' snatch my cell from off the nightstand, peeping the screen. Whoever it is, they aren't saved in my contacts, so that makes them insignificant. Chile, boom! I glance over at the clock. *Ohmigod!* It's almost nine o'clock in the evening. I stretch. I can't believe that I've slept the whole afternoon away. After I got home from serving my detention with Mr. Nandi's ole messy butt, I came home 'n' took it down a few notches. All I planned to do was take a quick catnap. *Not* sleep my whole day away.

Mmph.

My cell rings again. It's No Name again. "Yeah, how may I help you?" I answer with a lil stank.

"Yo, what's up? It's Cease."

I yawn. "Who?"

"Cease."

"Oooh. Ohhhkay, *and*?"

He chuckles. "Did I catch you at a bad time? If you want, I can hit you later."

I roll my eyes. "Well, I was kinda in the middle of a date with my boo. But you just killed my vibe 'n' jacked my happy ending."

"Oh, my bad. Don't let me hol' you then."

I suck my teeth. "Too late now. I'm up. So you might as well tell me what's so private that you couldn't tell me in school today."

"How you?"

I blink. "Um. Right now, aggravated that you woke me from my delicious dream. And you're about to hear the line go dead in five, four, three, two, one...if you don't get to the point so I can try to catch Trey Songz before some other *bish* steals him from me."

He laughs. "Yo, you wildin', yo. That's who ya date was wit'?"

"Yeah. In my dream, fool." I can't help but laugh with him.

"Hahaha. But, damn. I'm sayin'. You in bed mad early."

"Not usually. But for some reason bein' in detention staring in Mister Nandi's ugly face made me exhausted."

He laughs again. "Shoulda got to class on time."

I suck my teeth. "Whatever. Maybe you should start flappin' ya lickers 'n' tell me what you want before I hang up."

"Oh, right, right." He chuckles. "My bad, bae. Where you want me to flap these lickers?"

I frown, sitting up in bed, propping two pillows in back of me. "Hold up lil tiger, let me yank your chain right quick. Just because I'm on the line kee-kee-cooin' it up with you, I'm not ya *bae* 'n' you won't be flappin' ya lickers nowhere on *me*. Get it right, boo. Get. It. Right."

"Hahahaha. Yeah, a'ight. You got that."

"I know I do. Now, move along. What did you *need* to talk about?"

"Me 'n' you, yo."

I laugh 'n' cough. "Ooh, lies, lies, 'n' more lies."

"Nah, I'm dead-azz. I ain't even gonna front. I want you, ma."

Hmm. They all do.

I reach over 'n' grab the remote to my stereo 'n' press PLAY. My honey-boo JoJo's joint "Fairy Tales" seeps through my speakers. Ooh, I love me some JoJo! I close my eyes, easing back down onto my bed. "Why you want me, Cease? I know you don't even think I'ma let ya nasty azz smash."

He laughs. "Nah, nah. I ain't even on it like that wit' you. I mean, yeah. I ain't gonna front; if you let me hit, I'ma beat it up. But, nah."

Ooh, boo-daddy. Talk that talk! Beat it up, beat it up!

I swallow. "Then why you want me?" I ask again as JoJo sings her drawz off about how she used to believe in love 'n' fairy tales until her heart was broken. Mmph.

"Yo, c'mon. Don't front. You know you one'a the hottest chicks in school, hands down."

Yeah, I know, boo.

"And you *just* figuring that out?"

"Yo, c'mon now. You know I know what it is. Don't play me, yo."

"Mmph. So now you wanna bag me, huh?" I get up from bed.

"Yeah, sumthin' like that."

I twist my lips up. "Mm-hmm. Something like *that*. Boy, please."

"A'ight. I ain't gonna front—I wanna wife you up."

"Uh, no ma'am, no sir. Fiona ain't even signing up for that, boo." I walk over to my closet door 'n' open it, standing in front of the mirror hanging on the back of the door. I stare at my body, turning from side to side, admiring my bangin' curves. I make my booty bounce 'n' clap, watch each booty cheek pop. Pop, pop, pow! *Who loves you, boo?*

Yeah, that's what you wanna see, isn't it?

He chuckles. "Yeah, a'ight. Maybe not tonight."

"Umm, *maybe* not ever, boo."

"Oh, so I'm ya *boo*?"

I laugh, stepping away from the mirror. "No. What you are is getting on my nerves. You some boy tryna get him a taste of some'a this hot sugar. But I ain't offerin' none up, boo-boo. Just 'cause I do a lil hoin' here 'n' there, that doesn't mean I'm slidin' my goodies down every Tom, Troy, 'n' Cease's pole."

He cracks up. "Yo, Fee, you straight crazy, you know that, right? You stay wildin', ma. It ain't all about tryna get the panties with me."

"Uh-huh. So what is it about then?"

"It's about me 'n' you linkin' up—"

"*Linkin'* up? Uh-uh, boo-boo. That already sounds like some late-night booty call."

"Yo, chill-chill wit' that. Let ya future man finish his sentence before you start movin' them sexy lips."

Man? Ohhh, okay, boo-daddy. Talk that talk. I press my lips together, then say, "Not a word. Carry on."

He continues. "I wanna chill, nah'mean? Me 'n' you on some cool-out type ish, just vibin'."

I blink. Am I surprised he wants to chill? Nope. Am I surprised he's claiming not to wanna smash? Nope. Most boys stay lyin' about tryna get the cookie when they know that's all they really want. Buncha greedy, lyin' dogs. But, mmph. Fiona ain't the one you gotta lie to. If she wants to give you a lil taste, that's what she's gonna do. But not tonight. And not with Cease.

I change the subject. "So what were you doing before you hit me up? And don't even say playin' in ya man cave."

"Hahahaha, nah, yo." He tells me he was chillin' on his PlayStation doing whatever it is that boys do on that thing, like I got time to really care. I open my bedroom door, then head downstairs to the kitchen for a lil snackie-snack. Of course there's nada-goddang-thing up in here I wanna eat.

"So you hooked on playin' games, huh?"

He laughs. "Is that a loaded question?"

Of course it is. "It's whatever you want it to be." I suck my teeth, slamming the refrigerator shut. The least Ruthie-Ann could do is make sure there's food in here I can wrap my lips around.

"Oh, a'ight."

Mmph. Who can I call to bring me a treat?

"Well? Answer the question. You like playin' games?"

"Yeah, *video* games. It relaxes me. What about you? What relaxes you?"

Ooh, a chocolate boo-daddy with a set of strong hands 'n' sweet, juicy lips.

"Shopping," I tell him, rummaging through the cabinets. *And sex.* I open 'n' slam cabinet doors shut. Ohhhh—my—god! No chips. No dip. No lil Miss Debbie cakes. No sunflower seeds. Nothing but a buncha dang canned goods up in here. Who lives like this? This is nutritional abuse in the worst form!

"Oh, word? That's wassup. So how was ya day at school?"

I stop in my tracks. Excuse me? What? Wait. No boy has ever asked me how *my* day was, *ever*. All they've ever cared about knowing is how good the cookie is 'n' when they can come through 'n' chill. I blink, blink again.

"It was okay. Up until I got detention." I plop my booty up on a stool at the aisle counter. "Umm, how was your lil workout?"

"It was good, babe. Got it in, hard."

"Boy, didn't I tell you not to call me that? Ooh, don't get ya face slapped."

He laughs. "Yeah, yeah, yeah. And I tol' you I'm not a boy."

"Mmph. I can't tell. But whatever. Why you callin' me, again?"

"'Cause I dig you."

Yeah, right. You tryna dig in my cookies.

I laugh. "Ninja, you don't even know me."

"Yeah, but I'm tryna change that."

"Uh-huh. Well, don't hold ya breath," I say, reaching over 'n' grabbing the latest edition of *Cosmopolitan*. "I'm not givin' out interviews." I idly flip through the magazine. "But what I'm about to give you is the disconnect signal."

He laughs. "Yeah, a'ight. You stay talkin' slick."

"Whatever. Next." He asks if anyone else in my family has green eyes like me. I tell him no. He wants to know what I'm mixed with. I tell him I'm a mixture of none-of-ya-business 'n' I'm-not-tellin'-you. He laughs. But that doesn't stop him from wanting to know more. Am I the only child? Do I live with both my parents? If I have brothers 'n' sisters? He goes on 'n' on tryna pry in my dang business until I give him a lil taste. "No. I have four sisters. I'm the youngest. I live with my mother..." *Who I can't stand.* "And I haven't seen my dad since I was ten."

"Oh, damn. What happened to him?"

I shift in my seat. Swallow hard. Truth is, he was murdered. Shot three times in the chest—right in front of me. All he was was a white man walking his half-black, half-white daughter in the park, his arm draped over her small shoulder, him telling her how much he loved her 'n' would always be in her life, no matter what.

Then in the blink of an eye, he was gone. Shot down. Murdered. Three effen thugs took him away from me. I can still hear the gunshots. Still hear the screams. Still feel his blood on me. He died in my arms. His last words to me were, "No matter what, I love you, princess." That's what he called me. Princess.

I fight to keep my emotions in check. Tell Cease I don't wanna talk about it. He doesn't push it. And I'm relieved 'cause I really don't wanna start bawling. Not tonight. So I do what I do best. Shake it off. Press forward. And pretend—something I've learned to do real well.

I ask him about himself. Not because I really care at this very moment. But 'cause I'm not rude 'n' it seems like the right thing to do—even though all I'm really thinking about is what I'm gonna eat—but then he starts telling me about his family life 'n' about how he lives with both his parents 'n' has two seven-year-old twin brothers 'n' a three-year-old sister, his dad's an accountant 'n' his mother is a nurse (like my mom)—and I suddenly find myself hanging on to his every word, surprisingly. It sounds like he has a happy life.

I close my eyes 'n' take it all in. Oooh, 'n' I ain't even gonna lie, hun. Cease has a sexy voice. Mmph. Trust. Ooh, 'n' he's real lucky I'm not tryna click on my ho-meter 'n' give him the heat 'cause I'd drop it down on him, then send him on his way. But, nope. So not interested.

He lowers his voice. "You know I only called you tonight 'cause I wanted to hear ya voice, right?"

I pop my lips. "Of course you did, boo. I'm hot like that. Just don't be stickin' ya hands nowhere below ya waist 'cause I know you nasty like that."

He cracks up. "Nah, nah. I'll save that for you."

"Ewww. Not. Hand trollin' is not what I do."

We both laugh.

"Yeah, I hear you. But I'm sayin'...I know you say you ain't checkin' for a man, blah, blah, blah, but I'ma change that, yo. I know you're a whole lot more than them fly clothes you rock 'n' them pretty-azz eyes that got mofos droppin' at ya feet tryna get at you..."

For some reason that character Pecola in *The Bluest Eye* 'n' her desperately wanting blue eyes comes to mind. "Sometimes the prettiest eyes have cried the most tears," I say in almost a whisper, more to myself than to him.

"I feel you. Like someone with the biggest heart might'a felt the most pain."

I blink. "Yeah," I say solemnly. "I guess."

"Yo, let me ask you sometin'."

I press my cell closer to my ear. "Yeah?"

"You believe in love?"

What? Love? Ooh, this is my cue to end this call, right here, right now. This boy's tryna curse me! This diva has no time for none of that.

I take a deep breath, then say before ending the call, "No."

27

"*You keep tryna convince ya'self not to like him 'n' let me know how you make out.*"

Miesha's words ring in my ears as I glance down the hall only to see Cease walking in my direction with Lu-Anna popping her hips alongside him. *LuAnna! Ugh! Great! Just what the hell I need first thing this morning. Seeing him with that slanty-eyed trick!*

But why you care?

Oh, trust. I don't.

Lies!

I kneel down 'n' start rummaging through the bottom of my locker pretending not to have seen *him* with *her*, looking for something, anything, to seem too preoccupied to even notice. I stuff a few folders into my bag, noticing a piece of notebook paper folded into a triangle, the word *beautiful* scrawled across it. I frown, wondering who it's from. But my curiosity is quickly put on pause when I hear, "What's good, sexy?"

I look up 'n' it's Cease staring down at me with his dark chocolate eyes, grinning. He's alone. And I'm not sure why I'm relieved, but I am. *Ooh, this is soo not cute.*

I slide my eyes up over his body, then stand. Feeling my breath catch in the back of my throat. "*I'm* what's *good*, boo," I say, teasing.

"Oh, word? Let me sample it then."

I slam my locker shut, slinging the straps of my Michael Kors bag up over my shoulder. "Whoop, whoop! Come again. Fiona ain't on the menu."

He laughs. "Maybe not today. But you will be, soon."

I flick him a dismissive wave, heading down the hall. "Boy, bye. Lies!"

He walks alongside of me. "Here, let me take ya bag for you. It looks heavy."

I blink. "I got it, trust. But thanks. Where's ya lil girl-*friend*?"

"What girlfriend? I don't have one of those yet."

I twist my lips, cutting my eye over at him. *Sweet gawd! He's so dang fiiiiine. Mmph. And he smells ... delish.* Ooh, this boy is so lucky I'm keeping my ho-meter switched off; otherwise ain't no telling what Miss Fiona might do to him.

The first bell rings just as I open my mouth to say, "Well, lucky you, boo." I have five minutes to get to homeroom 'n' I'm not tryna be late. Not even for a fine cutie-boo like Cease. He's not worth detention. No boy is.

"Okay, bye now," I say, picking up my pace, my heels rapidly clicking against the floor. "Good day. Gotta go."

"Yo, chill." He laughs, keeping in step with me. "You not gettin' rid of me that fast. I'm walkin' you to ya home-room."

In spite of myself, I smile inside.

"Yo, whatchu doing Saturday night?" he asks, rounding the corner with me. I tell him I don't have any plans as of yet. "Oh, a'ight, cool-cool. Come to Luke's party wit' me. His parents are outta town again."

Ohmigod! That boy's parents are never home with him. They might as well just move out 'n' leave him the house 'cause it's like he lives on his own anyway. Ooh, why couldn't I be so lucky? Mmph.

I give Cease an incredulous look. "Go to his party with *you*? Like as a *date*?"

"Yeah. What's wrong with that?"

"Everything's wrong with it. Fiona's not tryna be no date 'n' she ain't interested in partying with anyone she has to see at school. Thanks, but no, thanks."

He laughs. "Yo, you mad funny. Why you do that?"

"Do what?"

"Always refer to ya'self in the third person like that?"

"'Cause that's what I do, boo. Why, you got a problem with it?"

He grins. "Nah, nah. I think it's funny, that's all."

I let out a sarcastic laugh. "Heeheehawhaw. So glad you find me funny."

"Nah. I find *you* sexy. I find what you do, funny. Big difference."

"Good day, sir." I smirk, stepping inside homeroom just as the bell rings.

"Yeah, a'ight," he says, laughing. "I'ma see you at lunch."

All through second 'n' third periods I find myself daydreaming, opening 'n' rereading the note I found in my locker this morning. It's another poem.

I See You

Every time I look into ya beautiful
green eyes
I see love
I see hope
I see my future
I see US
And I realize
You mean more to me than I ever knew
You are in my thoughts
I long to hold you in my arms
To kiss ya lips
And taste ya sweetness
Every time I close my eyes
I see you...

I close the note, folding it neatly for the umpteenth time, sliding it back down into my bag. I sigh, wondering who this new mystery boo is. *Ooh, he better be cute, too. Or I'ma slap his damn face for tryna do me!*

When the school day finally ends, all I can think about is grabbing my things 'n' screaming, "Free at last! Thank you, jeezus! It's Friday! Time to get my swerve on! Yesssss, *hunni*!"

But I keep it cute, sashaying down the hall, rounding the corner to the hallway where my locker is to gather my things. "Hey, boo, wait up," I hear in back of me. It's Miesha. I glance over my shoulder 'n' slow my stroll 'n' wait for her to catch up to me.

"Hey, *hunni*-boo," I say as she walks alongside me. "I didn't see you at lunch."

"I know," she says, pulling out her phone, sucking her teeth. "Ugh. I swear this woman gets on my last dang nerve sometimes. Like fall back, already. Damn."

I shake my head, unlocking my locker. "Girl, you know I know. What ya moms stressin' you about now, boo?" She tells me her mother wants her to go to Brooklyn for the weekend, but she's not interested unless she's gonna be spending the whole weekend hanging out with her girls. The thot pockets of Brooklyn.

I cringe, swinging open my locker. Mmph. *Them nassy hoodroaches.* "Well, why don't you wanna go?"

"Yo, Fiona," I hear in back of me. I don't even have to look to see who it is because I know the voice. It's Brent.

"That boy knows he has some sexy legs," Miesha whispers, eyeing him on the sly. I nod in agreement. Suddenly the image of my legs being wrapped around his hips quickly flashes in my mind 'n' I shudder, twisting my lips. "Mmph."

"What's up, Miesha?" Brent says when he approaches us.

"Hey, Brent," Miesha replies, her eyes darting back 'n' forth between the two of us.

He smiles at me. "What's up, Fee?"

"Nothin', boo." He's in his lacrosse practice uniform, looking too delish for his own dang good. Too bad I know he ain't as good as he looks in the sheets. Mmph. But I ain't messy, so I'ma move it along.

"What you getting into this weekend?" he wants to know. I tell him nothing much. "Oh, a'ight. I'ma hit you up later, a'ight."

Miesha raises a brow. "Should I leave the two of you alone?"

I roll my eyes. "Uh, nooo. You should not." I look over at Brent. "Okay, call me tonight around nine."

"A'ight, cool. I'ma get to practice. Check ya later, My."

"Bye, Brent," she says, eyeing me. She waits until he's halfway down the hall, then says, "Oh no, sweetie. What. Is. Going. On. Here?"

"What?" I ask, batting my lashes.

She wags a finger at me. "Oh no, heifer. I know you not even thinkin' about tryna ruin that boy's life."

I laugh. "Lies! I ain't tryna ruin nothing. Omigod! You stay tryna do me."

She smirks. "Uh-huh. Play innocent if you want. But I know ya kind, boo."

"And what kind is that?"

"A man-eater. I keep telling you that boy's too nice for you. You need you a boy with a lil more thug juice in his veins."

I crack up laughing. "Kiss my phatty!"

"Oh, it looks like someone's already tryna do that."

I wave her on. "Girl, bye! Yabba-dabba-boo-boo! Ain't nothin' poppin' off between me 'n' Brent. All that boy is, is eye candy, boo. Trust. *Annnnnny*way. Back to *you*. Why you all huffy with ya moms? Why you don't wanna spend the weekend in Brooklyn?"

She huffs. "Yeah, okay. Change the subject. 'Cause she keeps pressin' me about going home 'n' I keep tellin' her tonight I'ma be with my man."

I shrug. "Then go tomorrow."

"Uh, noo. Tomorrow night *we* are goin' to Luke's party."

I snap my neck in her direction. "Excuse *you*? Who's *we*?"

She rolls her eyes. "Me 'n' you. That's who. So, let me

shut you down real fast before you even start tryna do me. We goin'. Period. So get ready to get yo' life, boo."

I shut my locker. "Oh no, sweetie. Trust. Fiona already got her life. She ain't even about to be up in no house party with a buncha thots 'n' drunks. No ma'am, no sir."

We walk off toward the stairwell. "Well, *Fiona* better get her mind together 'cause *she* ain't even about to have *me* goin' up in there alone. So make sure *Fiona* gets *her* wears ready 'cause Saturday night *we* steppin' up in that party to turn up. Or Miss Fiona can put them heels to work 'n' hitchhike it home for the next two weeks. Trust."

I stop in my tracks, placing a hand up on my hip. "Oooh, you messy. You'd really do me like that?"

"Yup." She laughs, shouldering her bag 'n' heading toward the doors that lead out into the parking lot. And trust. Miss Fiona is right up on her heels. Me walk? Ha! I think not. She shoots me a look, smirking. "So are you walkin' or ridin'?"

I roll my eyes 'n' suck my teeth. "Ooh, *bish*! I can't stand nothin' you stand for right now. You stay tryna be messy."

We reach her car and she disarms the alarm, then opens the door. "Yup, messy as hell. Now pick a door. Walking or riding?"

I huff, open the passenger-side door, and slide in. "What time you pickin' me up?" I shut the door, eyeing her.

She laughs. "I knew you'd see it my way."

I roll my eyes.

Oooh, this hooker stays tryna do me!

28

Saturday night me 'n' Miesha are pulling up in front of Luke's big ole fabulous house in Jersey City Heights not too far from where Miesha stays with her aunt. And baaaaaby, *trust*. I am sooo not feeling this whole house party thing. Miss Fiona does college parties, okay. Not these lil kiddy parties. But okay. Whatever!

I'm here.

There are crazy cars parked outside 'n' a few kids walking up his driveway toward the house. I flip the mirror-lighted visor down 'n' check to make sure my hair is layed right. I toss my bang from outta my eye, then reach into my clutch 'n' pull out my lip gloss.

"I ain't even tryna be here all night," I say, gliding a fresh coat of gloss over my already sweet, juicy lips. "We need to dip in 'n' dip the hell out. Give 'em an hour of hotness, then bounce, baby, bounce. Fiona gots other things to do."

Miesha snaps her neck in my direction. "Girl, relax. We leave when we leave. Now let's go."

It doesn't take long for us to step outta her car 'n' make our way toward the house. And, *hunni*, trust. Fiona knows she's looking too cute in a pair of skinny jeans 'n' a slinky blouse that drapes off the shoulders 'n' a pair of heels that'll make you wanna slice a trick's face if she steps on ya toes. Oooh, my heel game is so sick, trust. Anywho. My boo Miesha's looking real cute, too, in her hip-hugging True Religion jeans 'n' multicolored blouse with the back cut out—her very own creation. I cut my eye over at how the fabric clings to her bouncy boobs. Ooh, I just wanna reach over 'n' squeeze 'em.

"Ooh, you got some nice juicy boobs," I tease, knowing she hates it.

She cuts her eye over at me. "*Bish*, don't get ya face slapped."

I laugh, slapping her on her butt. "Ooh, yesss! Slap me, mama!"

"Hooker, stop!" She laughs, swatting my hand away. "You play too much. Damn freak!"

"Ooh, don't be like that, boo," I coo, looping my arm through hers. "You know I'm a freak for you."

Miesha rolls her eyes, but she can't help laughing 'n' shaking her head.

There are some boys in back of us, whistling 'n' tryna holla at us. But we keep walking. But that doesn't stop me from glancing over my shoulder. *Ooh yes, gawd!* I peep a few buffed cutie-boos in the pack. "Ooh, there's some fine boo-daddies in back of us," I whisper, leaning into Miesha. Of course I wanna stop 'n' get my flirt on. But Miesha ain't tryna hear it.

"Girl, please. Not." She yanks me by the arm. "Keep it movin'. We ain't even pressed for them."

I suck my teeth, tossing a few extra shakes in my hips. I know I'm lookin' hot like fire. Trust. I decide I'ma save a dance for the three cutie-boos in back of me. But the two gorillas with 'em can go find a cave to wobble in 'cause Fiona ain't doin' wildlife. No ma'am, no sir.

I glance over my shoulder, taking them all in one last time before we make our way to the back of the house 'n' down into the basement.

Yessss, gawd! The music is thumpin' up in here 'n' the thought of grinding up on some cutie-boo's joystick on the dance floor got my honeypot flowing with excitement. I bounce my hips, hop, then drop down to Jay-Z's "Part II (On the Run)."

"Ooh, yessss!" I sway my hips, moving through the thick cloud of smoke. Weed. Milds. You name it, they smoking it. "This is my issssh!"

"Daaaaayum, yo, you sexy as hell," some nondescript boy yells in my ear over the music as a French Montana song starts playing. He has a blunt dangling from his lips.

I frown, looking him up 'n' down. He's not my type. At. All. Short 'n' skinny 'n' bright light with lil twists in his hair. But he has nice eyes 'n' big red lips. But all that don't matter 'cause I can tell in a few years them juicy lips gonna end up being all burnt 'n' crusty from smoking weed 'n' nibbling on bad batches of snatch-patch 'n' he gonna be all burnt out.

"Of course I am, boo. Glad you know."

"No doubt. You wanna dance?"

Of course I do. But not with you. I shake my head. "You

can't handle the heat, boo. Run along." I step off. Hand on hip, I slow-twirl it in the middle of the dance floor. I peep a few hoes tossin' haterade in the air, which makes me pop 'n' shake my hips real extra. *Yeah, hookers, boom-boom! Watch the phatty!*

When "I'ma Boss" starts playing, I really show out. I'm bouncin' 'n' poppin' everything blessed by genetics. Yesss, gawd, *hunni*! Miss Fiona starts turning it out. I spin around, then blink as a brown-skin cutie dances up on me. I drop down on him 'n' let him feel the heat just a taste while I scan the party. I'm glad there's not a buncha kids here from school, although there are more than I'd like to see; everyone else is from other schools 'n' outta town. I peep a few cutie-boos who might be worthy of a dance or two, posted up along the walls with they boys, holding cups overflowing with drinks, looking over in my direction. All eyes on me! *I see you checkin' me, boo-daddy!*

I see Tone—correction: I see the back of him—over in the corner with Miesha. Them nasty cows over there going at it like they already at a four-hour stay. He has her pinned up against the wall, grinding up on her. Her hands are draped up around his neck. Mmph. At the rate they going, her drawz'll be all sticky by the end of the night. But I ain't messy, so movin' along.

Everyone up in here is wetting up their throats, tossing back the drinks. I'm probably the only one up in here without a cup in my hand. Fiona don't toss back drinks at house parties. Oh no, boo. You won't ever catch me all lit up with my panties snatched to the side. No ma'am, no sir.

My gaze lands on Cease dancing with some brown chickie with a ginormous booty 'n' itty-bitty ant-size boobs.

And she's tossing 'n' shaking her cooties all up on him. Mmph. I keep eyeing them until his eyes finally meet mine. He looks surprised to see me here. As he should be. He smiles. I toss my hair 'n' turn up, like I ain't see him. But it doesn't take him long to make his way over to me, holding a cup in his hand, grinning.

"Damn, you lookin' mad sexy," he says, grabbing me around the waist with his free hand, pulling me into him. He smells of weed smoke 'n' alcohol. I spin outta his embrace. Tell him to tell me something I don't already know. He laughs. "Yeah, a'ight. I thought you wasn't beat to be here."

I smirk. "I'm not."

"Well, I'm glad you came. But I'm sayin' though…we coulda came together."

"No, thank you. I'm not tryna date you."

He grins. "Yeah, a'ight. That's what ya mouth says."

"Boy, bye. That's what it is." I bob my head to a Drake song, glancing around the party. Omigod! Luke is over on the other side of the room doing a nasty lil striptease for a group of thots, removing his shirt. He tosses it over his head 'n' they all start cluckin' 'n' clappin'.

I tap Cease, pointing over at Luke. "Ooh, you better go get ya boy before he ends up with his drawz off."

He shakes his head. "Nah, he's good. Let him do him."

"Daaaayum, ma," this dark-skin cutie-boo slurs, walking up to me. Ooh, 'n' he's real thuggish, too. But his eyes are all red 'n' half closed. He looks wasted. "You fine as *fuqq*." He licks his lips, straight dissing Cease, like he doesn't even see him standing here. Rude-azz. But Cease shuts him down real quick.

"Yo, my man. Chill, dawg. She's wit' me," he says, pulling

me into him, acting all protective 'n' whatnot, like he's my boo-daddy or something.

He belches. "Oh, word? My bad, son."

"Yeah, a'ight?" Cease says with attitude. Dude eyes Cease all hard 'n' whatnot, but Cease gives it right back to him until he spins off. I frown. Cease shakes his head. "Yo, you 'bout to have me run up in somebody's mouth, word is bond."

I laugh. "Boy, bye. Don't hate 'cause I got all eyes on me."

"Yeah, a'ight. But they better not have they hands on you. Or it's gonna be lights out."

"Oh no, oh no. Put the ego away. I am not—"

Before I can check him real quick, he pulls me farther onto the dance floor as August Alsina's "Let Me Hit That" starts playing, 'n' says, "Let's dance." I decide to eff with him a lil taste. I thrust my hips slow 'n' sexy, then press my booty into him. I let him grind up on me. He leans into my ear, places a hand on my hip. "Yo, keep it up 'n' you gonna find out how big my *ego* really is."

I smirk, spinning outta his embrace. "You ain't ready for this heat, boo." I thrust my hips at him, raising my arms up over my head, then run my hands through my hair. "I'll have you makin' babies in ya pants."

He cracks up laughing. "Yo, you mad funny, yo."

I eye him, feeling my body heat. I step into him, slip a leg between his. "Shut up 'n' dance."

"Yeah, a'ight." He gives me an intense look. Then pulls in his bottom lip. Jeezus! I gotta get my imagination 'n' these hormones under control. But I can't stop staring at his lips 'n' wondering if they are as soft as they look...

"Yo, you a tease, you know that, right?"

"I can back it up, too. Trust."

"Yeah, a'aight. You all talk, girl."

Now it's my turn to laugh. "Think what you like."

"Yo, why you be frontin', huh?" He playfully brushes my nose with his finger. Brow raised, I look up at him. Ask him what the heck he's talking about now. "Yeah, okay, play dumb."

I step back some. "Boy, boom. You're drunk."

He grins. "Nah. I'm nice, yo. But you know what'd be even nicer? You 'n' me, chillin'."

I stare at him, amusement 'n' curiosity dancing in my eyes. I know I should probably chop this right here, right now. But noooo. Fiona likes living on the edge a lil.

So, what's a diva to do?

I glance over 'n' peep LuAnna 'n' Chantel eyeballing me. Mmph. I ain't messy, but, trust, I know how to give a trick something to gag over. I reach up 'n' put my arms around Cease's neck. His eyes meet mine, 'n' he smiles. I hold my breath, suddenly realizing just how close we are. We're so close, our bodies pressed together, that I feel his heart beat.

And, for a moment, I forget where I am. I forget about all the other cutie-boos I promised in my head to dance with. Forget I'm not supposed to be liking this boy. But he's got my body rockin' 'n' all I wanna do is get filthy with him. Yes, gawd, *hunni*!

I swallow.

He's looking down at me. I'm looking up at him. And, uh, um, well...something's happening here. He leans in. Pretends like he's about to kiss me, then pulls back 'n' laughs. "Nah, you ain't ready for these lips, babe."

Oooh, okay! This nucca wanna play games. Let's play. I get caught up in the moment 'n' start poppin' 'n' droppin' it, showing him what I'm twerkin' with. Yes, gawd, *hunni*! I throw this diva heat up on him until I get him so excited that he's ready to turn this cherry out.

Then without warning, I step off, leaving him in the middle of the dance floor, his excitement stretching across the front of his jeans.

Boom-boom! Take that!

Don't. Do. Me.

How you like me *na*?!

29

"Hey, girl," LuAnna says, approaching me Monday morning as I'm stuffing another folded note left for me by my phantom boo into my back pocket, shutting my locker door. "You have a minute?"

I bat my lashes several times, then tilt my head. "A minute for *what*?" I say with a buncha stank. "You know I don't do you, boo."

She frowns. "And I don't really do you, either. Still, I wanna ask you something."

I roll my eyes. "Uh-huh. I know you don't do me, sweetness. But you *stay* talking about me, though." She opens her flappers to speak, and I shut it down. "No need to explain ya'self, hun. Or try to lie. I talk about you, too. Trust. The only difference is, I can say it to ya face. Now how can I help you?"

She huffs. "Whatever, Fiona. Are you messin' with Cease?"

Am I messing with Cease? Bish, GTFOH!

I laugh. Not admitting, not denying, just wanting this nosy chick to think whatever she wants to think. "Why? Is he ya man or something?"

She shakes her head. "No. But..."

I flick a strand of hair that has fallen over my eye outta my face. "Then you're not about to ask me *nothing*. Now, good day, ma'am." I shoulder my bag, then walk off down the hall.

Trick, please!!

Seconds before the bell rings, I slink inside my second-period class, sliding onto my seat 'n' dropping my bag, feeling slightly annoyed at myself for not finding out why she stepped to me, wanting to know if I was *messing* with Cease. And exactly what that *but* meant. I quickly dismiss the thought, remembering the note my phantom-boo left in my locker. *Oooh, why won't you show ya face, lil boo-daddy?*

I glance around the room, taking in the boys at their desks, wondering if I'd want any of them to be him. I frown. I'm in a room full of uglies. *No, gawd, please 'n' thank you!* I reach in my back pocket 'n' pull the note out, a slow smile easing over my lips as I open it.

<u>Pretty Green Eyes</u>

Exotic 'n' rare
Like a precious gem
I can't help but stare
deep into ya pools of green fire
Hot
Intense
full of passion 'n' desire

I get lost in the sparkle 'n' shine
Pretty green eyes
Won't you be mine?
You've got me under ya spell
My baby got them pretty green eyes
The kinda eyes that got me mesmerized
The kinda eyes that peer into my soul
'n' make me whole
pretty green eyes
you got me hypnotized

"So." Miesha leans forward 'n' looks at me with a slight sparkle in her eyes. "Are things *finally* heating up with you 'n' ya boo?" She gestures over at Cease, who is standing two tables over with his back to us, talking to Tevin 'n' two other guys from the football team. We're in the lunchroom eyeballing all the sights instead of stuffing our faces. "And *don't* even give me that *he ain't ya boo* mess. You might as well stop fighting it 'n' give in to the truth."

I roll my eyes, laughing. "Girl, boom! The truth is, Fiona ain't tryna let no boy try'n domesticate her. No, ma'am."

She laughs. "Girl, quit. Y'all were like hot fire all over each other at Luke's party, boo."

I feign innocence. "Ooh, lies, boo. We were just dancing."

"Yeah, okay, slutty-boo. I was there. I know what I saw." She grins. "Y'all look cute together, boo."

I laugh. "Girl, boom! Come again. We're *not* together. It was a party. I was there to dance 'n' have a good time. Not stand around taking up space."

She laughs 'n' shakes her head. "And this is coming from the grump who didn't even wanna go."

I shrug. "Well, since I was practically blackmailed into going, I had to make the the best outta a stressful situation."

She waves me on. "Lies. You were grinding all up on Cease like he was ya man 'n' the two of you were the only ones in the room."

I wag a finger at her. "Ooh, don't do me. You tryna be messy. My name ain't Wallflower, boo. I go to dance 'n' turn the party out. And okay, maybe I did let Cease *feel* up on"—I glide my hands over my hips—"all'a this goodness."

She laughs. "Well, the only thing I'm sure was messy that night was ya panties."

I can't help but laugh with her, giving her the finger. "Middle finger up! Ooh, wait. Let me tell you who had the effen nerve to step up to me at my locker this morning, wanting to know if I was *messing* with Cease?"

"Who?"

"LuAnna."

"Whaaat? For real? What you tell her?"

"Not a damn thing. That trick can go choke on a fat one. But it won't be his. Not on my watch. Trust."

She shakes her head. "Wait. I thought you *said* you didn't want him."

I buck my eyes. "Ooh, don't do me. I don't. But just because *I* don't want him doesn't mean I want *her* to have him. No, ma'am. I don't like that ho. So just on that alone, plus *knowing* she wants him, she ain't getting him. Not today, anyway. Check back in a few weeks, though."

She cracks up laughing. "Girl, you're a hot mess!"

"Uh-huh, but I ain't ever messy, boo."

30

A week later, I'm sitting across from Cease at Applebee's on 440, sharing an appetizer sampler 'n' sipping on a pomegranate lemonade. He's drinking a Sprite.

Oooh, you better not even try'n do me. But, um, well... Wait! Before you start getting messy 'n' getting all cuckoo-crazy, rolling ya eyes 'n' saying *I knew it*, I'ma just say it for you. Ever since that night at Luke's house party, Cease 'n' me been kinda, um, well... we been chillin' after school on the low-low 'cause Fiona ain't tryna have everyone all up in her business like that. Trust. 'Cause messy-azz tricks live to be messy 'n' I ain't tryna take a fist to nobody's head over no dumbness. No ma'am, no sir.

Um, hold up. It's not that serious. Trust. But over the last week, I don't know what's happening between us. Or what's happening to *me*! I mean, Fiona ain't ever been interested in knowing anything about a boy except for what kinda pet rock he's holding in his hand at night. But Cease... um, well... I don't know. I've learned so much about him. Things I never imagined. Like how he's scared to death of spiders 'n' lightning 'n' going through tunnels. That even though he plays basketball 'n' has acceptance letters to eleven different colleges 'n' universities, going to the NBA isn't one of his dreams. It's his parents', so if it happens he'll do it for them. But he'd rather join the Peace Corps after he graduates from college 'n' teach history in an underprivileged country. When I asked him why, he told me 'cause it's a way to give back 'n' help others less fortunate 'n' that it helped build character.

All I could do was blink.

Who woulda thunk it?

Anywho. Every time he tries to ask about me, about my life, about my dreams, I shut down. I find a way to flip it back on him. Shoot. It ain't none'a his business what I'm thinking, or what I'm feeling, or what I wanna do with my life. So why is he tryna be all up in my world? Please. Fiona ain't giving out interviews. The less he knows, the better.

But that doesn't stop him from asking. And it doesn't stop me from fighting myself every time to keep from opening up to him. Oooh, I shouldn't even be telling you this 'cause I know some'a you real messy, but the truth is, I don't know how to open up. I've never had to talk to a boy about me, or wanted to. Well, not about anything real, like my feelings, or my wants, or my dreams.

But, whatever. Yeah, okay...I'm kinda *liking* him. A little. Or maybe I'm just curious to see him without his clothes on. Not that I'm planning on giving him any of this cookie. Still...it never hurts to look 'n' touch, a lil. But I ain't even tryna get all goo-ga-ga over him like that. Oh no, hun, trust! No ma'am, no sir.

Anywhoo. All I know is, Fiona ain't tryna get all wrapped up in no boy.

"So why don't you believe in love?" he wants to know, bringing up a conversation we had the first night we spoke on the phone. I eye him as he bites into a boneless wing, wondering why he is even asking me this. I'm kinda surprised he even remembers me telling him that. It's not like boys remember most of what you tell 'em anyway, right? So why in the heck did he choose to remember that, of all things? I mean really? Why is he tryna be all up in my head about my lack of belief in that dirty four-letter *L*-word?

Love. Mmph. Ain't nobody got time for that.

Umm, I guess if I spit the truth, I'd have to confess that I've *never* loved a boy before. Never even think a boy's ever loved me. Yeah, they've loved this goody-goody. They always love that. Please. Fiona knows how to make it do what it do, boo. Trust. But I ain't messy 'n' I don't kiss 'n' tell, so moving along.

Um, can I say I've ever looked in a boy's eyes 'n' felt, or seen, *love* staring back at me? Nope. Well, shoot. I don't know if I'd even know what that *look* looked like if it were staring back at me, ready to bite me in my face. Ooh, no, no... not the face. But you know what I mean.

All I know is lust. Lots of it. That's all I ever see, all I've ever seen, anytime a boy looks at me. They love how I make them feel. Not who I am. And I don't—well, I've never wanted to—expect any more than that. Trust. I'm not like most chickie-boos. I ain't looking for love, boo. Just a nice, slow bump 'n' grind 'n' a hot, sweaty time. Fiona ain't ever been no fool to fall for the okey-doke, like some hoes do. No, boo. Mind tricks don't work on me.

You ain't ever gotta lie to me. I already know what it is. Trust.

Then why am I sitting here starting to feel some type'a way?

"Why you care?" I ask, eyeing him. I reach for my drink 'n' take a slow sip. I lick my lips.

He grins. "Maybe *I'm* tryna *care* about you."

"Uh-huh. And why you wanna do all that?"

"'Cause I think you're worth it," he says softly, burning his stare into mine.

I blink. See. This is why I don't let myself get caught up in this boy-girl ish. Boys like him too busy saying mushy stuff they know they usually don't mean. But the way he's looking at me—all serious 'n' intense—is kinda making me think he's serious. Sorta. Almost.

I shift my eyes. But he keeps looking at me, his eyes searching for mine. I fidget with the straw in my drink, re-fusing to meet his gaze. Refusing to get sucked into this boy's little fairy tale of sweet nothings. Oh no, boo. Fiona ain't tryna buy nothing he's pushing. Not today. No ma'am, no sir.

"I'd rather you not," I say, finally meeting his eyes. The warmth of his gaze makes my skin heat. I swallow, shifting in my seat again.

He frowns. "You can't tell me who not to care about."

I shrug. "You're right. I wasn't telling you. It was a warning."

He laughs. "Thanks. But I'm a big boy, bae. I think I got this."

"Suit ya'self. Now gentle reminder: I'm *not* ya *bae, baby, boo,* or *other*."

He smirks. "Maybe not today."

"Not tomorrow either," I shoot back. "Or the day after that."

"Yeah, a'ight. There's always next week 'n' the week after that. Fight it if you want. But I'ma still bag you."

"Ooh, you think?"

"Nah, I *know*."

I give him an incredulous look. "And what makes you so sure?"

He spreads his arms open. "'Cause I'm *me*, baby. Look at all'a this. Who could resist all'a this greatness?"

I roll my eyes 'n' suck my teeth. "Boy, bye. With ya conceited butt."

He laughs. "Nah. Never that. All confidence, boo."

"Mmph." I twist my lips. "Sounds more like confusion to me."

Cease stays silent for a moment. Across the room at another table I see these two brown-skin chicks arguing with some tall, lanky boy with dreads. They both have a hand up on their hips 'n' the other jabbing the air, neck-rolling it. Mmph. They probably caught him cheating on them with another chick. Oooh, I don't want that to ever be me.

"Listen. No lie," Cease finally says, leaning forward in his seat, resting his forearms on the table. "I'm tryna settle down, a'ight. I want a wifey. Somebody I can chill with on some exclusive type ish, feel me? I'm tired of the BS a lotta these silly chicks be into. I'm tired of trickin' wit' a buncha hoes. I want one shorty, feel me?"

I blink. Try to focus my sweeping gaze on anything other than him. But it's a struggle to not stare at his lips as he licks them. Ooh, this boy is really tryna do me 'n' I'm so not liking it.

"Well, good luck with that, boo. Let me know how you make out." I glance at my watch. I'm so ready to blow this joint 'n' get away from him before I snatch off my panties 'n' stuff 'em in his mouth.

He laughs.

"Why you laughing?"

He shakes his head. "You make me laugh."

I frown. "So what you sayin' is, I'm some kinda clown. Oooh, you tryna be messy." He keeps laughing. "Boy, bye. Laugh all you want. But trust. I'm not even tryna entertain you."

He stops laughing 'n' smiles, reaching over 'n' placing his big, warm hand over mine. "Yeah, I'm laughin'. You make me laugh, Fee. You make me smile, yo. That's a good thing, for real for real. I've never met a girl like you, yo. You different, Fiona. Special."

I swallow, pulling my hand from beneath his. *Dear-gawd, if this boy keeps talking like this I might wanna give him a lil taste of heaven. Or throw up in the back of my mouth!* No boy has ever told me I was special. And the way he says it sounds...I don't know, strange. In a good way, if that makes sense. But still, I ain't even about to fall for the trap. No, ma'am. Fiona ain't the one to get mind fu...

"Damn, I wanna taste ya lips," Cease says, slicing into my thoughts.

I blink, not sure of what he's just said. "Excuse me?"

"I wanna lean over 'n' kiss you right here," he says, staring at me. He grins. "But I'ma be a gentleman."

Oooh, kiss me, boo-daddy! Tongue me down, danggit! Girl, boom! Have several seats!

Not!

Mmph. Okay.

Oh no, oh no, oh noooo, ma'am! I'm not even 'bout to let this boy get up in my drawz! Not today.

"Ummm." I snap my fingers, waving the waitress over. "Check, please."

31

"I went out with Cease," I say all nonchalant, looking over at Miesha as she drives down the Ave. I leave out the part about how we've been either talking on the phone or Skyping practically every night until almost one, two in the morning.

"What?! *Lies*, boo! *Lies!*" She gets all hyped, bouncing up 'n' down in her seat 'n' banging on the steering wheel. "When, boo? When?"

I laugh. "Last Saturday."

"Ooh, you sneaky tramp!" She shakes her head, putting a hand up. "*Wait!* Wait. One. Minute! *Last* Saturday?"

"Yeah," I say, shrugging, like it's no biggie.

"Uh-uh, hooker; no, ma'am! And you just *now* telling me this? Ooh, so we keeping secrets now, huh? Is that how we doin' it?"

I wave her on. "It's not a secret. I just didn't wanna pump it up to be more than what it was."

She smirks. "Yeah, okay. You better give me details! And don't you dare leave a *gaaaawt*damn thang out! Nothing!"

I laugh, shaking my head. "Girl, there ain't much to tell. We went to Applebee's, then went to the movies afterward."

She eyes me all suspicious like. "*And?* What else y'all do?"

I laugh. "Nothing."

"Uh-huh," she says skeptically. "I know you, tramp. Ya middle name ain't Hot Box for nothin'. Don't do me. I know you did the nasty with him."

"Hahahaha." I shake my head. "Ooh, you tryna be messy, boo."

"Uh-huh. Whatever, hooker. I know you."

I keep laughing. "No, for real. Trust. I didn't give up none'a this honeypot. After the movie, he dropped me off home. I gave him a kiss on the cheek, then climbed outta his truck 'n' went inside." And, uh, um, well...then I raced my fast tail upstairs 'n' texted King to come over. I let him slobber on my cookie, getting it all wet 'n' soggy. Mmph. But she don't need to know all'a that. No ma'am, no sir.

Oooh, but I can't even lie. Cease's face kept popping up in my head, killing my dang vibe. I couldn't even enjoy myself. It got so bad I had to finally pry King's sticky mouth away from my treats 'n' show him to the door. Oh, it was so horrible.

I press my thighs together.

"So, are y'all talking now?"

I shrug. "Who? Me 'n' Cease? Ooh no, boo. We're just having fun, I guess." Umm, *hellooo*? *Helloooo?* Is anybody home? I know I said me 'n' Cease been kinda talking, but I'm not gonna tell her *that*. Oh no, hun. You can't tell everything, all at once. Some things you just gotta let marinate a bit, then pour it slowly. Like this. "You know me," I say, tossing my hair. "No strings attached, boo. I'm not even tryna get all caught up. Trust."

She eyes me, twisting her lips up. "Well, you need to stop the lies 'n' snatch that boy up before one of them lil birds swoops down on him. The thirst is real, trust."

I roll my eyes. "Who, you mean that big-titty *bish*, Lu-Anna?" Oops. The minute it slips outta my mouth, I cringe at how messy 'n' jealous it sounds. And trust, Fiona ain't messy or jealous of no chick. No ma'am, no sir. Never that. Still, every time I turn around LuAnna got her face all up in Cease's. A few times I had to fight myself to keep from running up on her 'n' snatching her edges out. Ooh, she's lucky I got saved 'n' changed my ways. Well, and the fact that I ain't tryna go back to jail again.

"Wellllll, since you mentioned it," Miesha says. "*Yessss*. She's one of 'em."

"Girl, boom. That chicken hawk can cluck around him all she wants. If he wants to pluck feathers, let 'im. We ain't in no kinda competition, trust."

"Oh, I heard that." She pulls into the school parking lot. And of course Miss Thing parks *way* too far from the dang school. I mean. All those empty spaces up front 'n' she parks *waaaay* back here, like she's tryna go hiking in heels. Mmph. Where they do that at? But since I'm the happy passenger I keep my happy mouth shut. But don't think I ain't rolling my eyes up in my head.

I flip down the mirror 'n' recheck my lip gloss before sliding outta the car 'n' shutting the door. I pull my shades down over my eyes, launching myself into the warm morning air.

"Ooh, I hope I don't wilt before I make it inside the building," I say sarcastically. "Fiona's too sweet to be out in the heat."

She gives me a dismissive wave, walking alongside me. "Girl, bye. Fiona better be lucky she ain't getting here on foot, okay?"

"Ooh, don't do me. You know I don't do messy. I can't wait to get my L's. Trust."

She laughs. "Um, sweetie. In case you didn't know it, you need to take the test first, then pass it."

"Ooh, you still tryna be messy." I pat her butt. "With ya ole big-juicy-booty-havin' self."

She snaps her neck in my direction. "Girl, I keep telling you I ain't into those kinda freak games. Don't get ya jaw cracked."

I giggle. "Ooh yes, crack it, boo. Crack it real good. Yes, gawd, *hunni*! You know I like it rough."

"Omigod! You so nasty!"

"Oooh, keep talkin' dirty, boo." I crack up laughing.

"*Bish*, bye," she says, stomping off, her heels clicking against the gravel.

When the fourth-period bell finally rings, I am the first one to snatch up my things 'n' hit the door, darting out into the hallway. And just as I get down the hall 'n' I'm about to turn the corner, I run smack into Brent.

"Oops."

"Oh, hey," he says, hoisting his book bag over his shoulder.

"Hey," I say back, letting my eyes roam up 'n' down his body.

He looks over my shoulder, then brings his gaze on me.

"Listen. I was wondering, if you're not doing anything later, if you wanted to chill after school today."

"You tryna feed me?"

He grins. "True."

"Oh, okay." I look down the hall 'n' see LuAnna walking up on Cease. I will myself to keep from rolling my eyes at the sight of that bird. I bring my attention back to Brent. "Call me when we get outta school 'n' I'll let you know if I'm free."

"A'ight, cool. I'll talk to you later."

"See ya." We go in opposite directions. Yeah, I might grace him with my presence. But I hope he doesn't think I'ma give him another round of goodness, 'cause he's gonna get his feelings hurt. You only get one shot at doin' this body right. If you flop, you get dropped. Sorry, boo-boo. The stairway to heaven is sealed shut from him. Trust.

"Yo, Fiona, wait up." I look over my shoulder, eyeing Cease as he run-walks his way up to me. I slow my stroll a taste until he reaches me. "Wassup, baby?" he says, grinning.

"Boy, boom. Come again. I'm not ya *baby*."

"Yeah, yeah, yeah . . . that's what ya mouth says."

I roll my eyes. "Whatever."

"Yeah, a'ight." He follows me down the stairs to the first floor. "Listen. I wanna see you tonight."

I blink. "Oh."

"Can you make time for me?"

I smirk. "Maybe."

"Yeah, a'ight. Whatchu mean, *maybe*?"

"It means what it means. Maybe."

"Maybe what?"

"*Maybe* I might have other plans."

"Cancel them."

"Mayyyybeee, I don't wanna cancel 'em."

"I'm worth it."

"Mayyyybeee, you're not."

He laughs. "Cancel ya plans 'n' come find out."

"Umm, no. Why should I?"

"'Cause I told you, I'm worth it."

"Not good enough."

"A'ight. How 'bout this." He stops at the bottom of the stairwell. "I'm tryna be ya man. Is that good enough for you?"

I blink, rapidly shaking my head. "Oh no, oh no. I already told you I'm not signing up for that. Fiona ain't looking for no man, trust. A boo-daddy with no strings attached, maybe. But you can cancel all that *I'm tryna be ya man* talk. It ain't happening."

He laughs. "Yo, here you go with the BS. I ain't tryna hear all that."

I smirk. "Well, you better hear it 'n' hear it good. Fiona Madison ain't the one. I already told you that." I swing open the door, then shake my hips on down the hall.

He laughs, following behind me. "Yeah, I know all about them lil diva rules of yours. But I ain't tryna hear all that. We 'bout to make some new rules that include me, starting tonight."

"Boy, boom! Come again. Not gonna happen."

We go back 'n' forth with this foolery 'n' him still tryna press me to chill with him tonight, all the way to the lunchroom. But I still ain't saying yes. And I ain't saying no, either. So he drops it, *finally*.

"Yo, you sitting with Miesha today?" I tell him no. She's spending her lunch with her boo in his car or hers doing whatever they do.

"Oh, a'ight." He holds open the cafeteria door for me. "I'ma go hit the weights real quick. But I'ma get at you later, a'ight?"

I look at him. "Okay, bye."

He blows me a kiss. "Tonight. Me 'n' you, a'ight? Don't play me, yo."

"Meathead, boom! Ain't nobody tryna play you. Trust. You couldn't handle me *playing* with you, anyway. With ya ole ugly self."

He laughs. "Yeah, a'ight. I got ya meathead all right. And lots of it."

"Middle finger up," I say, walking off, popping my hips. I feel his eyes on my phatty as it bounces 'n' shakes. *Yeah, watch it pop, boo-daddy!* I glance over my shoulder. And, boom! Just like I knew. He's still standing there at the door, grinning.

Oooh, he's really tryna do me.

32

The doorbell rings. I'm scrounging around in the kitchen looking for something to eat when I hear it. At first I think to ignore it. Shoot. Nobody has any business coming here without an appointment or an invite any-dang-way. And since I don't have anyone on my calendar or to-do list, there's no need to answer it, right? Wrong. It rings again 'n' again. And now I can only hope it's not my mother tryna get up in here 'cause she lost her house key or is weighed down with so many bags of groceries that she can't manage to get her key into the door. I have to laugh at that. Yeah, right. Picture that.

I'd hate to have to leave her out on the doorstep, but I will. Trust. I'm not messy. But I'm not beat for momma drama tonight. No, ma'am. The only drama I'm signing up for tonight is *Scandal* drama, *hunni*...yesss, gawd! Olivia Pope gives Fiona life, *hunni*! Trust. And Fiona ain't even tryna miss not one juicy morsel of drama over craziness. I'm a gladiator, boo. Boom! Thought you knew.

Still, the prospect of seeing my mother standing outside, locked out, in the pouring rain—although it's not raining out, yet—is delicious.

I sigh, grabbing the multigrain bread 'n' cheddar cheese, then taking a pan from outta one of the cabinets, finally settling on making a grilled cheese sandwich.

The doorbell rings again as I begin to prepare it.

WTF? Are you effen kiddin' me?!

I glance at the clock. It's a lil after eight o'clock.

The bells chime again. Now I'm annoyed. I slam my perfectly prepared sandwich into the buttered pan 'n' stalk off to the door, knife in hand, ready to slice a muthasucker down for tryna do me.

Can I live in peace? At least have the dang decency to call for an appointment. Jeezus!

I don't even bother to look through the peephole or peer out the curtains to see who it is 'cause I'm all the way turnt up on ready. But when I swing open the door, it's Cease standing there. And I don't know if I should be surprised, flustered, pissed, or frickin' embarrassed as hell 'cause I'm standing here with my bra-free boobs practically bursting outta a lil T-shirt with WET 'N' WILD scrawled in the front of it, wearing a raggedy pair of red boy shorts all hiked up in my honeypot—looking real trickalicious, holding a knife in my hand.

Ooh, this is sooo not cute imagery, right now.

"You got time for me?" He leans against the doorjamb, holding out a bouquet of flowers—the kind you find at ShopRite. "I bought these for you."

I blink. No boy has ever showed up at my door with flowers. Never. And now this fine, sexy boo-daddy is standing here offering me the cutest lil floral arrangement. So what do I do? I reach out 'n' take 'em, of course. Fiona ain't no fool, boo.

"Thanks," I say, bringing them up to my nose. I inhale. Oooh, they smell like me... sweet.

"You're welcome. So are you gonna invite me in?" His gaze quickly sweeps down to my melons, then drops to my cookie, then *alllll* the way down to my red painted toes, before sliding back up to the annoyed look I am sure he sees all over my face. But his eyeballing me is now making me feel increasingly naked 'n' heated at the same time.

I place an arm up over my boobs 'n' try to pull down my obnoxiously short shorts. "Um, no. How can I...?" I sniff. Sniff again. But this time it isn't the flowers I smell. Then I gasp in horror. Something is burning. Ohmigod!

I drop the flowers 'n' race toward the kitchen, leaving Cease at the door, to find the kitchen flooded with smoke. My grilled cheese is burned. The pan is smoking. The kitchen has turned into a four-alarm fire catastrophe. Okay, okay, I'm being overly dramatic. But still... there's a thick fog of smoke 'n' I coulda burned down the house 'n' I woulda lost all'a my heels 'n' handbags.

I quickly open a window, relieved 'n' pissed, snatching the burning pan 'n' my sandwich from off the stove, then tossing it into the sink, watching it hiss 'n' splutter all kinds of crazy. *Now what the heck am I gonna eat?* I open the back door.

"This is the fire marshall," Cease says in back of me, tryna disguise his voice. "I'm here to arrest the non-cooking cutie tryna burn down the crib."

I roll my eyes, turning to him. "Whatever, boy."

He laughs, placing the flowers in his hand on the counter.

"It's not funny." I reach under the sink for the dish soap 'n' scouring pad, so not interested in tryna wash this mess.

"I know," Cease says, still laughing. "But you shoulda seen the look on ya face 'n' the way you took off running. I didn't know you could move so fast."

I suck my teeth. "Boy, trust. There's a lot you don't know about me."

He grins, eyeing the smoky kitchen while walking up on me. "Yeah, I know," he says softly. He's now standing next to me at the sink. And *whyyyyyy* am I feeling all kinds of nervous? "But I'm tryna get to know you if you'd stop tryna reject me 'n' let me."

"Umm, did I invite you in?"

"You didn't have to. You left the door open for me."

"Oh, whatever, smart azz. You know what I mean."

"Yo, let me get that for you." He reaches his hand into the water with mine 'n' I ain't even gonna lie, I feel electric shock waves pumping all through my body. I shudder, snatching my hand from outta the water, glad to let him have at that burnt mess. He eyes me. "What was this supposed to be, anyway? Grilled cheese?"

I huff. "Yeah, something like that."

"I guess that's ya specialty, huh?" he teases. "Burnt cheese sandwiches."

I hit him playfully on the arm. "Oh, whatever. Cooking isn't one of my specialties."

He glances over at me, amusement dancing in his eyes. "Oh, word? What you good at, then?"

I cluck my tongue, tossing my hair. "You'll never know."

"Yeah, 'cause you stay runnin' from me."

I laugh. "Boy, boom. Ain't nobody running from you. Trust. Fiona runs from no one."

He shakes his head as he scrapes the pan 'n' tosses the now soggy burnt bread 'n' cheese mess into the garbage. I stare at him as he washes, then rinses out the pan. I'm not gonna lie, it feels kinda strange seeing this big ole bulky boo-daddy standing at my kitchen sink washing my mess. I almost wanna snap a picture 'n' toss it up on IG. But I think better of it.

When he's done, I take the pan from him, our fingers lightly grazing 'n' there goes them electric currents again. I try to ignore 'em as I dry the pan and put it back in its place in the cabinet.

"Okay, let me show you to the door," I say, suddenly feeling dizzy with a nervous energy bubbling up inside of me. I hastily walk outta the kitchen 'n' back into the living room—not caring that my booty cheeks are practically hanging outta my itty-bitty shorts, with him following be-hind me, getting his peep on, I'm sure. "Thank you for ya service." I swing open the door. "Now run along."

He laughs. "Nah, for real though, Fee. Why you be fron-tin' like you ain't feelin' a nucca?" He grins. "I think you big on me. Tell the truth."

I roll my eyes. "Boy, boom. Lies. I'm not even thinkin' about ya big head. Now, good night, sir."

He smirks. "Yeah, a'ight. I already know what it is."

Ooh, he's so cocky!

And sexy!

And so dang fine!

"Then you should know how to see ya way out the door. Out."

"Nah, I ain't leavin'."

I blink. "Come again. Excuse *you*?"

He repeats himself. "Nah, yo. You stay frontin', Fee. I wanna chill." He boldly plops his butt down on the sofa.

I blink. "*Chill?* Nucca, you ain't gotta go home, but you got to get the hell up outta here. My show is about to come on"—I glance at the time—"in an hour 'n' forty-five minutes, so—"

"*We* gonna chill for the next hour 'n' forty-five minutes." He grins at me. "So shut the door 'n' relax. Ya future man tryna chill wit' his future baby." He pats the space next to him.

Oh, no he didn't!

Oh, yes he did!

Oooh, he did that!

I stare him down in disbelief. And he is giving it back to me, only he's looking at me all warm 'n' sweet 'n' pleading 'n' there goes that irresistibly sexy grin of his that causes me to blink.

And just like that. He's won.

"Fine," I huff, slamming the door shut. "Let me go upstairs 'n' put on some clothes, then. But as soon as my show comes on, you getting the heck up outta here."

He grins again. "Yeah, a'ight, Fee. Whatever you say, ma."

33

"I'm really diggin' you, girl," Cease says, grinning that crooked grin of his. I swallow back nerves. And, *hunni*, trust. Miss Fiona doesn't do this. Being all nervous around some boy. Chile, cheese! I'm here on this earth to work the lil boo-daddies 'n' run circles around 'em. Not get worked over. Not get all flustered. Not get all goo-goo, ga-ga silly. But for the last two weeks, since that night he showed up at my house unannounced 'n' forced himself into my space on *Scandal* night, something crazy's been happening between us. We've been kinda, *chilling*, if that's what you wanna call it. I mean. He meets me at my locker in the mornings, 'n' we text.

And, yes, honey-boo, Fiona done broke down 'n' finally accepted his friend request. But I'm not all up on his Facebook page *liking* all'a his comments or being all thirsty up on his Instagram. And, trust. He ain't all up on mine. But he's slowly getting *allllll* up in my head.

And I'm not digging it. Not one dang bit. Trust. It's so not cute. But...

Cease pulls me into his arms. And it doesn't take long before he's kissing me 'n' I'm kissing him back 'n' forgetting that I'm supposed to be chopping this, this *thing*—whatever it is—before it gets *waaay* outta hand. Before I end up liking this boy waaaay more than my diva rules allow. Before I start getting more comfortable with him than I already am. Before he chips away at my heart 'n' starts to see the cracks in my life.

Never, ever, get too attached to a boy.

No, no, no! That is not the script I wanna be a part of.

But Cease, well, he's...I don't know. There's this gentle, sweet side of him that I didn't know he had. All this time I thought he was just a horny jock. But he's not. He's thoughtful. Compassionate. Affectionate. He's too good to be true.

Who woulda thunk it?

Oh, girl, stop!

What the heck is happening here?!

Chickie, stop! You know what's going on.

He's making me feel things I've never felt before. Special. Things I don't wanna feel. Butterflies. Things I'm afraid to feel. Vulnerable. Things I'm not ready to feel. That L-word. Not that *that's* what I'm feeling for him, but at the rate things are going, if I don't shut it down quick, fast, 'n' in a hurry, it could happen. Oooh, I'm so not liking this, this, new turn of events. They're unexpected. And so, so unnatural for me.

Ooh, damn him.

Damn this.

This does not happen to Fiona. Okay?

Oh no, hun.

I hump 'em 'n' dump 'em. I one-night-stand 'em. Not get all caught up. But shoot! We haven't even humped yet. And I'm already getting all sidetracked. Oh no. Oh no. He's gotta go!

Yes, girl, chop this up now.

Girl, bye! You know you feelin' him, so go have several seats!

Yeah, but I'm not tryna make him my boo-daddy. And I don't even know if I wanna have him on my BWB squad.

Girl, boom! Give him a lil taste of the candy, then show him to the door. Easy breezy!

Yeah, right. For who?

"I want you so bad, girl," Cease says, slicing into the mini discussion going on inside my cluttered lil head. "I don't know what you're doin' to me, but don't stop."

His lips are on me again. His tongue is in my mouth. My arms are 'round his thick neck. He's a good kisser. And I, um, well...I feel myself getting overheated 'n' melting in places that I didn't think kissing could thaw out. Ooh, this is sooo not cute, honey-boo.

What is a diva to do?

I force myself to peel away from our sweet lil lip dance, just so that I can catch my breath 'n' think straight before my ho-meter kicks up 'n' I end up pulling out my trick bag 'n' doing some things that might make this situation I'm already in worse—for him; for me.

"Uh, um, listen—" I begin, feeling the need to shut him down, this down, before he says too much, but...

"Sshh," he says, stroking my cheek, softly caressing my face, gazing into my eyes. "You're something else, Fiona. Damn."

"Cease, wait..."

"It's too late." He takes a breath. "I've wanted you since freshman year, yo. But I screwed up lip-lockin' it up wit' some busted chick."

I twist my lips. Fold my arms. And raise my brow. "Uh, correction." My neck swivels a bit. "With some wildebeest. Some hoof-toothed booga."

He starts laughing. I playfully nudge him backward. "Don't be laughin', boy. That ish ain't funny. Walking up on that nightmare scarred me for life."

"My bad, babe. I was stupid. Can you forgive me?"

"Nope," I say, smirking. "Forgiving you would mean letting you all up in my space."

He smiles. "Nah, ma, it's too late for that. I'm already up in it."

I'm already up in it.

Ooh, he tried it!

I roll my eyes. "Oh no, boo. It's never too late. I'ma drag you every chance I get for givin' up all'a this goodness for some endangered wildlife." He chuckles. Tells me that that isn't what he did. That I was what he wanted back then. But he was young 'n' dumb 'n' full of hot nastiness 'n' let his hormones get him caught out there. That it was stupid 'n' I shouldn't hold his dumbness against him. Mmph. Miss Fiona isn't big on forgiveness. But maybe, just this once, I might consider it.

But why?

I have to stick to the rules.

Why would he want to be with me? To want to love me?

I can't let him see that I'm really broken inside. That the girl he sees, that everyone sees, isn't really who I am. Not on the inside.

On the inside all I am is another Pecola. Ugly 'n' unwanted 'n' unloved 'n' not good enough. That's how I feel sometimes. That's what I am reminded of every time my mother looks at me. But then I gotta stand in the mirror 'n' look at myself, fighting back those demons, 'n' keep reminding myself that I am *pretty*, that I am *wanted*, that I am *loved*, that I am *good enough*. 'Cause that's what my sisters have always told me. It's what they want me to believe. And most times I do. But other times I don't. And that's when I have to smack on my happy face 'n' pretend to be everything my mother keeps telling me I'm not.

But how can I expect him to love me when my own mother can't?

Cease's voice slices into my thoughts. "Yo, what's really good wit' you, huh? Why you tryna run from something that we both know is good? I mean, damn, Fiona. I ain't tryna hurt you, yo."

I blink, fighting back tears. "You just can't. Haven't you paid attention to anything I've said?"

He smirks. "Yeah, I heard you. I listen to everything you say. But I ain't tryna hear all that. So you can cancel all that crazy ish you've been talkin', babe. You not gettin' rid of me that easy, yo."

I roll my eyes. *Ooob, this boy is really tryin' it. Who the heck does he think he is? Superman? Does he think he can come into my life, swoop me up off my feet, 'n' save the day?*

He grins, pulling me into his arms. He leans in 'n' kisses

me lightly on the lips. I swallow, taking him in, 'n' I have to fight to breathe; to catch my breath. He's *sooo* dang fine. And *sooo* much trouble.

Stand your ground. A diva has no time for love. No time for being chained down to one boy. Not even for the likes of this fine boo-daddy standing in front of you. He's gonna be leaving for college soon, anyway. Save ya'self the drama.

Girl, boom! Stop frontin'. You know you like this boy! Just give him a chance!

No, no, no! You can't!

I blink back more tears.

Cease tries to kiss me again. I jerk my head back. "I don't have time for silly games, boy."

"I ain't no boy. I'm a grown man, baby. And I know what I want."

Well, good for you.

I eye him. "Oh yeah? And what's that?" I ask the question, but I already know his answer. Still, I wanna hear it. Wanna be sure.

He pulls in his bottom lip all sexy 'n' slow, then finally says, "You."

I swallow. Close my eyes as he speaks—the sweetness in his voice, a gentleness that I swear I didn't know this extra-tall, hunky boo-daddy had. *Oooh, this boy is tryna do me!* Then I open them and gaze right into his. "Then whatever you do," I say softly as a tear rolls out of my eye. "Don't catch feelings."

34

"How was ya day?" It's Saturday night 'n' I'm up in my room with my door shut, lying across my bed doodling in my notebook with the stereo on low, listening to my boo Jhené Aiko playing in the background while talking on the phone with Cease.

"It was okay, I guess," I say, writing out the words to "Bed Peace" as Jhené's voice floats through the speakers.

Oooh, yessss. Let's get naked! This is my ish!

"Oh, a'ight. So, what you do last night after I dropped you home?"

"Boy, boom," I say, sucking my teeth. "Don't be tryna check for me."

He laughs. "Girl, quit. You know you want me checkin' you."

I roll my eyes, scribbling his name on my paper. "Uhhh, not!"

"Yeah, a'ight. You been thinkin' about me?"

"Umm, who are you, again?" I tease, sliding a fingernail

through my teeth, then clucking my tongue. "The number you have dialed has been disconnected. Try again."

He cracks up laughing. "Yo, Fee. You somethin' else, girl."

"I know I am. Now what you want?"

"You already know what I want. *You*."

"Well, sorry, boo. But Fiona lives by a set of rules that she ain't about to let no boy come in 'n' disrupt. No ma'am, no sir."

He chuckles. "Oh, word? And what lil rules is she livin' by?"

I slash a big X across his name. "Ha! Diva rules, boo. And rule number six is, never, ever, let a boy be ya life."

"Well, I ain't tryna *be* ya life," he counters, his voice dipping dangerously low. "I'm tryna be *in* ya life. Big difference, baby."

I swallow. "Well, it also says to love 'em 'n' leave 'em. And that's what I do, boo. Fiona has no time for getting attached or being attached to no boy."

"Nah, nah. I ain't diggin' that one. We gonna have'ta change that part. You not lovin' 'n' leavin' me, yo. It's me 'n' you, ya heard?"

I blink. "Okay, time's up. No ma'am, no sir. You not even about to do me. Let me get you the dial tone. We not even havin' this conversation."

He laughs. "Yo, chill. Don't make me put somethin' in that pretty mouth of yours."

Oooh, yesss, gawd, hunni! This boy is tryna be messy!

"Ooh, you nasty dog! Don't get ya face slapped."

He laughs. "See, there you go. I wasn't even talkin' about that. Get ya mind out the gutter."

When "3:16 AM" starts playing, I roll over on my back 'n' close my eyes, pressing the phone to my ear. I smirk. "Yeah, right. Lies!"

"Nah, word is bond. I wouldn't come at you like that. I respect you. But I'm sayin', though..."

"Boy, you sayin' *what*?"

"You like *that*?"

I blink. "Do I like *what*?"

"Yo, c'mon. Don't front. You know."

"Oh no, boo-boo. You got the wrong one. I receive it, not give it. Trust. The only thing goin' in Fiona's mouth is..."

"Fiona!"

I cringe.

My door swings open. "Why are there dishes all up in my sink, huh, girl? Why I gotta keep telling you the same damn thing over 'n' over, huh? You know I don't like see-ing no goddamn dirty dishes up in my sink."

I huff. "All right! I heard you! Get out!"

"Girl, who in the hell you raisin' your damn voice to, huh? Don't get cute."

I try to cover the phone to keep Cease from hearing this. How dare she embarrass me! A part of me knows I should probably hang up on Cease before he hears more than he already has, but I ain't ready to get off the phone with him.

Ooob, I'm about to turn up on her in ten, nine, eight...!

I hold my breath for a split second, then keep counting in my head. I am so frickin' done. I jerk up in bed. Then stare her down. "Ohhhkay! Dang. Can't you see I'm on the phone?"

She scowls, slamming her hands up on her wide hips. "Girl, I don't care about you bein' on no phone. I want those dishes done! I'm sick of saying the same thing over 'n' over."

"Then stop saying it," I snap, hopping up from the bed. "I *heard* you the *first* time. Now, *bye*! Please 'n' thank you!"

"I can't wait for ya lazy azz to get the hell up outta my house!"

"That makes two of us," I snap back.

She stomps out 'n' I slam the door behind her.

She yells, "Don't be slamming no doors up in my house, either!"

"Omiiiiiiigod! I can't stand that lady," I huff, putting the phone back up to my ear. "Hello?"

"Yo, I'ma let you go, a'ight? I don't want you gettin' in trouble."

I suck my teeth. "Screw her. Fiona ain't checkin' for nothin' comin' outta that bag lady's mouth."

"Damn. Sounds like you 'n' ya moms gets it in."

I blow out an aggravated breath. "You have no idea."

"You a'ight, though?"

I huff. "No, but I will be in a minute. She gets on my dang nerves."

"You wanna talk about it?"

"No," I say absentmindedly, walking over to the stereo 'n' changing the CD player to another track. "I'm used to her being messy 'n' tryna do me." I tell him this, but it's not really true. Cruella's jacked my mood. I mean, it doesn't bother me like it used to. But still...

I walk over 'n' lock my door, then flick the light off, wrapping myself in darkness, like the dang mood I'm now in. *Why the heck is she even home, anyway?*

"Yo, you can talk to me, Fee, a'ight? About anything. I got you, feel me?"

I plop back on my bed, hoping he can't hear the hurt in my voice. I close my eyes. "There's nothing to talk about."

"You sure? I'm a good listener. I promise."

I can't help but smile. "Thanks. But I'm good. Trust."

"Oh, a'ight. Why don't y'all get along?"

"She hates me 'n'—"

"Nah, don't say that. That's ya moms."

"No, trust. That lady can't stand me," I confide, surprised at how I am *sooo* not interested in pretending right now. "She's hated me for as long as I can remember. Always mean 'n' nasty." I've never, ever, shared this with anyone. Never even let anyone see this part of me. Yet here I am, unexpectedly letting this boy pry into pieces of my effed-up world.

"You don't deserve that," he says softly.

I choke back my emotions. "Yeah, you're right. I don't. But oh, well. It is what it is. No love lost. Trust. So moving on."

"A'ight. You got that. I can take a hint. So you miss me?"

I shake my head. "Oh no. Not this again. Next."

He laughs. "Yo, Fee, stop playin, yo. You miss me or not?"

I suck my teeth. "Not."

"See. You still frontin', yo."

"Annnnyway. Moving on. Have you decided which school you wanna go to in the fall yet?"

"Nah, not yet." He tells me that outta the eleven schools he's applied to, he's received three acceptance letters in the mail over the weekend. I tell him congratulations. Like, wow, that's really great. "Thanks. So, what's good wit' you? You know what you wanna do once we graduate?"

I blink. Shoot. Heck if I know. I tell him I don't have it all planned out yet. I just know Fiona ain't tryna be stuck up in here with that crazy lady downstairs. No ma'am, no sir. As soon as I graduate I'm outta here. Trust. I'll throw myself over the George Washington Bridge before I suffer another year in this death trap with her.

"I don't know," I finally admit.

"You need a life plan, Fee," he says thoughtfully.

"Yeah, I know," I say, suddenly feeling like I'm the big white elephant wearing a pink helmet, riding a tricycle with three flats. He wants to know what I'm passionate about.

"Ooh, that's an easy one. Cutie-boos, sexy heels, 'n' fly handbags." *And lots of hot, sweaty sex.*

He laughs. "Yo, Fee, you crazy, yo; for real, for real. But nah, seriously."

"I *am* serious," I say, laughing with him. Ooh, I can't even lie. I'm really enjoying being on the phone with him.

"Well, a'ight on the heels 'n' them handbags. But them cutie-dudes gotta go."

I shake my head. "Not cutie-dudes, silly. Cutie-*boos*."

"Yeah, a'ight. Them, too."

"Boy, bye. Fiona's always gotta have her a few cutie-boos on deck."

"Yo, you cancel that. Ya man's comin' through 'n' shut-tin' ish down. And yeah, you already told me all about ya lil silly diva rules."

"They're not silly," I say defensively.

"Yeah, okay. They are if you gonna let 'em keep you from opening up ya heart to someone."

I swallow. "Oh no, oh no, we not—"

"Nah, yo. Let me finish," he says, his tone dipping real low 'n' sexy.

I huff. "Fine. Say what you gotta say, then I'm hanging up."

"No, you're not," he says gently, but ohh so very firmly. "Stop tryna run from me, Fee. All it does is make me chase you harder. Is that what you want? Me to chase you?"

I suck my teeth. "Boy, bye. Ain't nobody asking you to chase me."

"I didn't say anyone did. How 'bout you be quiet 'n' listen sometimes, damn."

I blink. And I, uh, well, I um... crickets, okay? I shut up 'n' let him finish.

"All'a them lil diva rules you've made up are gonna have'ta change; word is bond, yo."

I laugh. "Boy, *boom*! Come again. *Not*."

"Aye, yo. Why everything always gotta be so difficult wit' you?"

I tell him I'm not being difficult, but I'm not gonna make it easy either. He tells me he wants to see me tomorrow, that his parents are outta town visiting his grandma in Arizona 'n' he wants me to come over.

"I wanna make dinner for you."

My mouth drops open. I can't believe he wants to *cook* for *me*. I've never even had a boy boil water for me, let alone wanna toss up pots 'n' pans in a kitchen for me. "Why?" I ask skeptically.

"Because, yo," he says softly, "I wanna show you how special you are."

I blink, caught totally off guard. I open my mouth to say something, but before I can get the words out, my mother is back at my door, banging 'n' yelling for me to unlock the door 'n' go downstairs to do them raggedy dishes.

"ALL RIGHT!" I scream back. "Get up off my door! Dang! I'm coming!"

"NOW, Fiona!"

"Omiiiigod! This broad's really gonna stress me out over some damn dishes that I ain't even put in the sink in the first place. I can't with this lady. Let me get off this phone before I have to get dragged outta here in hand-cuffs."

"Nah, yo, chill. Don't do nothin' crazy, a'ight?"

I tell him I'm not making any promises, then end the call, hopping off my bed, unlocking my door 'n' swinging it open, determined to give the crazy lady downstairs something to really scream about.

I'ma smash up every damn dish! That'll learn her!

35

"Yo, I can't front. I don't wanna see the day end."

I smile. "Me either." And it's true. I really, really don't. Ooooh, I didn't think this whole *date* thing was going to be all that. But, *hunni*, trust. It turned out to be real cute. Romantic, even.

Oooh, he did that, boo. Yes, gawd, *hunni*. The food, the low sexy music, the candles, even his company, is *waaay* more than I imagined.

So here we are.

The two of us.

Alone.

Now what?

Do I hop up, slip back into my heels, snatch up my satchel 'n' bolt for the door? Do I make a mad dash for the bathroom 'n' lock myself inside? Or do I sit here 'n' melt all over myself?

What's this diva to do?

Oooh, Fiona doesn't do well with confusion. Trust. And right now she's baffled outta her mind. Feeling these silly butterflies fluttering around in my stomach, like this is the first time I've been alone with a fine jock-boy before. Psst. I've eaten boys like him alive. I've had plenty. I've slayed more boys 'n' broken more hearts than I can count.

Please. I'm a seductress.

I'm sexiness at its best.

So why is *this*, being here with him, feeling so different?

This isn't supposed to be happening. Not to me. Not with him.

Not with any boy.

All at once, I stare down at my fingernails. And realize that this is the first time that I've ever felt so, so...vulnerable. So naked.

Ohmigod! What is happening to me?

My heart is pounding.

I gotta get outta here. But before I can find the strength to stand on what I'm sure will be wobbly legs, he hops up from his seat 'n' says, "Hol' up. I almost forgot. I got something for you."

I give him a confused look. He grins slyly.

"Oh, really? Is it long, thick, and hard?" I tease shamelessly. Oh, I know I'm such a flirtatious slore. Who said I was perfect? Don't answer that.

Annnyway...

He laughs. "You ain't ready for that. But, nah...somethin' else."

"Whatever, boo. You don't know *what* I'm ready for."

Lies! Truth is, I'm not ready for none of this that's happening right now. Maybe I could be if, if, I wasn't feeling so discombobulated. I need a lil get-right. Yeah, that's it. I

need a sip of yak 'n' a fat blunt to help get my mind together.

"Yeah, a'ight. Hol' that thought." I eye him as he walks
out of the living room and heads down the hall to the back
of the house. He returns a few minutes later holding just
what my nerves need. A bottle of Moscato. Yes, gawd,
bunni!

*This boy is about to have me toss my panties to the
side 'n' lose my religion.*

He pours us both a drink, then hands me a cup. I
quickly take two big gulps.

He laughs. "Yo, easy, easy. We got all night."

Oh no, oh no, oh... I ain't signing up for no all-nighter.
Not tonight. I take another sip. This time slower. He takes
a sip of his drink, then reaches over 'n' gently swipes a
curl away from my eyes.

"You pretty as hell. You know that, right?"

I turn to him, eyebrows arched. "Uh-huh. How many
other chicks you sayin' that to?"

"Only you." I tilt my head. Give him a look. "Nah, real
ish. You the real deal, yo. You already know that. You
know I been tryna holla at you for a minute. But you
stayed duckin' a bruh."

I roll my eyes up in my head. "Yeah, right. Tell me anything, boo. You still ain't getting no cookie."

He smiles. "Yo, who said I wanted some?"

I give him a look. "Oh, you don't?"

He laughs. "A'ight, a'ight. Maybe just a lil taste."

I suck my teeth, playfully nudging him. "Lies!"

He keeps laughing. "I plead the Fifth. But I'm sayin'
though. You mad sexy, Fiona."

I swallow, shifting uncomfortably in my seat. Yeah. I

hear that all the time. How pretty I am. How sexy I am. But not like the way he's saying it. No boy has ever said it 'n' looked at me the way he is. Like he means it. Like he's trying to dig down into my soul to see every piece of me. I don't know how to feel about that.

He makes me nervous 'n' excited at the same time.

I take him in, almost like I'm seeing him for the first time. And I'm suddenly distracted by the way his beautiful lips go slightly crooked when he smiles at me.

Why hadn't I noticed it before?

Because before you weren't tryna ride up 'n' down on his seesaw.

I blink, wrestling with the voices in my head.

Down girl! Stick to the script!

You better get yo' life, boo!

He already knows you a ho, so you might as well get ya ho on, boo.

Excuuuse you! Just because I've freaked a slew of boys, that doesn't mean I have to freak him.

"Yo, what you thinkin' about?"

I swallow. "Nothing, really."

Lies!

"Oh, word? Well, you wanna know what I'm thinkin' 'bout?"

No, not really!

"No. I mean..." I force myself to pause 'n' take a deep breath. "What are you thinking?"

He licks his lips. "I'm thinkin' 'bout how I wish I coulda had *you* for dessert. But that I'ma be a gentleman 'n' respect you... *this* time."

Oh, great! Like I really needed to hear this when I'm already feeling hot. Now I'm scorching hot. And if I don't cool myself down quick there's going to be a situation. My hot pocket is already starting to sizzle.

I press my legs together.

He scoots closer to me. This time, our legs touch and he hits me with his lopsided smile again.

I feel a flutter.

Oh, he ain't slick! I know what he's tryna do.

I know I should get up. Should tell him bye-bye. Good day! Good night! So long! See ya! But I don't. And when he leans over 'n' starts kissing me, even though I am caught completely off guard, it doesn't take long before my tongue slips into his mouth 'n' we start going real hot 'n' heavy at it.

I throw my arms around his neck.

"I want you, yo," he whispers all sexy-like, causing all kinds of freaky lil thoughts to pop into my head. His hands all over me, caressing 'n' stroking, making me feel like I am about to explode from the inside out.

This isn't how it's supposed to go down. This isn't in the script. But somehow this boy has managed to switch it up on me. I know I said he wasn't getting any of this honey, that I wasn't giving him an invite to heaven. But...

I can't hold out any longer.

He can't resist any longer.

We start clawing like two wild animals, tearing each other's clothes off. He looks into my eyes 'n' I look into his. Nothing more needs to be said. We both give in to the moment 'n' get lost in the pleasure.

All I can think now is, *Lights out! He's won again!*

36

*R*ead *'em for filth*...
*Ooh yes, gawd, hunni! Just the chick I been meaning
to check*, I think as I see Quanda coming outta one of the
girls' bathrooms on the third floor. One thing about me,
honey-boo, Fiona don't let nothing slide, okay? Trust. And
I don't always check a ho right away. Oh no, oh no. Sometimes I let 'em think they got it off, then I swoop in on
'em. Chickie hasn't been in school in over a week 'n' this
is the first time that I've caught her by herself since that
day she spotted me with Pauley in the hallway 'n' called
herself tryna bring the rah-rah.

I hoist my purse straps up over my shoulder, then run a
finger through my hair. I'm looking dead in her face, eyeballing her real hard 'n' reckless. She shoots me a crazy
look, then shifts her eyes.

"Yeah, sweetie. I *see* you, boo," I say, stepping right up
in front of her, blocking her way. "What was all that slick-

ness you were talking a few weeks back? Yeah, I know you thought I forgot. Not."

She steps back a pinch, putting some distance between us just in case things pop off with the hands. And *trust*. Quanda already knows my handwork. "Girl, bye. Not today," she says, putting a finger up. "I don't give a damn if you forgot or not. I'm not in the mood, okay. So go have a seat."

One foot in front of the other, I place a hand up on my hip. Tilt my head. "Sweetie, *boom*! I don't care about what ya mood is. I'm comin' to you like a woman to let you know don't ever step up in my face 'n' play ya'self like that again, especially over some boy."

She frowns. Tells me she'll come at me however she wants to come at me if she sees me or any other trick all up in her man's face.

I laugh. "Ooh, you done got you a lil taste of vanilla 'n' now you think you done snatched you a door prize. Haha-haha. Hoes like you stay delusional."

She sucks her teeth. "I don't *think* I snatched anything. I *know* I got that on lock. So I'ma need you to respect my relationship."

I keep laughing. "Then why are we standing here again?" I snap my fingers. "Oh, right. 'Cause you jealous of all this fabulousness."

She scoffs. "*Jealous?* Of what? *You?* Never that. We *standin'* here 'cause you stay doin' too much, obviously feeling some kinda way, get it right."

I toss my hair. "Sweetie, save all that yip-yap. All I know is, don't ever step to me about Pauley, or any other boy, again. 'Cause *trust*. Fiona ain't ever gonna be hard-pressed to mess with any boy after *you*. If these clown mofos wanna run up in that sewer hole of yours, then good for 'em 'n' good for you."

She rolls her eyes. "Whatever. Anything else? 'Cause if not, you can step up outta my face so I can meet my boo."

"Ya *boo*?"

"Yeah, that's what I said, *my* boo," she snaps. "So I'ma need you to save ya trollin' for somebody else's man 'n' stay the hell away from mine."

I laugh. "Med check, med check. Trick, did you just escape from da loony bin? That boy ain't ya boo. He doesn't even *want* you. All you were—all you *ever* gonna be—is an easy lay, boo."

The bell rings 'n' everyone is now piling outta classrooms into the hall 'n' now all'a sudden this chicken hawk gotta lil fan club situation going on 'n' she wanna turn up, talking with the hands 'n' cursing all loud 'n' crazy, like she's really 'bout that life.

"Like I said, *bish*, stay the eff away from my man or I'ma have'ta take it to ya face! You don't wanna see me, boo! So step aside 'n' stay in ya lane!"

I clap my hands. "Ooh, real cute performance. *Not.* Sweetie, you better go buy a vowel 'n' snatch a clue! You wasn't poppin' all that yippity-yap just a few minutes ago when it was just you 'n' me out here. Now all'a sudden 'cause the bell rang 'n' you got you a lil audience, you wanna grow wings. Hahaha. Booga-roach, bye! You better go fly ya bird-azz off a stoop!"

"Ho, please!" she snaps, rolling her neck.

I laugh. "Sweetie, *boom*! Come again. I know I'ma *ho*, boo. It ain't no secret around these parts that Fiona likes to get it in. And, *whaat*? But I ain't a desperate one. I ain't the one begging 'n' stalking boys. So instead of being on ya knees givin' out brain 'n' prowling the boys' bathrooms, you need to go find you a bottle of self-esteem, chasing behind boys who don't even want you. Trick, please. Where they doing that at?" I pause, covering a hand over my mouth. "Oops. I forgot. Only at Thots R Us."

A few kids laugh as they go by.

"What the hell y'all laughin' at?!" she barks. "Mind ya own damn business!" She snaps her neck, shooting her glare back at me, then starts going in with a buncha threats about how she's gonna take it to my face after school.

"*Bish*, you ain't gotta wait 'til after school. Leap now."

"No, I'ma handle you—"

"Ha! You gonna handle *what*?" I flick my fingers at her. "Poof, trick! If you not tryna go with the hands, be gone! No, better yet…" I drop my bag 'n' get ready to lunge at her 'n' take it to her face, when someone snatches me up from behind, wrapping their arms around my waist, catching me off guard.

I spin around to see who's yanking me up, ready to go off on 'em. But I kinda ease up when I see who it is. It's Cease.

"Yo, chill, chill. Why you snappin' off, babe?"

"'Cause that trick wanna turn up," I huff, tryna break free, "like she ready for some work. I'ma beat her skull in."

He grabs me tighter. "Yo, chill, chill. You lookin' too fly, baby, to be tryna tear up the school. It ain't worth it." Cease scoops up my bag. "Let that silly ish go. Eff fightin', yo! Let's go eat."

I bring my attention back to Quanda. "Thank this nucca right here for savin' you from these hands. But know this, skank: You got a azz-beatin' on layaway waitin' on you, boo."

"Yeah, whatever, whore!"

"Good day, ma'am," I say, waving as Cease is pulling me away from all the ruckus. "Bye, bye! Get ya IQ up, sweetie! Go read a book! Better yet, go have ya dumb azz several seats over in da whore section at the library."

The crowd starts breaking up as soon as they see Mrs. Dean, the vice principal, coming down the hall with two security gurards. "Okay, ladies 'n' gentlemen, let's get moving. Clear these halls. Quandaleesha, please tell me you're not in the middle of all this commotion."

Of course I don't hear what chickie says since Cease is run-walking down the hall, dragging me with him.

"Daaaaamn, Fee, baby," Travis, says as he walks by us. "You be wildin', yo."

"Boy, bye!" I snap. "When is ya face transplant scheduled?"

He sucks his teeth. "Yo, you stay talkin' slick. I got—"

"Yo, Tee-man, chill," Cease says all calm, draping his thick arm around me. "I got this, feel me?"

He cuts his eye over at me, then at Cease. "Oh, a'ight, a'ight. I got you."

The fourth-period bell rings.

"Boy, get ya arm up off 'a me," I say, nudging him away from me, "before you have these clowns thinkin' we got something goin' on."

He laughs, pulling me back into him. "Why you care what they think, huh? It's true, though. We do got something goin' on, girl. *You* the only one frontin' like it ain't."

"Lies," I say, laughing as we head down the stairs to the lunchroom. "I don't know what news feed you reading, boo, but you need an update."

He laughs, grabbing me again. "Nah, the only update I need"—he leans in, then whispers—"is you."

"Boy, boom! I keep telling you, Fiona ain't on the menu." I tell him this, but now I'm not sure if even I believe it anymore.

He cracks up laughing. "Yeah, right, right. I forgot. You got them silly lil diva rules."

I suck my teeth, rolling my eyes. "Whatever."

He holds open the cafeteria door for me. "I keep tellin' you, yo. I ain't tryna hear all that. You my baby, whether you wanna be or not."

"Come again. Lies, lies, 'n' more lies." I lower my voice, walking through the doors with him following behind me. "Just 'cause you had me all up on ya bedsheets 'n' I let you feel up on my goodies, that does not give you boo-daddy status. Trust."

He laughs 'n' shakes his head as he reaches for my hand. "Yeah, a'ight, Fee. Whatever you say, ma. Wit' ya sexy self."

Ooh, this boy is really tryna do me!

37

Oooh, Fiona doesn't ever kiss 'n' tell, but *baaaaaby*, trust. Cease finally got his mind right 'n' gave Fiona the business. Smack it! Flip it! Beat it down! Yes, gawd, *hunni*! And the last two weeks it's been nonstop. Every day after school. Outside, inside, my house, his house, in his truck, the old teacher's lounge down on the third floor, wherever the mood hits, it's been going down. Hot kink, boo! Ooh, thought you knew!

And somebody pull over 'n' blow the whistle! Fiona ain't even been checkin' for any of her other boos for the last two weeks. No ma'am, no sir. Cease has been the only one with unlimited access to heaven—for the moment, that is. 'Cause you know Fiona ain't one to keep the same boo around for long.

"Yo, what's good, Fee?" Pauley calls out, opening his locker as I walk by. "How you?"

I narrow my eyes. "Oooh, boy, you shouldn't even be speaking to me. Where's ya mutt today?"

He laughs. "Fee, you wild, yo."

"And that ho you smashin' is ghetto trash. But I ain't messy, so good day, sir."

"Yo, what up, Fee?"

"Ooh, *not* you in those Nike slides, boo." I shift my handbag from one hand to the other, sweeping my bangs from outta my eyes. "Good day, sir."

"Damn, it's like that? Ya boy can't get no love?"

"No, but he can get a prescription for some antifungal cream. I hear he's got a nasty case of jock itch."

He laughs. "Yo, Fee, you still my peoples. Word is bond, yo."

"Uh-huh. You still can't get no love."

"Yeah, a'ight."

"Fiona, wait up, girl," Miesha calls out in back of me. I stop 'n' wait for her to catch up to me. "Hey, girl."

"Hey, boo." We air kiss.

"Ooh, you real fancy now. You ain't got time for ya girl now that you all up in ya feelings with Cease."

"*Feelings?* Come again. Oh no, ma'am. Fiona don't do STDs, boo."

She twists her face up. "STDs? Girl, who said anything about some damn sexually transmitted disease?"

"Girl, hush. I know what you said. *Feelings* are the new STD, boo. Thought you knew. Don't catch that ish. That bug'll have you all effed up. Crying 'n' stressing 'n' losing ya mind. Ooh, no, ma'am."

She cracks up laughing, shaking her head. "Ohhhhh-miiiiigod! I can't with you!"

"Girrrrl, I'm serious." We take the stairs down to the third floor. "I'm staying far away from that mess. Fiona ain't interested in no parts of that nasty syndrome. That ish will have ya edges all jacked up. No, ma'am. I ain't signing up for that."

She smirks, eyeing me. "Mm-hmm. So you sayin' you not feelin' Cease?"

"Chile, what I'm sayin' is, I'm keeping my immune system up so I don't come down with nothing I can't get rid of. I'm not even about to have my hair falling out over no boy. Trust."

She chuckles 'n' waves me on. "Girl, stop. You know you feelin' that boy. It's all over ya face. And it's definitely all over his. And listen, girl, you ain't hear this from me," she says, lowering her voice, "but Antonio told me that Cease is real big on you, boo. You got that boy wide open."

I grin. "That's that diva heat, boo. Does it every time. Trust."

She cracks up laughing 'n' shaking her head. "Ohmigod, you a hot mess."

"Ooh, but I ain't ever messy," I say as we round the corner.

"Yeah, okay. You wanna hit the mall after school today?"

"I..." I blink. "Um..." I blink again. *Ohhhhh hell noooo!* I blink again 'n' again, hoping that somehow my eyes are playing dirty tricks on me. But they're not. My eyesight is perfectly fine. I narrow my gaze. And I know what the heck I see down the other end of the hall.

LuAnna 'n' Cease.

He's leaning up against some lockers with his back to us 'n' she's all kee-kee-coo-coo as he's talking. *Mmph. I wonder what they so deep in convo about.* LuAnna sees me 'n' Miesha just as we're about to turn the corner 'n' the *bish* starts grinning harder, touching his arm.

I grunt.

Miesha glances at me. "Girl, I know you not even tripping over that."

"Psst. Come again. Never that." I toss my hair. "That chick can't see me. Not even on my worst day, boo. Trust."

"Oh, 'cause I was about to say."

"Please, not a word. Cease can have whomever he wants up in his face. Fiona ain't even checkin' for him like that. Trust. It ain't even that serious."

She eyes me like she ain't really believing a word coming outta my mouth. And truthfully, I don't blame her 'cause I ain't trusting nothing coming outta my flappers right now, either.

"I shoulda ran up on him 'n' punched him in the back of his head," I mumble to myself, digging through my locker, yanking things out. "I knew I shoulda chopped this mess before I let myself..." I stop myself, shaking my head, disgusted at myself for not following my own dang rules. "That no-good motherf—"

"There's my sexy baby," Cease says, startling me, cutting into my mini-rant. He grabs me up, acting like he wasn't downstairs three periods ago with LuAnna's moon-face self. So what if *he* didn't see me. *She* saw me. That's all I've been thinking about. I didn't like the way she was looking at him. Not one dang bit. Her up in his face, all grins 'n' giggles, like he just got done beatin' it down. Trick, please. Even if it's only in my mind. Still...she's lucky I'm not a jealous chick 'cause I woulda dragged her.

Cease growls into my neck, his lips tickling my skin.

"Hmmmm. I just wanna eat you up. I've been thinkin' 'bout you all day."

"Boy, get up off'a me," I say, twisting outta his arms 'n' laughing in spite of myself. "You play too much."

"Nah, I ain't playin'. You are *my* sexy baby. You know that, right?"

Lies!

"Yeah, right." I eye him suspiciously. "How many other chicks you runnin' that line on?"

He frowns. "C'mon, yo. Don't start that. I thought we went over this already. There ain't no other chicks. It's *all* you, bae. You the only one I got eyes for. You the only one I been checkin' for. So chill wit' that."

Lips twisted, brow raised, I tilt my head. "Mm-hmm."

"Yeah, a'ight. You already know what it is. Don't front." He eyes me, then frowns. "Yo, why you lookin' all tight?" he asks, his finger sliding under my bangs, then down along my cheek, causing electric heat to shoot through my body. "Anything I can do to put a smile on ya face?" he asks, his hand now sliding around my waist. He pulls me into him.

"I don't wanna talk about it," I say, blinking away the image of that messy *mitch* with her double-Ds all pressed up on him as I melt, helplessly, into his arms.

Girl, don't play ya'self. Get yo' life!

Let this nucca know you ain't the one!

Chile, boom! Let it go. That chick ain't got nothin' on you, boo!

You are your own competition!

Besides, you ain't checkin' for him like that anyway, remember?

I swallow. Take a deep breath 'n' decide to let it go. Fiona ain't ever been that chick to go off on a boy about some other chick, 'n' she ain't about to go there now. Besides, do I really have a right, or reason, to set it off?

Nope.

Cease ain't my man.

Then why you standin' here feelin' some kinda way?

Cease stares down at me. "What you wanna talk about then?" he whispers, gazing at me.

I wanna talk about you 'n' that gray-eyed smut! Why the hell you have her all up in ya damn face? And are you hittin' that?

He takes his finger, the very tip of his index finger, 'n' slides it along my neck, then slowly traces the curve of my ear.

My lips quiver. Why the heck can't I stand my ground with him all of a sudden? Why does he make me feel so dang weak?

He grins, leaning in closer. His beautiful lips loom so close to mine that his mint-scented breath causes my mouth to water. And, yesss, *hunni*. I wanna slap up his face 'n' tongue him down all at the same time.

Oooh, this is soo not cute!

I glance away for a second, feeling stupid, embarrassed at myself for letting myself feel more than I should, for wanting to run up on LuAnna 'n' snatch her scalp off, for wanting to turn up on him. This isn't me. Caring. Second-guessing myself. Wanting to like him but not wanting to catch feelings for him at the same time.

Ooh, this is craziness. I go back 'n' forth between tryna

convince myself that it ain't that serious 'n' tryna pretend
that I'm really not that into him.

But I am!

I finally look back up at him, slamming my locker shut.
"I don't wanna talk," I whisper, holding my breath as his
lips meet mine.

38

Cease's cell rings five times. Stops. Then rings again.
It's Saturday afternoon 'n' I'm chilling with him at his
house. His parents are gone for the weekend. Again. And
Cease wants me to stay the night with him. Something I've
never done before. Stayed the night out at a boy's house.
Oh no, boo. Fiona ain't entertaining at home; she usually
does her dirt out, then takes it on back home 'n' climbs up
on her own sheets to savor the memory in peace. Waking
up to a boy is, um, well…that's taking things to a whole
other level.

"Yo, babe," he says, all wrapped up in some blood 'n'
guts game he's playing on his PlayStation while I'm BSing
on Facebook, "grab my phone 'n' tell me who's callin'."

I stop scrolling through my news feed 'n' reach over for
his phone. Maybe I shouldn't look, but I can't help myself.
I frown at the screen. It's LuAnna. *This trick!*

I kindly press IGNORE.

"Who was it?"

I shrug. "They hung up."

"Oh, a'ight," he says, his eyes focused on his game. "Prolly nobody I wanna talk to anyway."

I roll my eyes. *Mmph.*

A few minutes later, his cell rings again. I glance at the screen again, then hit IGNORE. *Ooh, this messy bish is really tryin' it.*

"Yeah, booyah! Take that!" he grunts, shooting the head off some dragon-type creature. I roll my eyes. Like, really? Mmph. "You wanna order something to eat?" he asks, his eyes glued to the fifty-inch Sony flat screen.

"I don't care." He tells me he's good with whatever I wanna eat. "Let's get—" His cell rings again. I grit my teeth.

"Damn, who is that?"

I toss him his phone. "Ya thirsty ho." It hits him on the thigh then bounces to the floor.

"*Who?*" He puts the game on pause, then snatches up his cell 'n' punches in his code. He checks the call log, sucking his teeth. "She ain't my ho. Why you say that?"

"Well, obviously she wants to be. Her stank azz keeps sweatin' you, like you her pimp or somethin'."

"See. Here you go wit' the BS."

"BS nothing." I narrow my eyes at him. "I'm sick of that chick. Why is she always in ya face? Are you screwing her?"

He frowns. "Hell, nah. Why you ask me that?"

"Because she actin' like she all stuck on silly over you." He laughs.

"Ooh, don't do me. I don't see nothing funny, boy."

He leans over 'n' tries to kiss me. But I mush him in his head.

"Nah. Chill, chill. It's not even like that," he tries to explain. "Ain't nothin' poppin' between us. I mean that on everything."

I tilt my head. Give him a *yeah, okay* look. "Well, then she must be putting in neck work 'cause she stays bobblin' her damn head all up in ya face."

"Word to mother, I ain't effen wit' that broad like that. We just cool, that's it. I don't even be lookin' at no other chicks like that. I'm good, yo. You all I need, babe. I already told you that."

I eyeball him, hard. "So you ain't ever beat that up? And don't even lie."

"Nah, not really. I mean, yeah. I ain't gonna front. I was tryna smash, but she kept frontin'. She topped me off a few times over the Christmas break, though. But that's all it was. So you ain't even gotta stress about that, ya heard?"

I tsk. "Psst. Trust. Fiona ain't stressin' over no neck bobbler. If that's who you wanna be with, then bye. Do you, boo."

He sucks his teeth. "The only *boo* I'm tryna do is *you*. Besides, her head game wasn't even all that." He reaches over to give me a kiss 'n' I push him away. "Oh, word? That's how you doin' me?"

"So where were you last night?"

He blinks, giving me a stupid look. "Last night?"

"Did I stutter? Yeah, *last. Night*. Where were you? 'Cause I called you 'n' you ain't pick up ya phone, not once. And so what you called me back."

And yeah, he told me when he called, four hours later, that he was over at Luke's 'n' didn't hear his phone. That *still* doesn't mean he wasn't with that trick.

Ooh, I can't believe Fiona is sitting here even questioning him about his whereabouts or about another chick.

This is soo not the move. But oh well. Fiona ain't feelin' that ho calling 'n' texting him, either.

"And before you even try to lie. Don't."

"Yo, I already told you where I was. I was chillin' with the fellas." I ask him if there were any chicks over there. He shifts in his seat. "Yeah. A few." I raise a brow, ask him if LuAnna was one of 'em. "Nah. Just some Spanish chicks from Bayonne that Luke be smashin' on the low; that's it."

I narrow my eyes.

"C'mon, yo. Don't do that. I don't cheat. And I don't lie. Straight up. If you don't believe me, you can ask him ya'self."

"Mmph. Then why is that ho *always* up in ya face?"

"C'mon, she's not always up in my face."

I twist up my lips. "Mm-hmm. Well, she's up in it more than she needs to be. You do know she's tryna get with you, right?"

He shrugs. "That's not my problem. I already told her what it is."

I tilt my head. "And what exactly is that?"

"That I'm not interested. I told her that you're the only girl I'm checkin' for."

"Ohh, so she just don't give a damn, then. And you not even tryna check her. But it's all good, boo. Fiona can go right back to her boo-daddy rotation 'n' slide you into one of the three slots. Trust."

He frowns. "Oh, hell naw. Don't play me, yo. I ain't even tryna hear that crazy ish you talkin', yo."

"Mmph. Well, you better hear it."

"Yeah, a'ight. Don't get nobody beat up, yo. I'm not tryna share you."

I tilt my head, stare into him trying to catch any hint of

him trying to play me. There is none. I breathe out a sigh of relief. But still...

"I'm not even gonna tell you who you can talk to, but I don't like *her* always up in ya face. It's disrespectful. But if you wanna play them kinda games, I can turn up. Trust."

"Yeah, a'ight. Turn up hell. Don't play wit' me, yo."

"Then stop havin' that girl all up in ya face."

He reaches for me, pulling me into his arms. "A'ight, baby. You got that. I'ma let her know."

I twist my lips, slapping his hands away. "Hm-mmm."

"Nah, word is bond. It's all you. Now give me a kiss."

"I ain't playin', boy. Don't do me. Handle that chick or I will. Trust."

He smirks. "Aww, my baby jealous." He tries to grab me 'n' I push him back.

"Come again. Fiona got green eyes, boo. But *trust*. It ain't from envy."

He leans over into me, his lips practically on mine. "Yeah, my baby got them pretty green eyes. The kinda eyes that got me mesmerized. The kinda eyes that peer into my soul 'n' keep me hypnotized. You got me under ya spell..."

There's something familiar about his words. Like I've heard 'em before. No. Read 'em. And I have. I pull back. Blink. Put a hand up. "Wait. Wait. Wait a minute. Come again. Those words...?" He offers me a sly smile 'n' starts reciting the poem. "Pretty Green Eyes." "*You*'re the one who's been leaving me those poems in my locker all this time?"

He grins that lopsided grin. "Yeah, a lil sumthin'-sumthin'. But you gotta keep that on the low. No one knows I like to write poems."

"Ohmigod...that's so..."

He raises a brow. "What, corny?"

I shake my head, feeling tears rim my eyes. "No, no…
that's so sweet. No boy has ever written me poems before.
It's beautiful. Ohmigod! Why didn't you tell me?"

He shrugs. "I wanted to keep you guessing. You're the
first girl I've ever written any for." He tells me this 'n' as
bad as I wanna believe what he says, something inside me
won't let me. He must see the look of doubt on my face.
"Nah, word is bond, yo. I been wit' mad girls, but I've
never felt like any of 'em were worth writing poems to.
Until you…"

And in hearing his words something inside of me kinda
shakes loose 'n' outta nowhere the tears start rolling outta
my eyes, but for once I ain't tryna check for 'em, so I just
let 'em roll out freely. I open my mouth to speak, but
Cease puts a finger to my lips. "Shh. I don't wanna talk
anymore. I wanna feel them sexy lips."

I smile at him.

This time when he tries to kiss me, I let him. He gives
me two quick kisses before his tongue slips into my waiting mouth, going in for the kill. Yesss, gawd, *hunni*! I love
the way this boy kisses. He cups my face in his hands, allowing the warmth of his kisses to heat through my body.
He leans back 'n' pulls me on top of him, his hands wandering all over my body.

Ooh, this boy's got Fiona feeling some kinda way. And I
can't help wondering, am I dreaming? Is this all too good
to be true? Or am I simply going cuckoo-crazy?

39

Now I know I said never, ever fight over a boy. Never! But, *hunni*...there's always an exception to every gotdang rule. And this right here is it. Now when I initially stepped to this chick in the hallway right after third period to ask her why she stays texting Cease 'n' being all up in his face, I came at her all sugary 'n' sweet. Yes ma'am, yes sir. I sure did. I asked this tramp real nice to ease up off the texting. Fall back a pinch. But the trick wanna turn up 'n' turn out, 'n' Fiona ain't the one for a whole buncha yip-yap. Oh no, hun. Especially when I'm comin' at you all cute 'n' classy 'n' ladylike.

"Why you care who I'm texting? Is he *your* man?"

I tilt my head. "Is he *yours*, sweetie?"

"Don't worry about if he's mine or not. Are you jealous?"

I laugh. "Come again. Girl, bye. There's nothing to be jealous of. Trust."

"Then why are you over here all up in my face? What,

you scared I'ma snatch him from you? I text 'n' call who I wanna. Take that ish up with Cease, boo."

"*Bloop!* Come again, hun. Take the *stank* down a notch. You can't take *nothing* from me. Trust. Jizz licker. You are no competition for me. Trust."

She grits her teeth. "Fiona, get up outta my face 'n' keep it moving. Before I turn up on you."

I laugh sarcastically. "Ooh, turn up, boo." I clap my hands with each word. "Turn. Up. Yes, boo. Turn. Up. Do me, boo. You're clown-shit crazy, a real riot, if you think I don't wanna see you go with the hands. Give me life, boo! Do me! Oooh, I want it. Trust." I tie the strings to my hat tight around my neck, then loop them into a knot. "You real thirsty, ole nasty ball licker."

"*Bish,* please!" she shouts, placing a hand up on her hip. Her neck starts rolling. "You're the thirsty one, coming at me all crazy. Screw you, ho! All you are is a slut! You done effed half the school and now you wanna put claims on somebody who would apparently rather be with *me.* Tramp, *please*! Take a seat!"

I keep laughing. "Trick, pull the hair outta ya teeth. *You* the one tryna get him to lick all up in ya gumdrop. He showed me the text. *You* the one tryna get all up in his lap, begging for another round, talking 'bout how good ya brain game is. So *you* go have a seat. Matter of fact, go have several. I'm not the one beggin' some boy to screw me. You are. Silly-bird."

Next thing I know, she lets her lil cheering squad put a battery pack up on her back 'n' now she thinks she got juice. She pushes me. Come again? Oooh, no, hun. The last thing you *ever* do is put ya hands on Fiona. Trust. In a flash, my right hand clenches, and my fist goes upside her head.

Whap!

Whap!

Two punches to her face.

She screams.

Her arms swing like a windmill, her hands trying to pull off my hat so she can wrap fingers into my hair. But the dumbo musta thought I was silly enough to step to a chick I know I'ma beat down, with my hair not properly tucked. A diva is always prepared, no matter the occasion. Okay? She shoulda known something was up when I stepped to her in sneakers. Everyone knows Fiona stays with a heel on, okay? So that shoulda been her cue right then to keep it cute 'n' not be all slick at the mouth.

But nooooo.

I hear the voices around me. Yelling. Coaxing. Cheering. Egging it on.

"Fight! Fight! Fight!"

"Oh sheee*iiiiiit*! It's goin' down! Fiona beatin' da brakes off dat azz!"

"Tear her up, LuAnna!"

Really? You think?

She swings wildly. But I duck just in time, feeling the swoosh of air as it passes over my head. I lean in close 'n' hit her hard. She stumbles back, and I charge her, grabbing her by the head 'n' kneeing her in the stomach. I am out for blood. This chick tried it. And ooh, that's a no-no!

We tussle hard, slapping, punching, scratching.

"Ugh!" she grunts, caving in to the pain of being hit in her ribs again.

This is no longer about Cease. It's about respect. It's about this ho crossing the line 'n' putting her hands on me. And it's about me reminding her 'n' every other chick that Fiona Madison ain't the one to eff with.

She stumbles backward, falling flat on her back.

"Oh, you a dead *bish* now!" I yell, standing over her and grabbing a fistful of her hair, drawing back my fist 'n' pounding into her face. I punch her over and over until I feel someone pulling me, kicking 'n' screaming, off her.

She had better count her blessings I didn't slash her face!

Next time I will.

"*Suspended?* Ten days? I gotta leave my job for this *bull-shit*?! Girl, have you lost what's left of your everlasting mind?!" my mother snarls as she slams her door, then starts the engine 'n' peels off. I'm so pissed that the assistant principal called her. I told that old hag to call Leona. Even though she wouldn't have been too happy about me getting suspended so close to the end of the school year, either. But having her beating me in the head with a lecture woulda been a hella lot better than this. Cooped up in a car, with this motormouth rattling on 'n' on 'n' on about nothing I wanna hear.

"All I ask is that you stay outta my damn hair! Don't stress me out! Don't inconvenience me! Graduate high school! And get the hell outta my house! That's it! But you know what? I'm done with ya lil grown behind! It's your life. Do whatever you want."

"You're right!" I snap. "It is *my* life! I've been doing whatever I've wanted for over five years. So what's so different now, huh? What, because you've had to be inconvenienced *one* day outta ya life 'n' come down here to get me? The lil screwup? Please. Don't act like you're doin' *me* some favor. I didn't ask you to leave ya precious job! Get it right!"

"Fiona, don't try me!" She grips the steering wheel and looks straight ahead. "I'm ten seconds from pulling this car over 'n' wearin' ya smart-azz out."

Ooh, I want you to. Please do. I beg you!

She speeds up, then hits the brakes all hard 'n' crazy, tryna keep from running a red light. Like her frantic driving is by some chance my fault. Lady, please. Take a seat! She rolls her window down. Then shoots me a nasty glare, shaking her head. She clenches her jaw. "How do you go from an honor student in your senior year to suspended for *ten* damn days, huh?"

I grit my teeth. Bite down on my tongue.

"Girl, you had better open your goddamn mouth before I reach over there 'n' knock you upside your head. Now I need for you to explain to me how the hell you got suspended."

"I *don't* wanna talk about it." *Especially not with you!*

She bangs her hand on the steering wheel, pulling off as the light changes. "You had better talk about it. NOW!"

I huff. "*They* already *told* you. I fought this trick."

She swerves over, slamming on the brakes. "You had better watch your tone with me."

I suck my teeth.

"And suck your teeth one more damn time 'n' see what I do."

Ooh, she had better have several seats way up in the

*nosebleeds 'n' leave me the heck alone before I turn allll
the way up on her!*

"You broke that girl's nose. Now I'ma be the one *stuck*
payin' her damn hospital bills. I shoulda left you there 'n'
had them lock you up!"

I shrug, taking a deep breath. Then cut my eye over at
her. "Yeah, maybe you shoulda 'n' maybe she shoulda kept
her hands to herself. But she didn't 'n' I tried to snap her
neck. End of story."

She grunts, finally speeding off. "I'm so sick of you."

Trust, hun, the feeling's mutual!

I press my forehead against the side window 'n' bite
down on my lip.

She can be pissed all she wants. I don't give a damn.
Fiona beat that ho down for a cause. And she stands her
ground. So if I gotta do ten days as just reward, then so be
it. It's worth every day of it. As far as I'm concerned, not
going to school tomorrow or the day after that, or the day
after that, is a blessing in disguise. I won't have to see her
big face 'n' I definitely won't have see Cease all up in
mine.

I fish through my bag, pulling out my buzzing cell. I roll
my eyes. It's him. I hit IGNORE, then toss it back into my
bag. I'm not tryna hear nothing he has to say.

Oh no. I've let him do enough damage. Disrupting my
life. Getting all up inside my head 'n' having me break all
kinda codes. Dissin' all'a my BWBs just to chill with one
boy. Breaking up nails 'n' going upside some trick's head
over some dumbness. Who does that? Oh no, hun. Trust.
Fiona ain't signing up for that. She ain't 'bout that life. No
ma'am, no sir.

Then what are you gonna do?

I blink, fighting back a buncha tears. My heart doesn't know the right response to that. But in my mind the answer is painfully clear. Trust.

I'm done.

He's gotta go!

40

*L*ove *'em 'n' leave 'em…*

"Damn, I've missed you," Cease says, standing in the middle of my living room. He scoops me into his arms, holding me close to him. I look up at him, tryna find the right words to *chop* this lil situation with the least amount of emotional agony. But the way he's looking at me, full of want, tells me this is going to be anything but painless. He lowers his head 'n' our lips meet for a kiss that I've wanted, but dreaded, since hearing his voice on the phone. Since the second he stepped through the door, I've wanted to pounce on him.

I've ignored his calls 'n' texts for a whole week. Tossing 'n' turning, fighting to keep him outta my head, to keep his voice outta my ear, first thing in the morning 'n' the last thing at night before I finally fall asleep.

It's so easy to let him draw me into his arms, to give in to the memory of his warm kisses 'n' the way my pulse

quickens every time I'm around him. The way it is rapidly
pulsing now.

But I can't. I have to dead this 'n' finally put this mess in
its casket. Then seal it shut. I have to fight myself to peel
away from his lips. But when I do, I am breathless. "I-I
can't do this anymore," I blurt out, still reeling from his
kiss.

He gives me a funny look. Scrunches his nose. "You
can't do what?"

I repeat myself. "This. Us. I think we should fall back
from each other."

He frowns. "*Fall back?* Are you serious, yo?"

I nod. "Yeah. I've given it a lotta thought."

He shoves his hands down into his pockets, giving me a
pained look. "Yo, you buggin', right?"

"No. I'm serious. I think we should go back to just
being friends."

He shakes his head. "I don't get it, yo. Where's this
comin' from?"

I shrug. "I've been givin' it some thought since I got
suspended. I gotta chop it. Now."

He's looking at me all confused, lost. "Why?"

"It wasn't gonna really be much of anything anyway,
right? I mean, you'll be going off to school in the fall. And
I'ma be doin' me."

He frowns, shaking his head. "Yo, I don't believe this.
You really gonna hit me wit' the BS? I ain't buyin' it. Keep
it gee. You eyein' somebody else? You wanna be wit' some
other—"

"No," I quickly say, not sure why I don't want him thinking there's some other boo-daddy in my life, although

there shoulda been. Fiona always keeps her a few boo-daddies on deck. But that's not the case, not this time. "It's not that."

He eyes me suspiciously. "Then what is it?

"I can't do this. Me, you . . . us. It has me comin' all outta character. Fighting chicks 'n' whatnot. Ain't nobody got time for that. Fiona doesn't fight chicks over a boy. No ma'am, no sir. Period. But I had to beat one down for tryna do me all kinda sideways 'n' crazy. Now I'm doing ten days' suspension behind that dumbness."

"Yo, c'mon now," he says defensively. "You can't blame *me* for what popped off between y'all. I wasn't even there."

I frown. "I'm *not* blaming you. I'm blaming *me* for getting dragged into this craziness."

He scowls. "*Craziness?* You makin' it sound like I *dragged* you into something?"

"You *did!*" I snap, shaking my head. "You dragged me into"—I sweep my arms open—"all'a this. Me 'n' you. Us tryna turn being friends into something more. I shoulda kept it movin'."

He throws his hands up, seemingly frustrated. "Everything's gotta always be about *you*, right?"

"*Your* words, *not* mine," I counter, tossing my hair. "But, yeah. It *is* about me. Yes! Me, me, me! It's my world, boo. Thought you knew."

"Yeah, whatever, man!" he snarls, eyeing me.

I shift my weight from one foot to the other. "Exactly. I mean. It's been fun. Kiss, kiss. *Mwuah*. It's been real. But Fiona ain't lookin' to be tied down."

"Yeah, 'cause *Fiona's* too stuck on a buncha dumb-azz rules."

"They're not dumb!" I snap. "And I don't care if you think they are. They're what I live by. Period."

He huffs. "Well, you need a new set of rules 'cause the ones you have are effen stupid." He sighs. "I don't believe this, yo. You really gonna squash us over a buncha dumb rules, right? Word is bond, yo. That's how you doin' it?"

I take a deep breath.

How can I tell him that I'm angry at myself for letting him get all up in my head 'n' creeping his way into my heart? This wasn't supposed to happen. Not to me! But it has, 'n' I'm scared, okay? But how can I tell him this? That I'm kicking myself for letting my guard down. That I'm hating him 'n' hating myself for wanting to be with him. That the way he's looking at me right now—his eyes all full of, of passion 'n' intensity, like I'm all that matters to him—is killing me softly.

Oooh, I so can't do this. Weak 'n' vulnerable is not who Fiona is. No ma'am, no sir! But this boy makes me feel just that: helpless 'n' pitiful. And I don't like feeling this way. It's so not cute. No ma'am, no sir! This is not what I do. Fiona does not get all goo-goo-ga-ga over some boy. No, no, no! Not me. But here I am. All teary-eyed 'n' mushy. Feeling all pink 'n' silly.

Cease reaches for me. But I break from his grasp 'n' turn from him. I can't believe that I am really about to cry 'n' have a mini-breakdown right here in front of him. And I have no dang clue as to why. I mean, I do. But I don't. Oh, heck no! This boy has me so flustered I don't know what the heck I'm feeling or thinking anymore.

I close my eyes 'n' take another deep breath. "Please don't make this any harder than it has to be," I say as tears roll down my cheeks. "There's nothing you can do except leave me alone."

He turns me to face him. I try to turn back away, but he won't let me. He keeps pushing, forcing me to look at *him*, forcing me to see *him*.

He lets out a frustrated sigh, staring at me.

"*Shit*," he mutters, running a hand over the top of his head, then his face. He shakes his head. "So what am I supposed to do now, huh? Front like I don't care about you? Turn the other way when I see you in the halls? Act like I ain't got you"—he takes my hand 'n' places it up to his chest—"all up in here, huh? Is that what you want me to do, huh?"

What does this boy expect me to do?

Carve out big hearts with our names etched in the center on some old oak tree? No ma'am, no sir! Not gonna happen.

Am I supposed to drop down 'n' get my bobble on 'cause all of a sudden he wants to whisper sweet nothings to me? Am I supposed to hop up in his arms 'n' smother him with a buncha sweet chocolate kisses 'cause he's standing here, looking all dang sexy 'n' delicious 'n' good enough to eat? Am I supposed to believe what comes outta his mouth? Am I supposed to trust a buncha empty words?

Am I supposed to believe I'm gonna find some happy-ever-after, wrapped in his arms? Am I supposed to drop all of my boo-daddies 'n' play wifey to one boy? No. I can't do it. I won't do it. I tried it for those two weeks 'n'...I can't trust myself. And I can't trust him. No. All that letting a boy be my life is a no-no. Fiona has no time for that. I close my eyes, inhaling as I silently repeat my mantra: Love 'em 'n' leave 'em. Never, ever, get too attached to a boy. I repeat it again.

I look up at him, feeling all lost 'n' scared. I don't like this feeling one bit. Don't like feeling helpless. Don't like feeling not in control. This is so, so bad.

"Let me love you, yo."

I'm not loveable.

I shake my head. "I can't."

"You mean you *won't*."

"I can't."

"Why not?"

I inhale. Hold my breath. Then slowly breathe out. "I-I-I...just can't."

He just stares at me. Silent. And, finally, I think he gets it. That I have a buncha baggage that he's not ready to sign up for. That I am not for him. That we can't be together, *ever*.

Never, ever, get too attached to a boy...

Cease looks into my eyes, seemingly unmoved. I'm feeling light-headed 'n' weak under his gaze. "Yes, you can. If you'd stop fighting it," he finally says, leaning in 'n' kissing me again. "I love you, yo."

I push back from him 'n' look into his eyes, my heart cracking into a thousand 'n' one pieces, realizing that I really do like this boy more than I pretended not to. "That's too bad," I say, steadying my shaking voice. "It's over."

41

"Oooh, you catchin' cabs now," Alicia says, smirking as I slide outta the gypsy taxi, slamming the door shut. "What, the high 'n' mighty Miss Fiona has fallen from grace with her bestie-boo?" She laughs. "Figures. You could never keep any friends anyway."

I take a deep breath. It's been a week since I chopped things off with Cease. And today, after two weeks, it's my first day back to school since my suspension 'n' I'm really, really tryna keep it cute 'n' not get hauled off in handcuffs this morning. No ma'am, no sir! But this chick right here is really tryin' it.

Yes, I caught a cab to school today. *And?* I did it to avoid having to ride with Miesha. I didn't wanna start my morning talking about *Cease*, having to explain why I shut it down with him. Why I won't give him a chance. Oh no, oh no.

It's bad enough Miesha was blowing up my phone all crazy with text messages 'n' phone calls tryna get at me, wanting to know what happened between us. Nothing happened. It was over way before it got started; now let's move along. Fiona doesn't have to explain herself to anyone. No ma'am, no sir. What's done is done. It's over. No biggie. Now let's move on.

I shoot Alicia a nasty look, slinging my satchel up over my shoulder. "Girl, bye! Move along, ma'am. Please 'n' thank you."

"Mmph. I knew that situation wasn't gonna last," she says smugly as I'm walking through the gates toward the school building.

I toss my hair, cutting an eye at her. "You knew *what* situation wasn't gonna last?"

"You 'n' Cease. I don't know why he even wasted his time tryna mess with you in the first place." She laughs. "Tryna wife a ho. Where they do that?"

I take another deep breath. Then kindly tell this undercover whore, again, to get outta my face. So *whyyyyy* is this messy booga-roach *still* skipping alongside of me poppin' her flappers? *Beeeecaaaaaause* obviously she wants to see me slip outta these heels 'n' go from hood classy to ratchet in zero-point-two-five-seconds 'n' drag her face over this cement. But I ain't gonna do it. Nope. Not today. No ma'am, no sir. I'ma let chickie keep her face in one piece.

Still, I'm convinced that this chick is really tryna provoke me into laying these hands on her, then tossing her in a casket. I take one final deep breath, stopping dead in my tracks. "Look, *bish*! Get the fu..." I catch myself just as I make my way into the building 'n' run smack into Mrs. Evans, who rolls out the imaginary red carpet 'n' welcomes me back to school.

"Fiona, it's good to have you back. I trust you'll get through the remainder of the school year without further distractions and/or incidents," she says sternly.

"Yes, ma'am. That is the plan," I say, tossing my hair. "Fiona is stickin' to the script. She's keeping her lips sealed 'n' her eye on the prize."

"And her hands to herself, I trust," Mrs. Evans adds, tryna be messy.

Alicia snickers. "Mmph. Good luck with that."

Mrs. Evans decides to check her before I do, sending her on her way. Then starts rambling on about expectations 'n' young ladies 'n' having less fights 'n' needing to have more self-respect, blah, blah, blah, but I am tuning her out. All I wanna do is get through this day. Get through having to eventually face Cease in the halls since putting the axe down on my lil situation with him that is suddenly starting to feel not so lil anymore now that I see Cease standing a few feet away from me, leaning up against a bank of lockers talking to Luke 'n' Justin.

I try not to look over in his direction, but I can't help myself. He laughs at something Luke says, but when his eyes catch mine his whole facial expression changes. My stomach churns. Cease just stares at me. Luke 'n' Justin stop talking 'n' both look over in my direction. They're giving me dirty looks. Or at least that's what I think I see.

I quickly shift my eyes. "Umm, Missus Evans," I say, cutting her off. "Not to be rude, but, uh, um, I really appreciate the welcome-back speech 'n' all but, um, I haven't heard a word you just said. I gotta go. Please 'n' thank you."

I bolt for the stairs, bumping into a few students, pretending not to see the bitterness in Cease's stare. Pretending not to feel his hurt. And all I can think as I fly up the stairs in an unexpected panic 'n' round the corner is, *What the hell am I gonna do now?*

The rest of the day is one big blur for me. It feels like I've been dragged through hellfire! I got my first C on an econ test I coulda aced upside down with my eyes closed 'n' my fingers crossed. But, *noooo*! I get a frickin' *C*! Fiona does not do damn Cs! No ma'am, no sir! Then, if that isn't enough, all this ducking 'n' hiding 'n' tryna avoid running into Cease in the halls 'n' dodging Miesha has worn me out.

I can't wait to get the heck outta here. Fast. I feel sick! I'm exhausted. And now I feel like I'm about to have a full-fledged panic attack when I look up from my locker 'n' see Cease coming down the hall. My stomach knots as I rise from my kneeling position, leaving my locker door open.

"We need to talk," he says.

I blink. "Cease, I—"

"Let me finish. You hurt me, yo. Like what the fu..." He takes a deep breath. "What I feel for you is real, Fee. It's not about tryna game you or get into ya panties. It's about what's in my heart. *You*. I really dig you. But I don't know what I gotta do, or say, for you to see that. I'm tryna figure out why you gotta be so stubborn."

"I'm not being stubborn."

He narrows his gaze at me. "Then why are you being stupid?"

"Stupid?" I blink. "I'm not stupid."

"Well, you're being stupid if you gonna let some ridiculous rules that you've made up in ya pretty lil head stop you from doing what you feel in ya heart."

I shake my head, blinking back tears. "Oh no, oh no... I'm not about to let you stand here 'n' disrespect me. I—"

"I miss you, yo, a'ight," he says, cutting me off. "And I'm hurt that you just shut me out. Like damn, yo. I could handle you wantin' to shut it down if I had played you or dogged you out, but you just dissin' me over dumb ish is crazy, yo."

I give him a pained look. "Um..." I don't seem to know what to say.

"Yo, what's good, Cease...Fiona?" David says as he walks by. I respond with a half wave, Cease with a grunt. Neither of us takes our eyes off the other.

He just stares at me, his gaze burning into my heart, then closes his eyes 'n' sighs. "So, we just gonna ignore each other when—"

"Heeey, Cease," Chantel says. I catch her outta the corner of my eye, smirking. Cease igs her. Three more chicks walk by 'n' coo out his name. He igs them, too.

I fumble inside my locker, dazed, lost, forgetting exactly what I need out of it. Nothing. I don't need a damn thing out of here. I just need to get out of here. Away from Cease's gaze. Away from the nosy, probing eyes of these haters. I slam my locker shut.

"I miss you, yo."

I blink.

Cease licks his lips, looking at *me* in a way I've never seen any other boy look at me. He wants to try again. But I can't. I mean. I want to. No, no. I can't. Oh God. I don't know what I want. Don't know what I mean. This boy has me so confused.

"I *am* hopeless," I whisper, trying to keep my emotions in check.

"Nah, you're not hopeless. And if you were, it wouldn't matter. I got enough hope for the both of us, a'ight? Give us a chance, Fee."

I hold my breath as he leans forward...

And then Samantha walks by 'n' whispers loudly to Quanda. "She didn't deserve a man like Cease, anyway." She glances over her shoulder. "Cease, boo, that ho don't deserve you." Quanda laughs. I glare at both of them. Ready to set it off.

"Yo, chill, fam," Cease says, frowning at her. "You outta pocket, yo."

"Oops, okay, boo," Samantha says, putting her hands up in mock surrender. "My bad. I just don't wanna see you gettin' hurt *again*. You know you can't ever trust a *trick*." She tosses a glare over at me, smirking.

"*Bish*," I snap, ready to light her up, "the only trick is ya bald-headed, drunk mammy with that one raggedy tooth in her mouth. Don't—"

Cease grabs my arm. "Yo, chill, yo. Let that ish go. This is 'bout me 'n' you."

I shake my head. "I can't do this, Cease. There is no *you 'n' me*! So please just leave me alone!"

I snatch my arm away 'n' hurry down the hall, fleeing from him 'n' the aching truth that I miss him, too.

42

Silence of the Heart

I listen
And I hear
The nothingness
That lingers deep
In the corners
Of my soul
Soft whispers that blow in the wind
And slip into the dawn of my dreams
I watch
And I see
Memories tossed in the air like confetti
Slowly falling
Disappearing
Into the pit of my own emptiness
I touch
And I feel

The pulse of a heart
That no longer beats
Because there is no you

Three days later, I'm standing at my locker, my hand trembling as I read the poem Cease stuffed in my locker for the second time. I close my eyes 'n' hold the paper to my nose, inhaling. Then...

Snap! Snap!

I blink. Miesha is standing in front of me, hand on a hip, fingers in my face.

I give her a blank stare.

She snaps her fingers in my face again. *"Bish*, get it together," she says, eyeing me all crazy-like. "You've been walking around here like a damn zombie all dang week, looking all lost 'n' crazy. Then you stay actin' all funny-style, iggin' my calls 'n' actin' like *I* burned a hole in ya damn drawz..."

She's right. I've done everything I can to avoid her. To avoid seeing her all hugged up 'n' all grins 'n' giggles 'n' full of...that dirty lil four-letter word that has crept up inside my heart 'n' screwed up my life.

Ooh, this whole mess is sooo not cute!

Why did Cease have to press his way into my head? Bombard his way into my heart? I didn't ask for that!

Didn't want it!

Why did he have to do that?

Make my life complicated!

Fiona was fine without him!

Snap! Snap! "Earth to Fiona!"

I blink. *"What?"*

"I'm talking to you, that's *what*. What the *fuqq* is going on with *you*?"

Cease is wrong with me!

Seeing you all lovey-dovey with Tone is what's wrong with me!

I want what you have!

Never, ever, let a boy get all up in ya head!

I miss him!

It's for the best!

You said you didn't want him!

I lied! I lied! I lied!

Never, ever, get attached to a boy.

But I want him.

"Oh, forget it," she says, snatching me outta the argument going on inside my head, before I can open my mouth to speak. "I know what's wrong with you! You're miserable without him. You know it. I know it. The whole dang school knows it. Just admit it, girl. It's all over your face. He's miserable. You're miserable. Swallow your dang pride 'n' go get ya man back. Why the heck did you break up with him, anyway?"

Ooh, she's comin' for you!

You better pump the brakes 'n' give it to her good!

I slam my locker shut, sighing. "I didn't *break up* with him. We would have to be going together in order for *that* to happen."

"Well, y'all *were* talking, *right*?"

I shrug. "Yeah, I guess. Something like that."

"Then why'd you dead it?"

I shake my head. "I really don't wanna talk about it." I turn to walk off, but she grabs me by the arm.

"Oh no, heifer. You not even about to spin off on me, boo. Not until you tell me what the heck is really going on here." She folds her arms, tapping her foot. "What lil thug-daddy bum are you chasing behind *now* that's got your mind so jacked up that you'd mess up a good thing with one of the hottest boys on campus, huh?"

"I—"

"And *don't* even try to lie," she hisses, cutting me off. "'Cause I *know* you. You always chasing after the next good time, always tryna keep ya boo-daddy stash up, so don't even try 'n' do me with the BS. You'd rather be a *ho* for a buncha no-goods than be a ho for *one* good one."

I blink.

Boom! Boom! Shots fired! Ooooh, she did that!

She's still tapping her foot. "Well? Don't just stand there staring at me all nutty. What the heck is going on, girl?"

My chest tightens.

I feel a buncha emotions bubbling up in the back of my throat. That I am sooo not tryna deal with right now.

Oh no, boo! Snap outta it! You better not dare drop one dang tear. Stand ya ground! This is what you wanted, so this is what you got! Now get over it!

I swallow hard. "Look," I finally say, sighing. "Fiona ain't the one-boo type, okay? So let's just drop it. It's over. There is no me 'n' Cease. There is no *we*. It was something to do, that's it. So move along. Please 'n' thank you."

She eyes me, long 'n' hard, then narrows her eyes to thin slits. We are both oblivious to the commotion around us, prying eyes zooming in on us as they slow-stroll by, sucking in the drama airing out between the two of us.

"Lies, lies, 'n' more lies," she snaps. "But, whatever. You

wanna spend ya life trickin' it up with a buncha boys, then
do you. I'm done tryna save a chick who ain't tryna be
saved."

She storms off, sweeping her rhinestone satchel over
her shoulder.

"Fine!" I huff. "Be done! Why the hell *you* care, anyway?!"

She stops 'n' turns to me. "*Bish*, because I'm your
damn friend! But obviously you wanna shut *that* down,
too. You're too stuck on stupid to even know what you
want. So, *trust*, hun. I'm done! You wanna be alone 'n'
miserable, then have at it!" She throws up two fingers.
"Deuces!"

I will my feet to move, but they don't. So I stand here in
the middle of the hallway—being bumped 'n' shouldered
by kids zipping by tryna get to wherever they need to be
before the bell rings—feeling lost, confused, 'n' ridicu-
lously outta place.

I'm fuming 'cause Miesha tried to do me. No. She did
do me! But the crazy thing is, no matter how pissed I
wanna be at her for servin' me—and oooh, *trust*. She did
that! The only person I can be mad at is *me*. For not sticking to the damn script! For letting that boy get all up inside my head! For missing him!

She's right. I don't know what the hell I want anymore.
Maybe I never did!

God, I feel so stupid!

Worthless!

Girl, boom! Because you are!

43

"Fee?"

I spin around, startled.

Cease's standing here at my locker. My heart flutters. Then sinks. I can't let myself get all caught up in him. Missing him doesn't mean I have to *be* with him. It means I just have to avoid him better, switch schools, relocate across town, to another city—anywhere other than being *here*. With him.

"Hey," I say softly.

"I can't keep doin' this, yo."

I blink. Shake my head, confused. "Doing what?"

"Pretending that I don't miss you. Pretending that I'm not hurting. I'm all effed up, yo."

I swallow. Him standing here is not helping my resolve to stay away from him. I knew coming to school today was a bad idea; especially after Miesha served me in the hallway yesterday. I shoulda played hooky. Played sick. Played crazy. Did anything to keep from being here. Standing here, looking into Cease's face. I've been avoiding him for the last several days, so this is the first time we've spoken since he approached me on my first day back at school.

"I-I'm s-sorry," I stammer softly. "I didn't mean to hurt you, Cease. It's just that…" I pause, looking away, tryna find the right words to tell him how I feel. How I don't wanna feel. I'm struggling to tell him how much I care about him. But how can I when I'm trying so dang hard not to? How can I be with him 'n' live by my rules, too?

I can't.

"Listen, yo," Cease finally says, lifting my chin. "I can't tell you how'ta feel or what to think. But I ain't goin' nowhere. If you scared, say you scared, a'ight? It's cool. Heck. I'm scared, yo. You think I wanted this to happen, huh? I knew I was big on you, but I ain't think I was gonna fall for you, yo. I didn't think not bein' wit' you was gonna hurt so much. Not like this."

He's fallen for me?

Ohmigod!

I bite my quivering lip. "I warned you not to catch feelings."

He pulls in his bottom lip, staring at me with sadness in his pained eyes, 'n' my heart sinks further down into the soles of my heels. "Nah. I ain't tryna hear that. It's too late. You already all up in my heart, yo. All up in my head. Now you got me walkin' around here feeling like crap."

"I didn't mean to…"

"You know we're meant to be together, so why you keep frontin', huh? We're good together, Fee. And you know we are. Tell me I'm wrong, yo."

I swallow, tearing my gaze away from his. "You're wrong.

I'm not good for you, Cease. I mean. I wanna be. But I don't think I can be."

"So it's all in my head, right? Is that what you're tellin' me? That I've imagined all this? Tell me I'm buggin' 'n' I'll spin off. Is that what you want?"

I swallow. "Yes. That's what I want. For you to just spin off 'n' not look back. Go off to college 'n' be happy with someone else."

"I'm not tryna be happy wit' anyone else. I wanna be happy wit' you, yo."

"I can't."

Omigod! Lies!

Ooh, I'm so confused. And, trust. Fiona 'n' confusion don't mix. My rapid breathing is in sync with my pounding heart. I feel dizzy. I want to cry. This is pathetic! I'm pathetic! This is so not diva-like. So not Fiona Madison. I don't do this. Crying.

Over a boy!

Over an aching heart!

And definitely *not* for all to see!

Ever.

Oh, girl, quit! Stop playing damn games 'n' just be honest, for once!

"I don't wanna hurt you, Cease," I say honestly. "I just..."

"Why don't you think you deserve to be loved, huh? Why can't you trust that I can love you, huh? I don't care 'bout ya past, I don't care 'bout how many dudes you been wit'. All I care 'bout is you, Fee. Why won't you trust me, huh?"

Because I can't trust myself.

"I-I'm..." I can feel tears beginning to burn in the back of my throat.

"You love me?"

I blink. Open my mouth to finally admit what I've been afraid to admit. That I've caught *feelings* for him. That that dirty lil *L*-word has snatched me by the throat 'n' sank its teeth into my heart 'n' now I'm scared to death—of hurting him, of hurting myself, of hurting each other. Oooh, no, no, no! Fiona ain't even tryna be all strung out on no boy. No ma'am, no sir. But I...I...I think it's already too late.

I *am* strung out on him!

The bell rings. Classroom doors fling open. Noise erupts. And kids start pouring out into the hallway. And I see it as my great escape. My chance to flee from him, again.

From my feelings.

From his.

Cease must sense that I'm about to take off running 'cause before I can make a speedy getaway he reaches out and cups my face, flicking away my tears with his thumbs. "You ain't gotta run from this, babe; from me. All you gotta do is trust me. Trust what's in ya heart. I know you feel it, too."

I shake my head. I feel myself starting to hyperventilate. "I-I can't do this, Cease. It's not you. It's me. Don't you see? I don't do *feelings*. I don't do *love*. I'm a heartbreaker. Not a *love*maker. Fiona ain't tryna let *you* or anyone else get all up in her head 'n' have her actin' all dizzy..."

"Kiss me," he says, ignoring my rant.

My breath catches in my throat. I rock back on my heels.

I blink. "Excuse you?"

"I said kiss me. One kiss. Right here 'til the next bell rings. That's three minutes."

I frown. Tell him I'm not about to stand here 'n' tongue him down. Not with all these wandering eyeballs all up on us. No ma'am, no sir!

"Nah." He steps in closer. "I'm not tryna hear all that. You don't wanna be wit' me, cool. I gotta learn to live wit' it. So, after today, you ain't gotta worry 'bout me sweatin' you or leavin' you any more poems. But I ain't gonna fall back 'til you kiss me one last time. That's all I ask. Then after that, if you still ain't beat to be wit' me, cool." His voice cracks. "If you don't feel what I feel, I'ma fall back, a'ight? I'ma let you do you. And I'ma do me."

Ooh, this boy is tryna do me. He's tryna be messy. And he knows Fiona don't do messy!

"Girl, you better get yo' life 'n' kiss that boy," I hear someone say. "Before I do it for you. Heeey, Cease!"

Laughter.

A small crowd is starting to gather for the spectacle that has become Cease 'n' me. I swallow. I don't want them to see me like this. Weak 'n' frickin' vulnerable. This is so not diva-like. I turn away, my face wet with tears. I don't want him or any of these messy onlookers to see me falling apart.

I close my eyes, shaking my head. Cease steps in closer. He wraps his arms around me 'n' nuzzles his chin on top of my head. "Let me love you, Fee. Don't run from this. I got you." A part of me wants to turn to him 'n' look at him. Tell him that I wanna trust him. But I don't dare.

"One kiss, babe. That's all I'm askin' for. You owe me that, yo." I swallow as he turns me to face him. "One kiss, a'ight?" He slowly leans in 'n' I surprise myself when I don't pull back. His lips find mine. He pecks them lightly.

But I push him back with the palm of my hand. "I can't."

He blinks. Then frowns. "Oh, word? So you really want me to spin off?"

"Yes," I whisper, refusing to look at him. I am crumbling inside, but fight to hold it all together. He shakes his head 'n' lets it drop for a moment. When he looks back up, he looks as if he wants to cry, but he doesn't. He's hurt. Crushed. And it's all my fault. "I'm—"

"Nah, save it." He swallows, takes a deep breath, pauses, then says, "I'm out. Have a good life, yo."

I eye him as he walks off. My hands shaking. Body trembling. Heart aching. My knees buckle 'n' I choke back a scream.

"Ohmigod, you stupid, bish!" I hear Miesha's voice in my head. *"You're really gonna let him walk away like that?"*

I can hear a few girls sniggering.

Someone says, "Mmph, good. I'm glad she doesn't want him. Now I can have him. She didn't deserve him anyway."

"Mmph. She's dumb as hell to let that fine boy slip outta her fingers."

Ho, stop the madness! You better get yo' damn life!

"Cease, wait!" I yell out. He keeps walking. "Cease, *please!*"

When he stops 'n' turns 'n' sees my face he must hear what's in my voice. Desperation 'n' fear.

Of being alone.

Of being with him.

Of being without him.

He just stands where he is, staring, waiting. His face expressionless. "What is it, yo?"

I drop my bag. Kick off my heels. And run to him, screaming out like some crazed loony tune, "Yes!"

He frowns. "*Yes*, what?"

I keep running full speed, leaping up into the air at him, hoping like heck he doesn't do me dirty 'n' let me hit the floor. Ooh, that'll be so messy. But if he does, I know it'd serve me right for being so dang stupid 'n' stubborn. Okay, okay, 'n' maybe a lil silly. But, whatever. Cease catches me in his arms 'n' tears spurt outta my eyes.

"I love you! I love you! I love you!" I keep saying it over 'n' over, wrapping legs around his waist 'n' my arms around his neck. I kiss all over his face. "Yes, yes, yessss! I love you, Cease! With all my heart!" I kiss his lips. And he kisses me back.

I'm not sure who pulls back first, or if the three minutes are up 'n' the bell has already rung. All I know is, I'm seeing stars 'n' feeling kinda dizzy. I blink. And Cease is smiling. Then grins that lopsided grin of his. And I feel my heart fluttering.

I pause for a moment. "I've *never* had a boyfriend, not a real one. I've never even known what *love* feels like until..." I close my eyes. Shake my head.

"Until what?" he says softly.

"Until you," I confess. "And it scares me. You have my heart, Cease. And Fiona is terrified. Of us. Of you. I don't wanna get hurt."

"I'm not gonna hurt you, Fee. Trust me. I got you."

And then, in the middle of McPherson High, fourth floor, west wing hallway, we kiss. And nothing else seems to matter anymore. Not my diva rules. Not the mess at home with my mother. Not even all these messy tricks gawking at us. Everything in me heats 'n' I feel myself melting. And it's as if the sun is peeking through the clouds for the first time in my life, shining down on me.

I hear a few kids whoop 'n' applaud.

I hear Antonio yell out, "Jeez, get a room! Freaks!"

Laughter.

But none of that matters, not this time. I'm with my boo-daddy. Yes, gawd, *hunni*! Fiona ain't tryna be no fool. And, hopefully, this diva's gonna keep her mind right 'n' not let her ho-ish ways mess things up between us.

Mmph. Maybe being with one boy won't be so bad after all. Maybe...

Cease finally eases me down to my feet 'n' leans in for another kiss. The kiss gets sweeter with each passing second. This time I let my eyes flutter shut 'n' melt into Cease's lips, so happy that I am gonna follow my heart instead of my silly lil diva rules. Wait. Ooh, don't do me. They aren't *all* silly. I mean, well...maybe a few of 'em will need to be tweaked a pinch now that Fiona's got herself a fine lil boo-daddy who she's about to let wife her up for a minute. Okay, okay, for as long as he can handle the heat 'n' doesn't get on my nerves. Shoot. After all, I am still fly, fabulous, 'n' too hot to handle. Boom-boom!

But now, drumroll *pleeeease*...I'm about to make a new set of diva rules for a diva in love!

DIVA RULES

Amir Abrams

ABOUT THIS GUIDE

The following questions are intended to
enhance your group's reading of
DIVA RULES.

Discussion Questions

1. Fiona Madison was a real feisty, self-proclaimed diva with a set of diva rules she lived by. What are your thoughts about these rules? Are there any you'd subscribe to? If so, which one(s)? And why?

2. What did you think of Fiona's relationship with her mother? Do you believe her disrespect was warranted? Is it ever okay to disrespect a parent, even when they've mistreated you? Have you ever disrespected your parent(s)? What were the consequences, if any, when you did? What was your reason for being disrespectful? And would you do it again?

3. Despite Fiona's volatile relationship with her mother, she seemed to have a very close relationship with her four sisters. What did you think of their relationship? Are you close to your siblings? Do you feel they understand you? If not, why?

4. Fiona was very flirtatious and had a reputation for lots of lip-locking 'n' making it pop with the boys. What are your thoughts about promiscuity? Do you know anyone who's like her? What did you think about her "love 'em 'n' leave 'em" mentality?

5. What were your feelings about Cease pursuing Fiona? How did you feel about her dismissing him after her fight? Why do you think she was so afraid of being with him? Do you think she's capable of really being with one guy? Why or why not?

The Girl of His Dreams

The rules are simple: Play or get played. And never, ever, catch feelings.

That's the motto seventeen-year-old heartthrob Antonio Lopez lives by. His father taught him everything he needs to know about women: They can't be trusted, and a real man has more than one. So once Antonio gets what he wants from a girl, he moves on. But McPherson High's hot new beauty is turning out to be Antonio's first real challenge.

Miesha Wilson has a motto of her own: The thrill of the chase is not getting caught. She's dumped her share of playboys and she's determined to stay clear of the likes of Antonio Lopez. But when she decides to play some games of her own, Miesha and Antonio find themselves wondering if love is real after all....

1

Antonio

No lie. Broads are good for only two things—well, three
...good sex, good brain, and keepin' my sneaker,
fitted-hat, and Polo game up—and not necessarily in that
order. They can scratch all the extras. I'm not lookin' for
love. I'm lookin' for a good time. And the only thing I'm
lookin' to do is give 'em this good lovin'.

Who am I?

Oh, my bad. Thought you knew.

I'm that hot boy wit' the spinnin' waves.

Antonio Lopez.

Dominican and Black.

Six-four, rock-hard body.

Smooth, suave, pretty boy wit' that mad swag.

A chick magnet.

The most popular dude at McPherson High.

Voted best lookin', best dressed, and homecoming king
three years in a row. All-star basketball champion.

Need I say more?

Not to pop my own collar or sound cocky wit' it or anything. But, real rap. I'm that dude, yo. Front if you want. Eight pack on deck. Nice chest, arms, legs, 'n' back. The chicks go crazy when they see this body. And I gotta mad assortment of colorful panties, text messages, photos, and phone numbers from thirsty broads who stay tryna get a piece of the kid to prove it.

Oh, you still don't know?

Let me put you on then.

I'm checkin' for them sexy dime-pieces who know how to handle a man like me. And oh yeah, I'll even holla at the ooga-booga as long as she gotta nice phatty, a whip, and a j-o-b. But I ain't ever gonna be seen wit' her out in public, givin' her no daytime airplay. Nah, them kinda broads gotta get it at night—*late* at night wit' the lights down real low. Better yet, they get the black light special. Once I'm bored wit' 'em, *chop!* It's on to the next.

So the moral of the story is, proceed wit' caution. And don't ever catch feelin's. And don't get too comfy, either, 'cause all good things gotta come to an end. And just like with tires and oil changes, chicks gotta be rotated and changed every three thousand miles—or in my case, every three weeks, otherwise they start gettin' real nutty, actin' like they own you. And after seein' the latest Facebook status I've been tagged on **To all you birds cluckin' 'round Tone. Back up or get ya feathers plucked! Get ya own man and leave mine alone or i'm snatchin lace fronts n slashin faces!**, I'm more convinced than ever before that most of 'em are straight-up psycho, like this chick Quandaleesha. My stalker. My worst nightmare.

I sigh, shakin' my head when I peep she has ninety-two

likes to her ignorant post and seventy-eight comments. All birds, I bet.

My pops peeped how triflin' Quanda was the minute he met her. And although he's never told me who to rock wit' 'cause he believes some things a man needs to learn on his own, he warned me about her. He said, "Tone, that girl's trouble. Don't give her too much of that Lopez lovin', boy. You hear? She ain't ready for it. Her mind's too weak. Give her one round, then get rid of her. And make sure you double-wrap."

"I got you, Pops," I assured him. "I'ma beat it down, then give 'er the boot."

He laughed. "Just like your pops. Give 'er just enough so that she'll never forget ya. But not enough for her to get crazy."

"No doubt," I said, givin' him a pound. See, Pops is mad chill like that. He stays schoolin' me 'bout life 'n' the honeys. So he's cool wit' me sexin' chicks and havin' 'em over as long as they bounce up outta here before eleven on weeknights, and by 1 AM on weekends. And for the most part, he's hardly ever home 'cause he's a contracted truck driver—he owns his own truck company—and spends most of his time on the road, goin' 'cross the country. And when he's not on the road, he's usually gettin' it in over at his main chick's crib or at one of his jump-offs' cribs puttin' in that work. Or he's here locked up in his room goin' at it.

I've had mad chicks up in here, over forty, and I've been havin' sex since I was thirteen. Pops made sure to it. It was the night before my thirteenth birthday. Pops walked up in my room and flat-out said, "Get showered and dressed. Tonight you become a man." I had no idea what to expect.

The only thing I knew is, it was goin' to be my rite of passage into manhood. And that, no matter what happened, nothin' would ever be the same for me.

An hour later, we were at his flavor-of-the-moment's crib—this thick-in-the-hips Dominican mami wit' big boobs and a real big booty. They were upstairs, doin' what they do. And I was down in the basement wit' her nineteen-year-old daughter, who was mad sexy, bein' welcomed into manhood. I smoked my first blunt, tossed back the yak, and then...she did all kinds of things to me that had my toes curlin', my eyes crossin', and my heart racin' so hard I thought I was gonna die. I was mad nervous as I fumbled around tryna find my groove, but that night I learned e'erything I needed to know about handlin' my business as a man. Then on our way home, Pops looked over at me as he drove, and said, "You a man now. You hear me? And a real man ain't meant to be chained to the hip of one woman. Men need variety. And it's in a man's nature to have lots of sex. And lots of women. That's what they're put here on earth for, to keep a man sexed and satisfied. They're not good for nothin' else. You understand me?"

I nodded, still floatin' from the weed, the drinks, and the memory of losin' my virginity to an older chick. But I was well aware of e'erything Pops was sayin' to me. That chicks are strictly for hit 'n' runs.

Now, I'm standin' here kickin' myself for not gettin' rid of Quanda sooner than later. Like I said, Pops had warned me. After all, he's had more than his share of nutty broads. So the one thing Pops knows is females. He's Mr. Playa-Playa, the original don. The Dominican panty dropper. And the egg donor—well, for a lack of a better title, the broad who gave birth to me—is Black. And ghost! But whatever! It is what it is. Anyway, back to Pops.

Truth is, Pops's a real smooth dude when it comes to the ladies. And he's been schoolin' me since I was seven years old, preparin' me for manhood. E'erything I know about broads—that they can't be trusted, that you can't give 'em too much of ya time, that you can't ever let 'em into ya heart, and the list goes on—I've learned from him. "I'ma give you what you need to be a man," Pops always told me. "And hopefully protect you from a buncha heartache 'n' disappointment. But there are some things you gonna hafta go through and learn for ya'self."

Like this ish wit' Quanda. Ever since I hit her wit' them discharge papers, like, just before the end of the summer, she's been runnin' around actin' like she's stuck on psycho. No lie, I dumped this broad three weeks ago and here it is the first week of September and this cuckoo bird is still cluckin' all up in my space, tryna block my flow. Talkin' 'bout I'm hers and she ain't lettin' me go. Real talk, she's outta control!

I get another Facebook alert. Now Quanda's tagged me wit' some more of her craziness. I click back onto my page, shakin' my head. It's a picture of her blowin' a kiss into the camera. **Stop playin, boo. u know u miss these sweet kisses! can't wait to see u in school!**

It's really too early in the mornin' for this nuttiness. I scroll through my FB settings and finally do what I shoulda done three weeks ago—I block her!